Also by Mac Griffith

Lyric River: a novel
Strong Hills: tales from the mountains

Above Your Raisin

a novel

Mac Griffith

Copyright

For Huck, Atticus, Carly, and Noah—sailors, home
from the sea.

A Note on Geography

Sometimes fiction makes me delirious with power, the power, indeed, to move mountains. I live in Summit County, Colorado, so it was natural to make my home the home of this book. I have always liked the small town of Frisco, a real place in Summit County. I have also roamed around lots of places in the Rocky Mountains, so it was easy for me to grab pieces of other settings for this book. Aspen, for example, has more than a few rich folks. Glenwood Springs has two big rivers. Having always had an unquiet relationship with the truth, I simply made up for this book a powerful river, which I called the Rolling River, and a broad river valley to go with it. For those who know Summit County geography, I put this wide, populated river valley down on top of tiny North Ten Mile Creek, thereby obliterating a narrow valley with a fine hiking trail. I did this because of that delirious power that fiction gives you. It feels wonderful to move people about at will and even better to do this to the great, lovely land itself.

Reader's Advisory

The characters in this book are fictional. I lived with some of them before in another book called *Lyric River*. Anyone who knows me will vouch for the fact that I could not possibly have known any Supreme Court justices or billionaires because such distinguished folk, people Huck Finn called "the quality," would have the good judgment to have nothing to do with the likes of me. Also, there is a real person in the book, a pope, about whom I made stuff up; I expect he would forgive me. Any resemblance to other real people is coincidental and beside the point of a work of fiction.

This novel has in it action, adventure, love, heartbreak, and redemption, true enough, but, contrary to proper form, it also has in it ideas. Sorry. Most of the ideas are straight-ahead goofy, but, still, they have no place in a novel. I blame only myself.

Chapter 1

My sainted mother, rest her, would have been happier than a dead pig in sunshine if she could've seen this Supreme Court justice pretending to drown in six inches of Colorado mountain river. This saying about dead pigs was not common, even in Alabama, but my mother was partial to it. I recall as a child trying to get its meaning out of her, but it was no good. Maybe she didn't know herself—maybe she just liked the sound of it. Sometimes all my thinking, all my questions, put her off, and times like that she clammed up and became cryptic; and then of a sudden one year she was busy dying. She may have intended to explain to me about the smiling pig but forgot in the rush that's always there when you're getting ready for a trip, so it was cryptic right on through. Much later, I came to know it was a simple pig rictus, dead lips drawing into a grin, hastened by heat, but I say respectfully I don't think she knew that. So, I still don't know for sure what she meant, but I came away at thirteen thinking dead pigs in the sun are happy creatures, maybe listening to some sweet, silent melody, maybe forever, like Greeks on a brown urn. At least it makes me happy to think this, same as it makes me happy to dust off some childhood memory of her, hardheaded though she surely was.

Back in Muscle Shoals, Alabama, they called me Tree, for reasons that are convenient for me to forget, unless you have a brown jug of whiskey on you, which might get you more of the truth. The part of the whole truth I feel like telling right now is that I used to be a janitor at R.E. Lee High School, and with that knowledge you might think I am not an educated man. I am not, that is right, but I worked nights in the library and was not always faithful to my duties. And, more besides, I could check out any book I wanted, and did (always leaving Marge, the librarian, my friend, a note). So, call me Tree, which I like, or call me Vernon Purcell, which I don't (and neither would you). I was a plain man and often alone, so I had time to read and space to talk to myself about things of keen interest. I wondered often, and widely, just wondered, just for the joy that was in it. You may wonder why I say I "was" a plain man. It's not that I think I've become more (or less) than plain; it's that Julie loved me for a while before she died and that made a difference to me.

"Perchance to dream"—I always liked that. There is a perchance to life that has been my friend, my enemy—it is a puzzlement that hurts to think about. I am a man who was loved by a certified English teacher at R.E. Lee High, a lovely Julie with red hair, who married the school janitor and passed, thereby, all my understanding. She then got hurt and quickly passed on to another understanding of things, where I have not yet followed, not yet. But consider this odd perchance: I did not know that Eunice, my cousin, my remaining family, was going to shoo me from Alabama to find a new life after Julie. Out of a bag of possibles, I happened to stop in Colorado, a fetching place. One little job followed onto another and then I was swamping the fancy floors of a huge barn belonging to a rich guy, who hung out, of a summer's evening, with a justice of the Supreme Court. And, as it happened, Julie, who lived in all my days, had never liked this Justice Grasso. She was unusually particular about her dislike, as she could be at times. I don't mean to suggest that she would have called upon me to drown him in the Rolling River; she was always opposed to suffering, and at the end she dreaded mine more than hers.

On the other hand, I think my mother would have been happy at the spectacle of Associate Justice of the United States Supreme Court Dominic Grasso on his back in a bitty part of the Rolling River. She would have been happiest at the sight of him slipping and falling and flailing about, judicial dignity having taken flight like blackbirds from a pie. She would have admired Grasso because he was godlier than a prayer meeting, but she would have also liked seeing him fall because the fall of the mighty was satisfying to her. Powerful Yankees getting a comeuppance—the Alabama heart sings.

My sainted mother, like Julie, wouldn't have approved of me letting a Supreme Court justice drown although she might have made an exception for a liberal one, which this one was not. This one was beached in six inches of Rolling River water that was cold but not deadly. He was too fat to drown in so little water, and he seemed content to lie there and let the clear water wash feebly at his sins; my thought was that he needed a deal more water for a thorough job. I was raised amongst full immersion Baptists in Alabama, and they would have been calling for more water (more, more), pinching his nose shut, and pushing down on the bald spot on top of his head. For now, he seemed content to lie where he had fallen, his large belly offered to the sky and his eyes offered to me in mute challenge.

Sandra was in charge and trying mightily to pull him up, but it was me, up on the bank, he stared at, like he suspicioned that my heart did not fly fast enough to him when he fell. Sandra was in distress because she was responsible for taking Justice Grasso fly fishing on this early July day when court was on summer vacation. It was Sandra's bad luck to be a good fly fisher and in full possession of the confidence of our boss, Willard Jordan. Our friend Grasso was a bad fly fisher and not spry in any way you would notice. And, more besides, he was brash far beyond his abilities (truth, I kind of admired that). It's just my view, but he had no business wading in fast rivers, even the shallow parts where Sandra kept him to keep this kind of badness from happening. In the world of the rich, divided always into orderly parts, I was only in charge of leading the horse along the river because there was wine and food in the saddlebags and because the horse and I were part of the scenery.

Sandra tugged on Justice Grasso, but he was determined not to be helped by her or by himself. He was waiting for me to help because, as nearly as I could get it, it was his due and my place. So, if that was his attitude I thought it proper to leave him there for another ten months and let the spring runoff float him out. But I couldn't let Sandra get fired, so I waded in and took both his hands and gently rolled him forward. He gave me his hands like he was offering me a ring to kiss, and I let it pass because Sandra needed this job. It was a happy thing that he liked Sandra because she got a raise, which was welcome to her, and I got fired, which was welcome to me.

Until I got myself fired, Sandra and I both worked for this goofy little man name of Willard Jordan, who had, among other stuff, this huge ranch in the mountains of Colorado, which he bought for a ton of money and then had a few billion dollars left over, so if he wanted to buy some assorted ranch supplies down to the feed store he could do that. Jordan and the justice were not childhood friends but got to be pals after Jordan had some billions of dollars and after Grasso got to be a Supreme Court justice. Some people might say these two had things they could trade with each other, even over and beyond the joy of pure friendship. It was the kind of true friendship that caused old white men in helicopters to gather at the big house, hidden (from me) on the other side of the forested ridge. Sandra sometimes cooked at the big house, and she told me the rich old men got together and talked about how friendship was the truest of all true things, and she left it up to me whether to believe her or not.

I believed in true friendship because I had a few such friends back in Alabama and was making some in Colorado. None of us had a helicopter, though, except for Marcos's little boy, and it was made of blue plastic and crashed a lot. I was happy at Marcos's house, teasing Maria and helping Javier swoop his helicopter under the coffee table. Marcos and I moonlighted cleaning resort town condos and spent evenings plotting our own cleaning business. My mother had been resting a long time, but she was a faithful friend, and I still missed her and wished I had understood what the grinning pigs meant to her. Did she think that being dead was such delight as made you smile? I missed Eunice and her two little children back in Alabama. But Eunice had kindly run me out of Alabama so I would forget Julie, which, God love that Eunice, she thought would be possible for me to do. My mother belonged in Alabama because she always voted a straight God-and-money ticket and would have been shocked to hear they were separable—she was confused that way. Eunice and I believed another way, which made us fish on bikes in Alabama, which was, I guess, another reason to leave. Southern people have always been peculiar, and it would be a fine thing if that was all they were. But, ofttimes, they are also mean.

Sandra was fussing over Grasso and exclaiming over how he must be cold and ordering me to spread a blanket and open a picnic basket, and His Honor was thawing out and perking up.

Justice Grasso liked Sandra fussing over him and he liked me busy with a task.

"What did you say your name was?" he asked me. I hadn't said because he hadn't asked.

"Vernon, Your Honor."

"Don't 'Your Honor' me. We're out fishing. Call me Nico."

"I couldn't…"

"Call me Nico! That's an order of the court." He thought this one was plenty rich, and I thought underlings had been laughing at his jokes more than was good for him (as I set about to laugh at his joke). I peeked at Sandra to rule on whether I should call him Nico and she nodded.

"Yes, sir, Nico." The judge sighed at the "sir" but was satisfied.

"Where you from, Vernon?"

"Alabama, sir."

"Ah, that explains it." There was a pause, which grew, while I was left to ponder on exactly what being from Alabama explained to an Italian from New York. And then he tried (barely) to smooth it over by adding, "I thought I heard an accent."

I stayed busy because I could see Sandra was still alarmed although I was too new to know exactly why. I didn't know the way of things here, so I figured if alarm was right for Sandra it was right for rubes like me. I knew how to fetch things, so I emptied the saddle bags of wine and dainty finger food, which His Honor ate without daintiness. I offered to ride to the guest house and get him a change of clothes. Sandra, smarter, said no; I could ride up and bring a truck down to fetch the justice up to his room so he could change. She didn't want me going through the judge's things and didn't want the judge having to change clothes in the bushes, and I slowly got it. Sandra had a way about her, and I said she was all the way right and I could be back with a truck in two shakes of a lamb's tail, which expression I calculated would be Southern enough to satisfy my new pal, Nico.

Nico did not want a change of clothes and that was another order of the court. He wanted just a taste of the grape for his digestion. He threw down canapés like popcorn. I admired his appetite. I told him that in Muscle Shoals we appreciated people who lived with gusto. He slapped me on the back and said I was pronouncing it wrong, and he kept saying, "goostow, goostow," and I missed his joke, but happily he didn't waste time on it since there were more canapés.

Nico went into the bushes and then wanted to fish. It had gotten on in the day and fish were rising all up and down the river. Nico's eyes were big as Sandra rigged his fly rod with the right fly. I tidied up the picnic leavings as they waded into the river. Sandra stayed at Nico's left elbow. She quietly coached him about where to cast. She kept her hip pressed against him to help him balance, and I could tell that Nico did not mind this. I admired the work Sandra was doing. She had to keep Nico from falling over. She had to watch the river and tell him where to cast. She had to watch Nico's fly as it flew; sometimes she threw up her left arm in front of both of their faces so that justice was not inadvertently blinded. Sandra was a busy person, and even still she got Nico to catch a couple of nice fish, big rainbow trout. The river on Mr. Jordan's place was full of large fish because he bought only big ones from a private hatchery and fed them Purina fish chow to ensure their loyalty. My belief is that Nico thought it was a great country because anyone could go out anywhere and catch such fish, and I guess wine and dine on the richness of canapés and lean your hip against Sandra's to keep from falling in. It was a beautiful vision and all a billionaire or his dear friend had to do was reach out his hand.

Nico and Sandra took a break, and this time Nico wanted a beer. He was entertained when I called the bottle opener a church key, and I could tell Sandra didn't mind because Nico was catching fish and happy, and I was providing local color, which was my role, which had gotten lost in the unhappiness of Justice Grasso falling colorfully on his behind. I admit that Sandra got tense again when I produced a small, damp paper bag full of boiled peanuts I had made myself. It occurred to me that she might be regretting picking me for this job. But the judge loved the soft, salty peanuts with the beer, and Sandra was seeing her way clear. The judge lay back in the tall meadow grass, amongst the columbine and paintbrush and fireweed, and was lost in thought and maybe even happy—it was hard to know.

He took his break, and Sandra asked him if he wanted to fish more. He studied the water and the rising fish and pointed to a place far out in the river, on the other side of a deep, fast channel, and said, there, there was where he wanted to fish. I could see Sandra getting tense again, just as she had begun to see hope for this day, which the Lord had already made, so all that was allotted to her was to make the best of the Lord's leftover doings.

"Your Honor...Nico...we're going to have to wade through some heavy water to get to those fish. And they're really not any bigger than the ones..."

"I can see the water, young lady."

"How about we send Vernon for the truck and cross the bridge to the other side?"

"Sandra, Sandra." He patted her knee. It was actually a place up considerable from her knee, but he likely just missed his patting aim. "The thing is, I want to fish over there." He smiled.

"Besides, I have a plan. Vernon can help. You can both guide me across the river."

I knew it was bad at that moment without knowing exactly how. It was just bad and I wager it was what he had been thinking about when he lay in the grass and flowers and stared at the blue sky and deep drifts of cumulus clouds and drank beer and ate my boiled peanuts.

"But Vernon's no use to us. He doesn't have waders or wading shoes. He'll be swimming before we will."

"Oh, nonsense," said the judge, "he's young and strong." And that settled it and we set about to wade the river.

I was just happy to be wearing sneakers. They were still wet from when I went in earlier to retrieve Nico, which was not much matter. What mattered was that I had started out the day on Sandra's bad side because I showed up to work in sneakers, when she wanted me in cowboy boots. She explained to me that I was scenery, and the scenery was supposed to look Western, and she had no, none, zero interest in the excuse that I did not own any cowboy boots. This was the like amount of interest she had when I reminded her that there were maybe forty real wranglers with cowboy boots on the place, and I was not one of them. I was the janitor for one of the barns, which was itself about the size of R.E. Lee High School, and which contained startling expanses of rustic wood floors, alongside the hay-covered horse stalls. The job was mostly OK, but the barn needed a library for all the times I had nothing to do. As it was, the wranglers were in loafer's paradise, and I could know this because so was I. Willard Jordan was an answered prayer for the local cowboys because he didn't have any informed opinions about how many cowboys a person might need for a ranch this size. It was just bad luck for all of us that he impulsively bought a herd of actual cows before the foreman could distract him, and now the wranglers were all gone off trying to figure out something to do about the cows, and I had to lead a horse around in sneakers (I know, I know, but the thought of a horse in sneakers makes me smile). The thought of me in sneakers did not make Sandra smile, but she let it slide, and now we both got to be happy that I was not leading us to a watery grave in a worthless, slippery, filled-with-water pair of godawful cowboy boots.

Because leading us is what I was doing. Sandra had Nico follow me with a hand on each of my shoulders. She took from him his fancy creel and draped it over my neck so I could look down and see the two nice rainbows Nico had caught. She carried his fly rod and kept a hand in the small of his back for balance. It was a good plan because Sandra is a smart one, but smart sometimes comes up shy, which it did when I got out into the edge of the deep channel with the strong current. The water rushed up to my waist and I slipped but found a new footing and stood still for a moment testing the current. I thought we might make it, but I worried about Nico's weight and how hard it was going to be to pull him out if he got swept down in the strong current. Already the current was pushing and rocking me in fitful bursts, trying to lift my feet from the bottom, and I could feel Nico's hands tightening on my shoulders as I swayed in the water.

It turned out all good and I had no need to be troublous over pulling Nico out because he stopped where he was, in the calmer water, and gave me a mighty shove. I was surprised he had the strength for such a shove, but he got his considerable weight behind it, and I reckon he was inspired. I gave thought later to what he was inspired by. The simplest explanations almost always go best—he got mad when I didn't jump fast enough when he fell in. He decided to squash me when he found his chance, and he found it and for certain sure did it.

I went spinning down the current, kicking along with my sneakers. The water was icy, but Nico was right. I was young and strong. I heard Sandra yelling and I put up a hand and waved, but I didn't look back and made no attempt to make it to shore. I stayed in the main current and paddled like a bluetick hound with my nose sticking out of the water. I tucked the fancy creel against my chest because it had some air in it and was buoyant. So, Nico's creel was my makeshift raft, and I was satisfied with the all-around of life. I was sure Nico had some act planned for when I swam to shore, and I was happy to miss it. I was happy thinking (wrongly) that I was all done with the likes of him. I expected I owed Sandra a beer for the trouble I caused her, but I thought she would be OK—it was me Nico wanted to drown. I went around two bends of the river and came to the bridge from the ranch to the main highway, where I climbed out of the river and shook off in the sunshine. I smiled as I walked back to town, with the water squishing in my sneakers, thinking about Nico's feet flying up and his arms beating the air like helicopter rotors, beating so fast that it seemed like it might actually work, his arms might beat fast enough to suspend him permanently, so that he never squashed the clear and innocent water of the Rolling River with his ponderous behind.

When he fell, I was startled, as anyone would be. But I swear I didn't laugh; my mother taught me better than that. But, spare me, maybe I did smile for a moment, just long enough for Nico to notice; maybe I grinned then as I was grinning still, walking to town in the sunshine, thinking pigs.

11

Chapter 2

In the outskirts of Frisco, I stopped at Peak One Coffee and Chai Emporium, which always put me in mind of Kansas. Robert, the owner, had told me twice that it was not his intention to remind me of Kansas, and the second time he said this I reminded myself not to be overwhelmingly irritating by going back for thirds on Emporia, Kansas. After this, also, I decided not to ask him what a chai was, even though I couldn't help being curious. I remembered, to my credit, the lesson of wearing my mother down with questions. Though, truth, I was not now so curious about anything as I once was about everything.

I held open the door and pointed to my wet shoes and ordered a coffee. I took a table outside in the late afternoon sun and Mindy brought my coffee. My clothes had dried as far as damp and I thought they might be completely dry by the time the evening chill came on. The sun and the coffee warmed me.

"Have you been fishing, Tree?" Mindy asked.

I was confused until she pointed to the creel at my feet.

"Huh, I guess I have."

Sandra pulled in, driving my old truck. Rick, her husband, who also worked at the ranch, pulled in behind her, driving their new truck.

"I want that creel," said Sandra.

"It's yours. Can I at least have the fish?"

Sandra pulled up a chair. "Actually, you can have the creel and what's in it. The creel belongs to the ranch, not to Nico. Call it a severance package."

"I thought as much. They didn't fire you, did they?"

"I'm the hero. Nico pretended to slip down again on the way back to the bank, mostly by falling over on top of me, and I pulled him to shore as he struggled feebly. God, he's a drama queen. I know he's an old man, but he wasn't very feeble when he shoved you in the river. I'm the hero. You're the villain. Nico's the victim."

"So, seriously, they're not going after your job?"

"Just yours. Sorry. I'm golden."

"Jobs come and go. You can always find a job cleaning things that are dirty, if you can once make up your mind to be happy with the pay."

"It still sucked that he got you fired. I can try putting in a good word for you when I get Mr. Jordan alone. Today wasn't the time."

"No, no, and no. My work there is done. I may just take off for a little while. The rangers in the national forest can't draw a bead on my camper long enough to charge me rent. I've got a little money set by. I'm golden, too. I'm glad I didn't cause trouble for you. Is Rick going to join us? How about coffee?"

"Thanks. We have to go." She tossed me my keys. "It was pretty funny when Nico went in."

"How about when I went in?"

She laughed. "Yeah, that, too."

"I figured. Floating down the river, I got this picture of the headline, 'Redneck Drowned by Supreme Court Justice.' It was my only chance in life to be famous, and I blew it by surviving."

Julie, I thought, would have loved it. I called to mind the time she pushed me into Pine Creek. We were standing on a little bluff

13

over the creek and I couldn't seem to find a good moment to stop kissing her and she pushed me in to cool me off and it worked for some little while that was likely restful to her. My thought was that the other reason she pushed me in was because earlier I had the bad judgment to ask her aggravating questions about Miss Eudora Welty, and Julie brooked no nonsense on the sacred writings of Miss Eudora, even if this same Eudora was a lowly Mississippian and not a highly Alabamian (like the great Miss Harper Lee). Julie wanted to put together a book for her high school students that included some of the stories of Miss Eudora, and it was a thing that Julie did not get to do in her one life.

Julie was, I guess you'd say, my sacred subject. A part of me knew that it might now be to my betterment if I had known Julie long enough to get sick of her aggravating ways. Maybe I would have gotten tired of her with the trudging years and the regularity of marital tribulation. I could imagine the idea, but it didn't seem very real. In the leastways, I missed the chance to find out. In the gym at the high school, I herded debris with my push broom and you don't expect, ever, to make a turn on the gym floor and have your gatherings, gum wrappers and paper clips and love note confetti, drop off the keen edge of the world—and you, falling, too. A body naturally does not prepare for such doings.

I was hungry from Supreme Court swim class, and I craftily decided that if I showed up at Marcos's apartment with two fish I could turn this into a welcome and a dinner. I passed the snug library overlooking the river and I had time to stop in but my shoes were still squishing, and Sally, one of the librarians, had thin lips when it came to me. If Thomas were on duty I would be fine, but in this time of long, peaceful shadows I didn't want Sally to gripe on my day. Marcos's apartments were behind the library.

They were rundown but fine unless you were a member of the Junior Debutante League. The heat in the building worked, according to Marcos, so a family could stay warm in a cold land.

I knocked on the door while Maria was yelling at Javier and she opened the door without slowing her yelling. The lecture was in Spanish except for "your butt." She smiled at me while continuing to chew on Javier. She motioned me to lean over so she could kiss me and then announced my presence to Javier and Marcos. I suspicioned that she left off abusing Javier in Spanish and started in on me, but it was hard to know, even though I was working on my Spanish. Whenever I tried to use it, Maria covered her ears and begged me to stop.

In high school, I had a French teacher whose name, truth, was Miss French. She was old then and dead now. She was what they called a maiden lady, a forever bride of only France. She had lived and studied in Paris in her twenties and later glowed at the mention of this time, this feast for her heart. Her father, who was, in almost fact, a hardware store, and a good one, paid for her years in France, and she came home and cared for him when he got sick, and when he died she stubbornly refused to sell the narrow shell of a building in which the store and her father had existed. There must have been in this a decision that split the heartwood of her life. She stayed, against all reason, in Muscle Shoals and taught French, while the years blurred Paris into a mirage. I came to know her story a little bit in the way you come to know the stories of people in small towns. Their stories, slowly excreted, become things separate from the person, shells that sometimes fit and sometimes chafe. Miss French did not go back to Paris, and my supposing is that she must have thought that teaching young people this language and teaching about this Parisian oasis she had loved would make rich her life. At the time

I knew her, she was old and wiry and bitter and batty. It was one of those Southern lost causes that could not be let go. She broke her dreams on Southern redneck kids (me), who could not pronounce words correctly in any language, English first amongst them. Depending on how you take these things, it was tragic and comic and predictable to everyone except the one who needed the sound of that beautiful, remembered tongue, needed it like love.

So, when I said to Maria, "*Zapatos agua*," I was proud, but it made her ears buzz. She was happy with my fishes and gave me a knife and sent me to the river to clean them. She sent Marcos and Javier with me with instructions not to let me speak any more Spanish. Outside, Javier wanted to see the fish, and his eyes widened that I was a man to catch such fish. Javier was seven and full of movement and chatter. He walked on his father's feet and leaned against him and talked over him and the only notice Marcos paid was to tousle his hair. Marcos spoke slowly and carefully, which gave him dignity and a little extra time to find the right word. He smiled and allowed they were great fish and wanted to know where I had "lifted" them, which was the word choice of someone who was a born diplomat, and a good thing, too, because his welcome on this land was uneasy.

I knelt by the river and cleaned the fish, and Marcos sharply instructed Javier to pay attention and learn. I explained a little to Marcos about my day. He whistled softly. I think he didn't believe me, but he was not going to have an opinion about some high federal official Marcos did not know and did not want to know. Javier wanted to inspect the fish guts, and he let them slide slowly through his fingers. Javier asked what would happen to the fish guts I flung into the river, and I didn't know because there were no janitorial catfish in this high country to sweep the river bottom after the littering likes of me.

I had no experience of such a fancy creel. The outside was a buttery, dark leather, and the inside was flexible plastic, so the leather didn't get discolored by fish scum. I rinsed out the inside in the river and asked Javier if he wanted the creel. There was only going to be one answer to that question, so I checked the creel to be sure there were no dangerous judicial pocket knives anywhere. I found a waterproof compartment with a book of matches. There was also something like a letter or brochure, but I couldn't tell much about it in the fading light, so I stuffed it and the matches in my back pocket and hung the creel around Javier's neck. We took the two fish inside. I offered to cook them because I also can be a diplomat, and Maria handed a beer to me and one to Marcos and made us sit at the kitchen table while she cooked. Maria admired Javier's new creel and said sure, he could use it as a book bag if he wanted, but he had to scrub it out with soap.

Maria wanted to know where I had gotten the fish, but she used the word stolen rather than lifted. I aimed for a lofty dignity when I said if she thought they were stolen she should not eat them. She gave me the finger, which required no translation, although Javier yelled at her for using bad words, and she said she didn't use any words, and they had an argument over this that was deeply satisfying to both. When the argument was winding down, Javier turned his back and Maria gave him the finger. He sensed something and whirled, but she was tending the fish and Marcos was smiling dreamily into his *cerveza*. I told Maria a little about how I had gotten the fish, and I was not surprised to learn from her that this entire day was my fault. Not only was the stuff with Nico my fault, but, also, I had caused Javier to get in trouble at his summer reading program—I had done this in ways I did not fully understand, but I did understand that I could choose to argue, or go without dinner, up to me all the way.

Maria breaded the fish and filled the air with a cloud of spices and set the pan on the burner to fry while the laggard spices in the cloud were still settling over the counter. Maria got herself a beer and joined us at the table.

"So, how could you get yourself fired? I told you not to go to work for that rich guy. There's something wrong with those people."

"I don't care about getting fired."

"I know you don't. But sometime you will start caring again and then you will wish you had listened to me. Just listen to me and do exactly what I say. Don't listen to Marcos. He doesn't know anything. Just listen to me until you get better."

"I'm better. I know what I'm doing."

"Save that bullshit for Marcos."

"Don't say bullshit, Mama."

Maria cuffed Javier gently on the top of his head. "You think that telling me not to say bullshit makes it OK for you to say bullshit? I know that trick. You don't say bullshit."

"So, who's this guy you pushed in the river?" she asked.

"I didn't push anybody. He pushed me."

"You sound like Javier. Of course, you didn't push anybody."

Maria leaned across the table and cuffed me on top of the head. "Not Tree, *mi ángel*."

"It was a judge."

"You pushed a judge in the river?"

"A Supreme Court justice."

Maria looked at Marcos, who shrugged. "Big," he said.

"Are you crazy? And you stole his fish?"

"No, he pushed me."

"What difference does that make? Who cares? You made some big *jefe* mad. You don't care about anything. That's dangerous."

"Maria, wait. I didn't push anybody. He pushed me in the river because he thought I laughed at him. He got me fired. That's all. It's over. He won—that's the main thing. If I had won, there might be a problem. Now, he will never give me another thought unless it's to tell stories about me swimming down the river. It's done. And I'll get around to looking for another job, just to make you happy. Maybe Marcos and I will start that business."

"I don't know. Maybe I don't want Marcos in business with you right now."

She saw this hurt my feelings because she touched me on the arm and said one day, one day, and in the meantime just do everything I say. And then she turned to Javier and said that goes for you, too.

"So, what about Papa?"

"San Marcos? San Marcos? He already does everything I say." Marcos continued smiling dreamily into his beer bottle.

Maria got up to check the fish and fix some sides. I began a question about helping with dinner, and she cut me off and said no and stop asking because the answer is not going to change. She told Javier to set the table, and he promptly went to work. I had learned that Javier talked back about everything but a chore. Maria brought the steaming fish and rice and a salad to the table. For me, she had nuked a slice of French bread because she knew I liked this whole puffy wheat thing. She gave me water to drink because she drew the line at making sweet Alabama tea.

Irina knocked and entered with no seam atwixt the knocking and the entering. Maria had Javier set another place. Irina made the rounds and kissed Marcos and Maria and Javier and gave me the kind of chaste air kiss safe for a leper, and I could see Maria narrowing her eyes. Irina apologized and said she didn't know they had company and she couldn't think of staying as she swept open her napkin and pulled up the chair next to mine.

Irina was Marcos's younger sister. She lived with their parents in an apartment across the courtyard. She was family and had privileges, which grated on Maria.

"I'm glad you could eat with us tonight, Irina," said Maria, "especially on a night when Tree is here."

"I'm always happy to see Tree," Irina said politely. "And Javier, my favorite in all the world."

"I asked her to drop in," said Marcos, helpfully, and Maria rewarded him with a special look.

My thought was that Irina was just bored, or maybe trying to aggravate Maria for reasons of her own. I mean, I got what Maria was thinking, but it just seemed like a TV show or something else not quite real. I was always struck by how the stories in books, good ones, seemed real to me, more real ofttimes than life. The stories on TV, however, seemed like a nice high school play. On TV, when an actor turned and sighed, I could not get out of my mind that they were turning towards the camera. Maria could suspicion all day, but that did not make Irina interested in me by any stretch. At thirty-two, I had my full growth and was all done getting better looking. Irina was twenty-five and gorgeous and for all I knew might get more so with passing time.

And, same, none of that made me interested in Irina. Julie was six months gone. I counted the months in my head to see if that could be. January in Alabama and four months stunned like a bad fighter. I got to this high piece of Colorado the first of May, with snow everywhere and nothing but some shy intimations of green grass, and Billy let me park my camper beside his house and sometimes let me tramp around the ridges with him. I found a family table with Billy and Lena and the kids, and then I met Marcos on a landscaping crew and soon had another family table. Truth, I was grateful, but most of the time I didn't want a family table and needed to be, had to be, alone, to try to read and to fold my hands firmly over my solar plexus, which wanted to be held in. So, when the snow crept farther up the hills, Billy helped me find a place in the national forest where I could camp for free, and I suspicion maybe he asked the badges not to notice how long I stayed. Billy drove a snowplow and other heavy equipment, and he knew everybody. What did I know of the mountains? It stood to my kind of reason that the snowplow driver was the most influential citizen in town.

But still, Irina. She was not interested in me and the same the other way. But once when she leaned for the salt and brushed against my shoulder I was confused. And later, driving home, I watched the headlights suspend like a bridge over some steep drop-off in this tricky terrain. I watched the path of the headlights and called to mind the words of Mr. Charles Dickens, that great life-giver, who said, mysteriously, "Recalled to life." My education was as random as the scratching of a drunken hen, but I did not often forget what people told me, especially when they talked to me direct like Mr. Dickens. I wondered if I would be recalled and in what way. I was recalled already, if reading books counted—and it did. During the time I was stunned, I could not read a book or remember having read one. Before Julie, reading books was mostly what counted, along with tramping the Alabama woods; those were alone and peaceful years, in which there was the gentle rocking of small hopes and small sorrows bobbing off towards the curving of the earth.

So, books called to me. In calling me his uncle, "*Tio* Tree," Javier also called. Tramping the hills with Billy, or, yes, Irina brushing against my shoulder, these were calls. Maybe I was called, recalled, to life, without yet knowing what that life might be. But Julie called, too. And she was as much (more?) a part of life for me as these other callings. Truth, I was making a life with Julie. OK—not the one we planned. But we talked like before. We laughed. She teased me out of being sad, if I just let her. I did not tell people this although this was part of what Maria guessed. I was right when I told Sandra you could always find a job cleaning things that were dirty, and mostly you did these jobs by yourself. So, Julie could be with me at work and when I walked the hills and sat by a fire in the woods. We could talk about books and take turns picking a book so I could be sure it was not going to always be the great Eudora (no disrespect). These were things that made me happy. I knew Maria would not approve, but just because Maria had this lovely confidence in herself did not make her right. I felt called by Julie, called to a kind of life, and when I felt that call, I felt a kind of joy.

Chapter 3

In Alabama, what with all the Protestants, the pope was less than big, but surely more than small. I'm just saying, setting aside what you think you know of bumpkins, I had heard of the man. More than once. I admit that, looking at the letter, I got confused because, having seen the return address on the envelope, my mind rushed into a spin on why the pope was writing me. Theological advice, mayhap? Unitarian? Trinitarian? Vegetarian? Vexing questions, all. Surely, he had better advisors, though, unless maybe it was about hounds, which someone named Francis could rightly take an interest in. I liked to think I knew as much about bluetick hounds as anyone in Muscle Shoals, but the thing is I personally knew a couple of guys who were plenty good with dogs and were Catholic to boot, so you could see why my mind was spinning.

Maybe the letter was a job offer from some maintenance crew chief at the Vatican, using the company stationary, and not from the pope at all. So perchance they had heard about my work at R.E. Lee High and were looking for an assistant janitor in the Sistine Chapel. I felt clear I did not want St. Peter's Square because I had seen pictures, and it would be a long, dusty pilgrimage for one man with a push broom. I was fetched up by the fancy Vatican stuff on the return address. The whole envelope was that thick and soft it could have been cream cheese icing on a carrot cake; this thickness is why I remembered thinking it must have been a brochure when I took it out of Nico's creel in the dim light the night before and shoved it in my back pocket, and why I suddenly knew to look at the addressee, who was not Tree Purcell, and, more besides, I could now stop worrying about sweeping St. Peter's Square. I was embarrassed, but alone in my embarrassment, which is always best.

I tossed the letter onto the big rock that was my coffee table and poured myself a refill from the new, blue, speckled pot that was made to look like an old-timey, blue, speckled pot. The coffee was stout and good and my granite coffee table really was granite, a boulder half-buried in the ground, requiring no hot pad to protect it from the heat of the coffee pot. This granite coffee table had been fired in the earth's stern heat miles below and eons before and pushed to the earth's surface just in time to receive my blue, speckled coffee pot, with matching cup. I was pleased with the timing because a million years, plus, minus, and I would have had no coffee table.

I drank my coffee and set about to admire the morning. I liked Alabama, and it was full of good country, but it was more laid flat, so if you wanted to see how many oak trees were in the next acre you had to arise, as the Christians would have it, and walk. In Colorado, it was as if someone big, someone like my friend Billy Mapp, reached long fingers into the earth and tilted the display case up so you could sit and have your coffee and count the trees from the comfort of your camp chair beside your granite coffee table. It was convenient, except when some moment came when you had to stand and walk up one of those hills, then less so.

My new friend Billy was teaching me about hiking in the mountains, and I can't allow it was restful. I said to Billy that I wanted to find a loop trail through these hills that had its beginning and its ending at the exact same spot and was an easy downhill stroll all the way. Billy reflected on this and said that a trail like that would be good and a life like that better.

There was a long view in the mountains that made for good postcards. All this tilting of the land meant you could see far, but the bad was that far could see right back at you, and I didn't always want to be seen, to feel seen. The wide, open spaces that the cowboys loved sometimes made me tremulous. I didn't know much about cowboys, but I suspected that they were rarely (publicly) tremulous. Before Julie left the world, I never saw fit to think much about what my public thought, or whether I even had a public; and, after she left, I couldn't work up much interest in the opinions that others might have of me. So, I was now free to be tremulous at will. I was training myself to cope with the open spaces, but, truth, I liked the little narrow bunk in my camper. I had this habit when sitting of folding my hands under my solar plexus and pressing gently up—it was a comfort.

Sitting in my ragged camp chair, looking at the wide, open spaces, made me feel like my own molecules might separate, each from the other, and drift randomly up and away, like they did not have enough mass to stick against the earth. And then I might not be able to corral again my dancing dust motes. I did not want to be scattered to all the contrary winds, did not want my molecules to dissipate into the void. I did not want this at all except for the times when it was all I wanted.

This was the time of the morning when I sat outside and had my coffee and sometimes talked a little to Julie. About nothing in particular. Maybe she wanted to hear about the junco that perched on my coffee table to eat my bread crumbs. I liked these little mountain birds. Billy had taught me their names. I liked the chickadees in prim shades of gray and black, who also favored my bread crumbs. The juncos were best, though, because they had feathers colored slate and rust (but they didn't put on airs about it). A chickadee scrambled over the Pope's letter and pecked an inquiry at a thickly embossed "S" and learned, I suppose, that it was not a worm. The chickadee left behind a tiny blob of shit, which seemed OK to me because a bird has got to shit somewhere. I was always struck by the way birds just shit on the go. Foxes and rabbits and other such creatures paused to shit, maybe so they could concentrate. And while studying on it, it came to me that bird shit was white and those pausing creatures had brown shit, as best I knew, and I was happy that there was this new stuff to think on even if there were not going to be a big lot of people sharing my interest in the color of shit. But Eunice had told me, rightly, that it was a welcome sign whenever I took an interest, and I had no reason to think that this principle of living excluded bird shit.

I tried to make myself wonder what His High Pope Holiness wanted with His High Honor Nico, but nothing as interesting as bird shit came to mind. I knew that Nico was a bigtime Catholic but could not recall how I knew this, likely from Julie. As I said, Nico was on Julie's shit list although I could not call the particulars. She just scorned him, plain and simple, scorned him through and through. I called to mind her ranting about his hypocrisy, and I know we all hate hypocrisy so much we will take trouble to hide our own. Julie was a good person and didn't have much hypocrisy to speak of; however, she could be righteous about how clean she kept our house. In light of my love for her, I found this to be a trespass easy in the forgiving. When she got going on this, she seemed blind to the fact that dirt was my trade, that I knew more about dirt than, say, most of the learned English teachers at the high school. I was amused that she seemed to see no connection between the dirt at school, whose removal and replenishment formed my livelihood, and the dirt in our home. Her unexamined assumption was that I would know nothing about housecleaning, and she sheltered me from it. I went along with this. Out of love. Besides, if this was all the hypocrisy she had, it was worth preserving. As to my own hypocrisy, I was none too troubled by it and thought it more loving to first help others with theirs.

I supposed it might be natural, the pope writing to Nico. They had Catholic stuff in common and maybe they both liked to whittle those little wooden Santos that made Catholics feel to home and that made Protestants feel like killing Catholic human beings for hundreds of years, give or take on the time, and, of a truth, both ways on the killing. More truth, I didn't start with any strong feelings about Nico one way or the other. I laughed at him a little bit for falling in the river, and he caught me at it and pushed me in the river, and he likely laughed about that, so forget about that part of it. But here's a thing, a thing I thought on as I was swimming down the river—it was pure good luck that I could swim. That was not a thing Nico and I had discussed before he pushed me in the river because it would have, you know, ruined Nico's surprise for me. The current where he made me walk the plank was fierce and the water in places deep. So, I guess it was all good fun to Nico, and it turned out to be so to me, but no thanks to my pal, Nico.

I expect Nico thought (rightly) that I was an ignorant hick. Fair enough on that, and turnabout on my opinion of him is still fair play. So, I was happy to forget about Nico except for his letter, still sealed, lying on the planet's old granite, with a speck of pale bird shit on it. I thought about hunting up Sandra to return the letter, but then I came back to the idea that Nico and I were even up and maybe I was even owing him one for not asking to see my swimming certificate. If he wanted the letter, he could hunt me up and come after it. He hadn't bothered to open it, so he may have thought of it as junk mail, just another papal solicitation for the Little Sisters of Infinite Mercy, tossed absently into the creel and forgotten. I found that I was interested in the question of the bird shit more than the contents of the letter.

Julie, though, Julie. I found in the way of talking to her that was my habit that she was interested in the contents of the letter, sealed or not. Not only did she scorn Nico, but she was more likely than I to see politics as personal, or I guess you could fairly say to see things in politics that I was sometimes blind to. I was stuck between Julie and my mother on this one.

I should have done right but did not—instead, I read the personal mail from the pope to a justice of the Supreme Court. I fetched a kitchen knife to stand in for a silver, jewel-encrusted letter opener, because it seemed fitting. I have always been a quick reader, and, in that moment, I was like a swift barn swallow that banked left to intercept a rising mosquito and flicked it seamlessly from the air. My mother would say that barn swallows reading other people's mail are sinful creatures, no matter how richly colored their feathers, no matter how ringing their flight path against the dusky vespers sky. Julie would say, Tree, shut up with the barn swallows and tell me what the damn letter says.

The pope made out to be not angry but sad in the face of the sinful Nico. This "more sad than angry" thing is an old cross, and passing heavy. My mother, physically small person that she was, used to lift one end of this metaphorical cross with two hands and drag it across the floor and lash it right to my back. I wondered at not falling clean through to China under the black singularity of its weight.

I do note well that Christians, no matter how they might wish it otherwise, do not have exclusive rights to "more in sorrow than anger." If the Christians did own this copyright, the other religions would have no chance, and Jewish mothers would be bereft of purpose, once again the aimless desert wanderers of the old times.

Other than sorrow, the pope himself showed no real style in the letter; a little liveliness always goes good, but maybe he really was too sad to be lively. An angry man, puffing and pawing and snorting, is a better friend to style than silent tears. The pope called Nico his brother in Christ, which I believed mainly was hokum. Maybe it was ritually hopeful language, like calling high government folk "The Right Honorable." Some might be honorable, I guess. Depends how strict you are on the grading. Julie was a stickler on grading, but she was so loved by her students she made them happy to get a "C," and she made them see the correctness of it, because the bar had been set by Miss Eudora Welty, so they understood it was a right honor to be judged on the same scale as Miss Eudora, and passing miraculous to belong to her same species. That Julie could make you fair see.

So, this letter from the pope was short but no more to the point than I am. The pope proved himself a master of indirection. He never got around to saying right out that Nico had sold his soul to Willard Jordan for thirty pieces of silver, silver sliding down some silent electronic wire to a bank beside an island palm. If Judas could have gotten his money wired silently he might have saved his reputation, and there might be children today named Judas. Can Judas come out to play? The pope mentioned the poor and mentioned the rich, and the pope was sorry that so many chose to minister to the rich. The pope was sad because Nico, in the zealous and pharisaical pursuit of his job, protected with one hand the rights of the poor from unreasonable search and seizure, and with the other hand made sure they had nothing but a copper penny and a marijuana cigarette worth seizing. And for Willard and his friends, Nico performed benedictions of gold and silver that made nice their lives. Those damn Pharisees—ye will have them with you always.

I confess straightaway that I am paraphrasing—pharisaical was my word and not the pope's although I like to think the pope might have used this lively word were not his sadness so heavy on him.

That was mostly it for the letter, all implication, and no movie evidence, like a Swiss bank account number. The pope allowed he suffered at the wrongdoing but offered only his suffering as proof of Nico's misdeeds. The pope encouraged Nico to pray for the strength to do better. As I thought on it, Nico might hate having my letter (I had come to think of it as mine) made public, but it probably wouldn't kill him or make him lose his job or make him stop being pals with Willard Jordan.

Dear pal Nico, who baptized me in the clear, chilly waters of the Rolling River—I don't believe I'm too crazy about you. What's more, Julie scorned you; the pope isn't looking to wash your feet; so, you had best see to your own self...Pal. Me and Julie and the pope might just smite you, hip and thigh, for so long, at least, as I can make myself care.

So, my thought was that I would let this letter lie and see if more little birds decided to shit on it while I admired this big open country and pressed my hands against my solar plexus for the safety that was in it. Despite the fearsome open spaces, I liked these mountains although I couldn't figure out how I might survive the winter in my trailer. A question for another day. For today, I gave some thought to groceries and firewood and the guest list for dinner. Sometimes the guest list was just me and sometimes more and I marveled that I had such a fancy thing as a guest list.

.....

I was regaining the power of speech although always it seemed it was a power that came into and left my life according to its own whims. Some of us used to go fox hunting or raccoon hunting at night with our hounds in Alabama. We liked it and the dogs liked it and the foxes tolerated it because we and the dogs were cunningly ineffectual. We were ineffectual at wildlife harassment because we liked to sit around the fire and drink whiskey and tell stories. When the power of speech was upon me, and the power of whiskey within me, I was pleased to tell a story. My belief is that the dogs sensed our lack of interest in the hunt. On chilly nights, the dogs would call off the hunt early and sneak back to the warmth of the fire and doze. Sometimes they would yip happily in their sleep, as if they had just bitten, snicker-snack, through the fat, bushy tail of brother fox. And even those of us without dog genes understood the yips. Because the dark and the crackling fire and the whiskey made us feel, also, that catching foxes, of every kind, from that moment forward, would be, for us, the merest leaping play of a child.

In those years before Julie, I was a solitary person. My dogs liked me and my mother liked me, before she left the world, and Cousin Eunice was always there. My hunting buddies liked me, but, truth, they weren't many, and, more truth, if they weren't misfits they wouldn't have been sitting by a fire with the likes of me. My hunting buddies and Eunice liked my powers of speech, which I think it not bragging to say could be lively. My speech was often best under the stars, beside the swirling sparks of a fire.

And I might as well say it here as anywhere. My speech and my thoughts mostly lived separate lives. I could for sure talk about dancing dust motes with my hunting buddies, but I had a care not to mention that this was part of the science story of Brownian motion, a conversation about atoms that Einstein jumped in the middle of in 1905. I knew this from finding a physics book in the library of R.E. Lee High, when I was supposed to be dusting the shelves. Interesting stuff that made a wonderment in my head, but best kept silent, so I could be free and easy with my hunting buddies and they free and easy with me the same. Alabama mostly does not favor scholarly janitors. From an early age, my speech lived the one life and my thoughts the other, and the separation made getting on with others a smoother thing, but sometimes made a clanging within myself. And then Julie came to me, and I could be all one. Thanks, Julie.

I speak of my hunting buddies in Alabama, Robbie and Jeff, because my life was finding this pattern again in Colorado, which seemed odd and unexpected to me, yet a comfort. Maybe there are just lots of people who like to sit around a fire of an evening and take a sip of whiskey and tell a story should one come to mind. I liked it that none of these gatherings were planned. People just showed up or not, with only the certainty that I would have a fire going, mostly small so as not to frighten the stars into hiding. The stars in this high country drew me up and out but not in a way that frightened me like the big open spaces of the day did. The difference between day and night made no sense, but there it was. As I was surprised about the stars, my surprise was no less for the people who came to my fire. Unlike Alabama, there were women as well as men. And sometimes children.

Billy came often, sometimes with Lena and their two boys. Their boys played with Javier even though Javier was much younger. The three boys left camp heading up the dirt road and an hour later showed up from the opposite direction, having circled around us in the dark hills like Jeb Stuart's Confederate Calvary. Billy's boys were casual about this feat, but Javier ran to Marcus, bursting. I studied Marcos and Billy and saw them to be alike as parents. When fit, they gave the boys the gift of ignoring them, so they were free to wade in streams and to throw errant rocks at arrogant ravens.

Sometimes Billy brought his friend, George Monroe. George loved a campfire and talk and whiskey. When George was there, he took charge of the fire and built it so high that it scared away the distant fire of the stars. I liked a small fire, but it was worth it to see the happiness George took from a bonfire. George was the editor of the local paper, and he talked smart but didn't look it. I thought newspaper editors were supposed to wear white shirts, even if the armpits were yellowed, and a tie with ketchup stains. I don't know; that's how they looked in Alabama. But I had run into George in the daytime in town, when he was working, and he was just the same scruffy as when he was drinking whiskey and building bonfires to defend my campsite against attack from marauding stars. George brought his wife once, and she was nice, but I don't think she liked so much the bathing in wood smoke.

Once a woman named Iris came, a friend to all these friends. She kept wanting me to talk, but I could not think how to talk and fear her all at once. I don't mean to say she wasn't polite to me, but she was Cleopatra all through. I was happy I met her because it was going back through time. I had this notion, and I'm still not ready to give it up, that all you need do is lie in wait and you will meet all these people from history that you have read about. Cleopatra. Samuel Johnson. George Washington. They are all still around in one guise or another but no longer driven to greatness by the hard press of circumstance. My hunch was always that Washington would be less stern with less responsibility. I met Washington once, farming sixty acres in Winston County, and he did seem content and had an easy smile. I don't think he even knew he was George Washington, but I was of no mind to intrude on his privacy by asking. It made me happy to think of all the famous folk I had yet to meet.

I made no headway figuring out why these new friends had anything to do with the likes of me. I was no George Washington or, thank goodness, no R.E. Lee. But they liked me some, and I was happy for it. I called, too, that Julie liked me, in this same way that was not to be reckoned. Julie was also above my station—certified English teachers don't marry the school janitor, especially not in Alabama. But she was happy with me even when I was not happy with myself. These Colorado people seemed happy with me although I could not be sure about Iris. They were above my station, except maybe for Billy, the snowplow driver, and Marcos, the always worker. For reasons I was not exactly sure of, I had the notion that Billy would be a forever snowplow driver, but that Marcos could wind up being governor of Colorado, or maybe Chihuahua, depending on the eddies of fate, unexpected eddies I knew of more deeply than I wished.

In one such eddy, Julie fell in love with me because she happened on me reading aloud from *A Tale of Two Cities* by Mr. Dickens (a great man I still hope to meet). It was October and a Tuesday and dark and Julie wandered into the gym with the notion of shooting some baskets instead of grading papers. I was alone with my push broom in one hand and in the other a book. I liked the sound of the words rising into the big empty space, and I liked the soft rasp of the broom. Julie sat quietly in the bleachers and listened and forgot I was a janitor with a plain face. There came a time when I tried to explain to her about my station and hers, but she was deaf to good sense, and I gave it up (eagerly) because she was the most beautiful woman in the whole history of there being women. I considered that maybe it was Mr. Dickens she loved (in fair, the words were his), but I made up my mind not to mind. If a big man like Mr. Dickens can't give a small man a hand, what's the point of bigness? And here's the other thing. Once I decided to accept my good luck, I could see no end to it. No one young and in love does. Mr. Dickens in his book about the two cities leaves the lovers in peace after their troublous times. But I had lived some and read some and should have known better. In this life, I never knew my father, and my mother died too early. And in my life of reading, Mr. Shakespeare stood aloof and let there be a forever end to the good luck of Romeo and Juliet. Mr. Homer, for his part, gave not much rest to those young Greeks of old times. I knew all this. I had shed the tears of a lonely person over their sadness and some sadness of my own. I knew all this and forgot it in the firelight glow of Julie's red hair. As anyone would.

In these Colorado mountains, I had more or less decided to go on, but it's strange to go on with no notion of who you are or who you might become. These people around me who I liked seemed to live in a purpose. I don't know if they lived for a purpose— that's not what I'm talking about. They lived in a purpose as I had with Julie. And now I lived apart from purpose, but I was getting so I could be amused at such a strange pass to life. Kind of amused. And kind of amused at myself that pressing gently upward on my solar plexus was a comfort.

Chapter 4

There was a blackened fire ring, and I started a small, shy fire with kindling from my burlap sack, full of paper food wrappers, copies of George's small newspaper, and dry sticks from the aspen forest. Later, with the fire burning bold, the gang began to filter in, and I was happy, happy to have company, while yet alone. George showed up and began to turn the fire into a bonfire that would chase away the stars, and I didn't mind.

It was maybe not a fancy garden party, but it was a nice little group on a cool, summer evening in the mountains. My granite coffee table had two whiskey bottles on it and a bottle of brandy. I sampled the brandy and decided that its unknown provider was a Prince of Colorado. Also on the table were a bag of corn chips and some suspect dip, both provided by me, as I tried to grow towards culinary refinement. I had thought about making a bowl of grits, but I knew the explanations would be wearisome and the jokes all corn and pone and Alabama. There was a galvanized bucket with ice and beer, and Javier's blue helicopter floating on its side. And then a sheriff's car pulled up, red and blue lights flashing, and Iris (*née* Cleopatra) got out on the driver's side and a big man in uniform got out on the passenger side. The little band of partiers switched from cheers to boos when he reached back in and turned off the flashing lights.

This was going to be Hector Morales, the sheriff, a person in my life. I got that he already was Hector when he arrived. I got that Hector did not pop into existence at that moment, that things and people and teeniny light photons all existed apart from me, stuff to wonder about while you're buffing the long high school halls. I got that what we see of the world is most likely real, though I am not perfectly resigned to it.

I remember calling to mind the queer notion of quantum entanglement at some point after Julie died but before much good sense had returned to me. The way I thought I understood it was that two subatomic particles (teeniny rascals), struck by the same figurative cue ball, can afterwards spin in synchrony, no matter that they carom in different directions, no matter how much cold, dark space comes between them. And, more besides, those two billiard balls, prowling separately across the undulating fabric of space, have somehow managed to escape time. (Mr. Einstein, not time's fool, found it spooky that things might escape time, and disapproved.) But by this entanglement notion, in no time, outside of time, the one spinning ball always instantly conforms itself to any change in spin of its distant mate, so that billiard ball synchronized spinning can continue right on across the cold reaches that make a body feel alone. (And, no, it doesn't seem to matter whether the billiard balls are solids or stripes.)

It's a beautiful metaphor for entangled yet parted lives, and it's a much more plausible explanation for communion with the dead than anything else on the market. I liked it. I remember thinking our tiniest pieces, Julie's and mine, knew each other so deeply, were so entangled, that they spun as one across the gnawing void. And in my pain, because of my pain, there were these ecstatic moments when entanglement took over my mind. Mostly, though, time passed (thanks, Einstein), and I gradually remembered that entanglement might be true for spinning wavicles, but for me and Julie it was only a metaphor. Wait...fix that. It was not <u>only</u> a metaphor—it was <u>simply</u> a metaphor, lovely and perhaps even timeless. But man cannot live by metaphors alone (even mixed ones)—I knew that, while still not knowing what it was that man could, alone, live by. At least that's how it came to my understanding in those dark Alabama times.

I assumed I was about to be rousted by Hector because as such things go there's always a rule against something you're doing. Maybe illegal camping (for sure illegal camping) or illegal firewood or illegal blue helicopters in the beer tub. The one thing I wouldn't cop to is littering because I hated it for professional reasons. I was pretty much guilty of everything else and content to plead it so. Hector, whose existence I granted but whose name I did not yet know, was in no hurry to roust me if that was his goal. He wandered slowly through the gang, shaking hands, trading hugs, patting backs, doing nothing if not taking communion. Billy brought him a beer, and, standing together, Hector was still a big man but now dwarfed by Billy. They liked each other, which cheered me, even if I was about to be rousted.

Hector finally got to me as I sat in my camp chair. He took off his jacket and dropped it on the coffee table. He sat on the ground, which I did not expect, with his back against my coffee table.

"Are you the Tree?"

"My nickname chose me before I could do anything about it, Sheriff Morales." I was reading by firelight from his gold nameplate.

He stuck out his hand. "I'm Hector. No nickname. No title. When I was a kid, I wished my friends would call me Heck. I can't remember why."

"Are you here to roust me?"

"Hah. I'm here to write down your driver's license number and check you out. I could roust you for about ten different things, none of which I much care about. Here's how I do. When there's a mind-bending party, or even a dull one like this, I just show up and have one beer. You'd be surprised how much that calms people, and calms the party. I visit with my people and ask about their kids. I've been sheriff a long time. It's how I do."

Hector wrote down my driver's license number and handed it back. "Do you have kids I should ask about?"

"No kids."

"I heard your wife died. I lament your loss."

"As do I. A guy in a book, an Italian major, lost his wife and said it's hard to resign yourself. True enough." And I thought the major also angrily meant that the peace of resignation was impossible, but I did not say this because it did not cheer on a conversation.

"Billy says you sit out here all day and read books unless he makes you go hiking with him."

"Yes."

"Good. Book readers mostly don't cause me a lot of trouble. Take Billy. Think how much trouble he could cause me if he took his nose out of a book and went on a rampage with his snowplow. Or without the snowplow, for that matter."

We both looked over at Billy, towering over Iris, and smiled.

"Then take George," said Hector. "You expect the newspaper editor to know everything, and he does, at least compared to me. But he caused me many problems when he was younger and liked to fight."

"When was that?"

Hector took off his baseball cap and scratched through his thinning hair. "Thursday?"

"How about you?" I asked.

"I hate to fight."

"Reading books."

"Louis L'Amour westerns on Sunday afternoons while I'm watching baseball."

"Do I need to move my camper?"

Hector shrugged. "Not now. Depends who complains. I'll send word through Billy. Or maybe I'll get a new Louis L'Amour and come sit in the sunshine with you."

"That would be good."

"But only if your driver's license checks out. Otherwise I'll come tomorrow and throw you down and step on your neck and arrest you." A warning. And, also, an offered chance to leave in the night for another county that Hector was not sheriff of if I knew he was going to find something bad on my record. Perhaps a wise sheriff.

"How about if I just surrender?"

"That works."

"Iris was driving your car. She scares me by half and makes me curious by the other half. Do you have a thing with her?"

"Huh, maybe book readers can be trouble, after all. I know you all of five minutes and you're asking me questions that are none of your business."

I grinned. "Maybe I'm just being the Tree of Knowledge. Your nickname seeks you out."

"You're starting to piss me off. Be careful the sheriff doesn't seek you out."

"I'm easy to find, Hector. But I've known a couple of mean Southern sheriffs, and you're not one of them. I watched you move through the group. These people love you. If I'm a bad guy, you'd put your boot on my neck. But not for getting into your business with Iris."

"You're pretty damn sure?"

"Pretty sure. Plus, I'm just exactly 50-50 on whether I care if you put your boot on my neck or not. There's always the question of whether I have anything else I care about losing."

My new friend Hector was silent and shifted around to free his pistol where it was wedged between him and my coffee table and jabbing him in the back. "I am sorry...and sorry I never knew your wife."

"Julie."

"Julie. I will remember. And your rude question about Iris. Old friends, I guess. Do you know the right way to describe all the people in your life? With her, with anybody, I'm a slow mover. I think, unlike you, I want to keep caring what happens to me. As you may know, people who no longer care can be dangerous. I don't want to have to resign myself to any more loss if I can help it. Maybe that's smart—maybe no."

Javier came up, looking for his helicopter. I told him to have a beer and he vehemently told me his mama would not let him drink beer, and I told him OK, but he could at least look at the beer, that much solace was allowed even unto a child, and, in that moment, he remembered where he left the helicopter. He fished it out and shook the water from it. I asked him if he knew the sheriff and Javier shook his head and was shy but, also, could not take his eyes from Hector's gun.

"Hector, this is Javier—a good guy."

Hector put out his hand and they shook.

"Maybe I will show you the gun sometime but only if your parents say it's OK. Guns are dangerous. Don't ever touch one by yourself."

Javier yawned and crawled with his helicopter into my lap. "*Tio* Tree, a story."

Marcos and Maria had come up in Javier's wake to be sure, I suppose, that Javier did not say bullshit in front of the sheriff. Iris trailed behind them and taunted, "Yes, *Tio* Tree, a story."

"Hector?"

"Of course, a story."

"No. I was talking to Javier. Do you want a story about Hector?"

"Isn't this Hector? With the gun?"

"No, a story about a long-ago Hector."

"OK."

"Hector lived in place called Troy, a long way from here. He was a great warrior."

"How far away?"

"Let me think. Across half a continent. An ocean. A big sea. Then a small sea."

"Did Hector have a gun?"

"No, warriors in those days fought with light sabers. Troy was a place that was full of magic. There was a mountain in Greece, across the small sea, where powerful magicians lived and looked down on battles. There was even a woman named Iris, like that woman over there, who brought messages down from the magicians to the warriors. Hector's country was invaded by Alabamian Greeks. Their greatest warrior was named Achilles. Achilles was his last name. His first name was Tree. Tree Achilles. His friends called him Tree, and his very best friend called him *Tio* Tree. Tree got in a fight with Hector outside the castle. They ran around the castle and fought all night and you could see their light swords flashing, just like the sparks from my fire."

"But why were they fighting?"

"Oh, right. They were fighting over a woman. The most beautiful woman in the world. Her name was Queen Helen Maria of Troy. She was the mother of Prince Javier and the wife of King Marcos. Everybody just called her Queenie." Maria looked at me and scratched her nose with her middle finger.

"How could they be fighting over her when she was married to King Marcos?"

"Well, good point, I should have figured it all out ahead. But here's what happened. Tree Achilles said something mean about Queen Helen Maria, about how her fajitas were yuck and needed more guacamole. All the Alabamian Greeks were shouting for more guac. Guac! Guac! Guac! And Hector was like a brother to her and he stood up for her and told Tree Achilles to take it back or he was going to fight him with his light saber and Achilles wouldn't take it back and instead jumped in this blue helicopter and flew up high in the sky and dropped huge rocks down on Hector." Hector let the tiny pebbles that I arced at him bounce off his sheriff's cap. "Achilles brought the helicopter in low over Hector to drop more rocks and Hector jumped high and grabbed hold of the...the runners...these things on the bottom of the helicopter. And then Hector pulled himself up, and he and Achilles were fighting inside the plane...the helicopter...and the helicopter was about to crash and just then Queenie came out and called Hector and Achilles to dinner, and they went inside to wash up and have fajitas and they were the most delicious fajitas ever because Queenie is the bomb."

Queenie leaned in and gathered up Javier, who was barely awake. But he held on to the helicopter.

"Put him down in the camper," I said.

"The story did the trick," said Iris.

"I never have figured out whether bedtime stories should be exciting or dull," I said.

"Or just confusing," said George, from the background. "You actually stunned him to sleep. No disrespect, but I don't think Homer meant for the *Iliad* to be translated into the Alabamian tongue."

"I liked it," said Hector. "It wasn't Louis L'Amour, but at least I got to be the star."

"One of the stars," I said.

"I finally got to listen to you talk a little," said Iris. "Everybody says you're a talker. But when I came out here before the cat had your tongue."

"Where does that come from?" I asked. "How can a cat get your tongue?"

"Who cares?" Iris asked.

"Me."

"Me, too," said George. "I care about that."

"But you're right. The cat had my tongue. I was telling Hector that you about half scared me."

"Well, good," said Iris. "You should be scared of me."

"By any chance, do you recall ever being Cleopatra in a past century?"

"Do you recall ever having good sense?"

"The very question my sainted mother, rest her, used to ask me."

After Iris wandered off, George took over my interrogation.

"What's with you and Justice Grasso?"

"Ah, my dear friend, Nico. I helped Sandra take him fishing."

"And?"

"Are you asking for the paper?"

"Hell, yes. A Supreme Court justice in Summit County. That's news. I get hungry for real news in this backwater place."

"We went fishing. Or he went fishing."

"Sandra says he pushed you in the river." Hector said nothing, missed nothing, and let George do the work.

"George, I wish you wouldn't make a story out of that," I said.

"Sandra says she'll be fired if I use her as my source. She says it should come from you, since you already were fired—for pushing the judge in the river."

"What?"

"That's the official story. You pushed the judge, but he didn't press charges because he's a hell of a good guy."

"What does Sandra say about me pushing him?"

"She knows how to roll her eyes."

"George, just let it alone. It was all just good fun. I simply took a notion to go swimming. Turns out I'm a good swimmer."

"Except Justice Grasso has decided that maybe you stole something from him. A letter."

I looked at Hector. "He made a complaint?"

"All news to me. But my people lead interesting lives."

"Tell me the story," said George. "I'll make you the same deal I made Sandra. I won't quote you unless you say OK. I just want to get filled in on what's going on here."

I looked a question at Billy, and he nodded.

"There was a letter. It was in the creel I had around my neck when I went for a swim. Later, Sandra gave me the creel, not knowing there was anything in it but fish."

"What kind of letter?"

"A letter from the pope to Grasso."

"Holy shit."

"You read this letter?"

45

"I did."

"And? And? Tell me what it said."

"The pope said, 'Dear Tree, it's not nice to read other people's mail.'"

"Damn it, you're not going to tell me, are you?"

"Not now. I have to figure out what to do."

"Where's the letter now?"

"Safe."

"OK, you want to be difficult. You don't want to share it with me. Why not just return it? You're an Alabama farm boy. These are big time people."

"Julie thinks I can put it to good use."

"Julie?"

"Doesn't matter. But I'll tell you why I didn't return it."

"OK."

"Nico didn't know me, except that I was an Alabama hick, and true for him on that. But this afternoon it came into my mind that one simple thing he didn't know about me was whether I could swim or not. That river's dangerous in the heavy channel. So that was in my mind when I read the letter. It's mine now. Kind of a keepsake of my trip down the river."

There was a silence where people decided at the same time to stare at the fire, a good thing that fires are for. I looked at the sparks darting high against the black mountain and decided that if you had maybe a drink or two of whiskey and closed one eye and squinted the other that there could be warriors with light sabers on the high hills. Javier had not had a drink of whiskey, but he had the advantage of a child's imagination, so maybe he did see light sabers. I allowed that whiskey could have become my substitute for childhood imagination, but I decided no, not true, because even sober I traveled an orbit that only intersected reality on certain leaping, quantum occasions, which advantage was that I didn't have to see more of reality than I could understand.

I poured myself another thimble of whiskey, maybe more like a tumbler. I liked looking at George's bonfire and the unruly sparks. I liked looking at the bright side of faces, with the other side in cool, imagined shadow. This business with Nico was becoming more real, more substantial, than I liked. I didn't trust Nico, and this was beginning to be my own opinion and not just Julie's. I was a stranger in this up and down Colorado land and didn't know whom I could trust (except for Julie—I knew to listen to her). The closest I came to a touchstone was Billy. That's why I looked to him to see if I could trust George. Billy had no suspicious angles about him. He spoke rarely and briefly and told the truth. Marcos, I trusted, but he was a shrewd diplomat. I gathered that his place in this country might be risky, and I knew that his wits were tuned entirely to keeping his family safe. Good luck to anyone who got between Marcos and the safety of his family. If I got in trouble, I could become a risk to him, and I did not plan for that to happen.

I liked Hector, but I knew our purposes might run in different directions. I had the feeling that Hector and George and Iris were some sort of tag team. But they were all too deep for me. Billy was part of this team, but I trusted him because he was like me, even though he was mostly silent and I was mostly not. I didn't know what things were like among them although I knew I was out of line in questioning Hector about Iris. I could see now that I just wanted them to be a couple because they were of an age and, like a young girl, my mind was in a place where it wanted to see couples, to think about couples. And even I could figure out why my mind would go off in that direction, but I needed to apologize to Hector. I had not been sufficiently respectful, but that was no new thing. I had the redneck chip on my shoulder that made me flare up at my betters and made me go off by myself and read and study and wonder how you got to be not a redneck or whether being not a redneck was even a consummation to be wished. Another thing I wondered was whether even a backwoods guy like William Faulkner also had a chip. I mean we're talking Mississippi here—lower than which there are only some countries whose names end in "-stan"—how could he not have a chip? I would have to track down a Faulkner biography.

Marcos and Maria were now perched on the edge of my coffee table as Hector sat on the ground at their feet. It came to me that likely he did this with everyone, and it didn't add up to genius but was deeply smart. He had told me he had been sheriff a long time and I was thinking small wonder if he sat at the feet of his people. He and Jesus would both wash your feet although Hector would also step on your neck. Hector and Maria and Marcos were speaking Spanish for what privacy it gave and maybe for a comfort. Hector was not looking at driver's licenses and Maria was not tense. I heard Javier's name mentioned, and later, mine.

George and Iris were several feet away. She was tall and spare and regal and he was short and solid, and she had her arm draped on his shoulder, as she leaned her weight against him. He was talking rapidly, and she was listening by maybe half, just enough to see if he said something that was not entirely predictable to her. I was not yet ready to give up the idea she was Cleopatra although I think maybe Cleopatra did not live to be as old as Iris. Iris thought I was being weird, and I thought that was probably right. Because, like Faulkner, how could I not be? Weird because

I stole letters from the pope. Weird because I felt called to make a match in my mind between Hector and Iris. This is what Maria saw when she told me not to do anything without checking first with her. But things were catching my interest, things besides just the sweetness of my conversations with Julie. When Eunice sent me away from Alabama she wanted things to catch my interest. And here they were. Not so much this silly letter from the pope. Not so much this silly Nico. But yes, for Marcos, for Maria, for Javier, for Billy, and Hector and Cleopatra. And George, a scrivener, writing bonfire sparks across the sky.

Chapter 5

Maria and Marcos ended their conversation with Hector and headed towards my camper to check on Javier.

"I was wrong to get into your business with Iris," I said.

"Yes, you were," said Hector.

"Sorry." I was full of virtue for apologizing, which was probably a worse sin than the original sin of failing to mind my own business. I was not a fan of Christian hoorah and flapdoodle, but my mother was, and it would have been mostly less than possible to grow up with my sainted mother in Alabama without swimming in a greenish stock pond full of snapping turtles and Christian rules. Pride was bad and false pride was worse and praying in public was base sin unless it was you the one doing it. I think...maybe. I sometimes didn't listen sharp enough to the rules to master the subtleties that my mother could go on and on about if asked or not forcibly stopped.

"I have to confess something else, Hector."

"Go ahead, but if it's a crime, and I have to get up and arrest you, I will be pissed. I'm content right where I am."

"I can't promise I won't get in your business again...it's how I do."

"No shit."

A big car jostled up the dirt road, and it was a Suburban or such like and then there was another of the same behind it. People coming to my campfire did not drive cars like this. I was in my camp chair facing the dirt national forest road. Hector, seated on the ground and leaning back against my coffee table, had a view down the road and had been watching the lights come up. The first car was black in the firelight and appeared to have seating enough for a choir of angels. The front doors opened and two stout men in matching black windbreakers got out and praise Jesus if they didn't have Ghostbuster sunglasses on. The second car was identical, and the driver, a man in a white cowboy hat, no sunglasses, got out by himself. When the interior light went on in the second car, I could see more cowboy hats. I was entranced, or maybe a little drunk. One of the Ghostbusters held the backdoor open and out rolled my pal, Nico, the director of the choir of angels. The other Ghostbuster took a powerful flashlight and played it over the group, and George told him to turn that fucking thing off, and the group muttered, as pre-riotous groups will do. I looked over at Hector; he was still seated but now holding his jacket in his lap, maybe preparing to get up. The Ghostbuster with the light said United States Marshall and told George to shut up, and I noticed that George moved a step closer to him and said Howdy, Marshall Dillon, which was borderline disrespectful. Hector did not move but softly said George's name, which seemed to work because George stopped. Marshal Ghostbuster Dillon asked, "Where's the officer that goes with that police car?"

"That's me."

"And you are?"

"The sheriff. You can call me Hector."

"Well, get on your feet, Hector, and pay your respects to Associate Justice of the Supreme Court Nicholas Grasso."

Hector waved and pointed to the galvanized tub. "Hi, Judge. Have a beer." Hector did not get up and the marshal sharply nudged Hector's outstretched foot with his own, trying to get him up and moving, but Hector really was content where he was.

The marshal seemed confused and angry although it was hard to know because of the dark glasses. My limited experience is that law enforcement prefers not to let on to being confused. It's just that this was, by God, a real, live Supreme Court justice, and who doesn't leap to their feet for one of those? And the most reasonable answer to that question was: Hector. And me. Most everyone else in the group was already standing, so they didn't have to be nudged with the marshal's foot.

"Who the hell do you think you are?" asked the marshal of Hector. Even with the sunglasses, I sensed belligerence, and I was sorrowful for any ghosts that might show up, what with this ghostbuster on the job. I thought at this odd time of Julie. Maybe I was a little drunk.

The man in the white cowboy hat from the second car had come up to the fringe of the group.

Hector ignored the marshal. "Is that you, Al?" asked Hector.

"Hector? I didn't know you were going to be here."

"How's Alice? The kids?"

"Good, thanks."

"Listen, Al. It looks like you've got a crew with you from the ranch. That big car is full of big cowboy hats. You came prepared."

"It's what you taught me."

"That makes me proud. Another thing that would make me proud and happy is if you would take your wranglers back to the ranch. Not that I wouldn't like to have a beer with all of you, and we'll do that for sure another time. Right now, you've got a car full of cowboys, and I've got George, a famous hippie, and it's oil and water because they probably all like to fight. I know George does. I also know he's too old to be much good at it."

52

"Hi, George," said Al. "I see you've also got Billy, who is good at it."

"And Iris," said Hector.

"Oh, Jesus," said Al. "I didn't see Iris." He waved. "Don't forget that beer."

"And you don't forget to give my regards to Alice. The marshals and I will look after the judge. But I doubt he needs looking after." Nico was fishing a beer from the tub and seemed entertained.

The belligerent ghostbuster ordered Al to stay, but I guess Al didn't hear because he got in his black Suburban and drove down the hill. Hector explained helpfully that Al used to be one of his deputies, but I guess the marshal was another one that didn't hear. It was Julie's opinion that I was a good listener and that was true as far as it might throw. But here it is: I listened to her because I was all the way in love and wanted to get the directions to her favor straight. I confess that I paid not nearly so much mind to others. This seemed to be a night that put me in a confessing frame of mind, and it was either because of this pope business or mayhap the whiskey.

"Well, Vernon," said Nico. "Sandra says your Southern name is Tree. I like it. The last time I saw you, you were doing a nice dogpaddle down the Rolling River. There was just the back of your head to wave goodbye to. I did wave, but you didn't wave back." Nico looked around. "Are these all Alabamians, Tree? Friends of yours?"

Once again, I didn't care for Nico's tone. It seemed like it might be more arrogant than strictly necessary, and, more, it seemed like the tone was kind of fixed in place—it grated. I had gotten that tone some before, back home. You would expect that tone to sometimes go with my station in life, and, true, it sometimes did, but not as much as all that because I was skilled at staying away from people. There was once at R.E. Lee High an assistant principal who did not like his janitors literate. He had a tone with me, and with the students, and my thought was that I could stand it better than they could. I call the time he caught me reading a book styled *The Republic*. He didn't like it much (me reading), but it evened out because I didn't like it much, either (*The Republic*). That really was an excellent job because I could always claim to be on break when reading and no one the wiser. The principal was wise to me, but he was wise to everybody and didn't care if I needed to, had to, finish a chapter so long as I got my work done at some time before school started in the morning. The assistant principal soon got a better job, and, too soon, the principal, Ed Pollard, got sort of permanently tired but continued kindly to me and I earnestly hope vice versa. But, no mistake, I knew enough people with the tone, and it was a main part of why I liked being a janitor because the job sort of works the same as that wonderful Harry Potter's invisibility cloak.

Nico looked down at Hector. "And this is local law enforcement at its finest?"

"Pull up a chair, Judge. Take a load off." Nico looked around and didn't like it that there weren't any chairs (except mine), and he was being made fun of. I liked it, but I had no idea what Hector was up to.

"Did they ever teach you that the proper form of address is Mr. Justice Grasso?"

"Thanks, Judge, good to know. Here, I will slip over and you can snuggle up beside me and lean back against this rock."

Truth, Nico was ready to shit or go blind.

"Sheriff…"

"Call me Hector."

"Are you an old friend of Tree's?"

"The way I get the story is that you and Tree are old friends."

"You didn't answer my question."

"Yes, sir, I didn't."

Nico tried to adjust. I could tell he was trying to adjust. I tried to understand what was going on without much luck, but I did catch on that Nico and the marshals were on the same page: There must be a law against what was happening, but what was it, exactly?

Hector continued, "Judge, we're happy to have you. As a courtesy, I want you to know that George over there, the one who didn't like the flashlight, is the publisher and chief reporter and receptionist and janitor of the local paper. So, don't threaten the overthrow of the US government because George would take that as news." Hector seemed satisfied he had Nico boxed. I know I was satisfied. Finding out about folks like Hector, about how they do, is a fine entertainment, passing fine.

"No press. I don't allow press. I want him out of here."

"I'm with you, Judge," said Hector. "There are so many things I want that I can't have, though. Just ask my county commissioners at budget time."

"I want him gone." Nico was speaking now to the ghostbusters.

The original ghostbuster turned to George. "You heard the justice. Move it."

"Fuck you," George explained, tenderly.

The other marshal was quiet and apparently thinking, "Uh, Mr. Justice, I'm not sure..."

"Think, Judge, think," said Hector. "I'm trying to help. Nobody invited you here. Nobody's got to leave. Nobody's got to stand up. People can call you anything they want. Think."

There was what seemed to me a long moment, grave with possibility, and then Nico did think and reverted to charm and called off his ghostbuster, who, it turned out, did not want to be called off. "I'm a United States Marshal," he said to George, "you can't talk to me like…"

"Yes, he can, Marshal. George tells me to fuck off about once a week. I wish it was against the law, but it's not. So back off and please take your right hand away from that gun. That's just way beyond silly."

The marshal reached farther inside his jacket and Nico quickly said no to him and then there was the metallic click of a hammer being pulled back under Hector's jacket, which was still in his lap, as the sheriff continued to take his leisure on the ground, with his back against my coffee table. My strong guess was that this was the sound of a gun and not Hector fiddling with his zipper. Marshall Ghostbuster agreed because he twisted and looked at Hector (possibly with wide eyes, who could know?), scuffed at the ground with his shoe, and went off to kick the tire of the big, powerful car.

Nico, to my deep interest, stayed with the charm. He dropped down on his knees and turned to sit beside Hector. He did not do this gracefully but, by God, he did it. All due credit.

"I don't get out enough. I'm used to people treating me like royalty, and to tell the truth I kind of like it. There are only eight people in the world who get to disagree with me, and they do so at their peril, because, by God, I will rip them a new one." He turned his attention to George. "Is this a story for you, Mr. First Amendment?"

"Oh, I'm happy to know it, even if it's just feature page fluff. But it's not a story for me. I'm old school. Officials get to let their hair down when they're not being official. If Hector arrests you, it's a story. If you and Hector get drunk together, that's just touching and heartwarming, and I don't write that shit. You want to talk about your job? I'll write that."

"Maybe later. What I really want right now is to have a private word with Hector. Did you know, Sheriff, that there was once a famous warrior named Hector?"

"No shit," said Hector. "I tell you what we can do. We can walk off down the road, or you can just whisper in my ear."

Nico did just that, probably to avoid the struggle to get up, and it was OK with me not to hear, and George shrugged and got himself another beer. The others had crowded around at first but drifted off because a Supreme Court justice was a fleeting thrill but beer a storied blessing to pass on to your children. Nico whispered and Hector interrupted a couple times to whisper back.

Hector turned to me. "The judge thinks you have a letter that belongs to him. It has religious significance for him because he's a Catholic. So am I...supposed to be. Anyway, the judge wants the letter back, in original condition."

I saw Julie, then, a wavy ghost up in the campfire where the flames and smoke joined. It was the exact place where ghosts were supposed to hang out. I knew to look for her because I had seen her there before. I worried about the ghostbusters, but they seemed to have other thoughts to occupy them. Seeing Julie made me feel like Mozart. Julie and I once saw this movie about Mozart, and it made him out to be this guy who had this whole big symphony in his head and all he had to do was scribble down the notes that were sort of floating before him in the air. That's how I felt because the story I wanted to tell was there in the flames, whole, and all I had to do was get it told. But not in a rush. I had to pay attention to the pauses. I am a talkative man, but I know words gather their power from the void, the pauses; cadence is the child of silence.

And so, I began: "Your letter from the pope, Nico, was in the creel. It was almost like holding in my hands a letter from God. I even wondered if the pope could divine somehow that I was the one holding it. I don't mind telling you I looked over my shoulder a time or two. I held it in my hands, and the Christian thought came to me that maybe it was a sacred relic that had the power to heal. I knew that was silly, but the desire to be healed is strong in some folk. So, you can't blame me, and I won't blame myself for that. At first, I had no curiosity about what was in the letter. I figured it was probably not from the pope, anyway, but from some low-level bureaucrat, thanking my pal, Nico, for his generous donation to the Little Sisters of Transcendent Mercy. I was going to give it to Sandra so she could return it. I admit it did pop into my mind to open it, but my mother said no."

"Your mother?" asked Hector.

"Dead. But she still bosses me, if you know my meaning."

"I know. Brother, don't I know."

"And then it popped into my mind again to open it, so I just went right on and did that. Curiosity. The curiosity that tripped up the cat, same for Adam and Eve. It was always hard for me to let well enough alone, my mother used to say."

"You read a letter addressed to me," shouted Nico. Once again, I sensed anger.

"I did. Interesting letter. Stilted, though, like it had been written in Spanish and then translated through Latin and Italian and German, before it got to the monk with the quill pen that does English." Frankly, I was inspired. And proud. Monks with quill pens—that was a nice touch. Nothing sells a story like details, especially ones that are wholly irrelevant. I carefully avoided eye contact with George and Hector.

"You read my mail from the pope. You are a...a..."

"A rascal. Yes. That's what my mother always said. She could really get pissed, for a Christian woman. But, here's the main thing. Francis, Big Frankie, your pope, is not that happy with you, Nico. 'Gravely disappointed,' as I recall his words."

Nico's jaw was clenching and unclenching, and his bushy eyebrows were flying up and down, but were in nowise synchronous with his jaw; my thought was that the eyebrows moved separately, more contrapuntal-like, but what did I know—being fresh out of Muscle Shoals, Alabama, where Confederate General John Bell Hood crossed the Tennessee River on his literal last leg at the very losing end of the Lost Cause, and I, a sinner, in no position to call down on anyone, was still thinking that Hood and all his men should only have drowned in that shallow, clear water in the fall of 1864. Maybe as an object lesson for Nico and the plantation economy.

I could see the wrinkles in Hector's forehead relax as he went from confusion to a glimpse of where I was going. Oracular is how I felt, once freed from the surly bonds of truth. I did not dare look at George. Sometimes I could see Julie in the fire through my smoky vision. This story was, after all, for her.

Nico said, "I'm going to tear you a new...Do you know who I am? Who I really am? You're such a hick you have no clue."

"I don't know anything about you, Nico. But Big Frankie, your own pope, seems to think he's got you figured."

"You dare to..." Again, with the jaw and the contrapuntal eyebrows.

"Big Frankie mentioned that his church owned a bank. I never knew that. He said one bank out on an island somewhere let slip to another bank that you have become rich in the judging business. Out of all proportion to your salary. Big Frankie said money slid quietly down a wire from one Willard Jordan of Summit County, Colorado, my former employer, into your pocket. And the amount Big Frankie mentioned was way more money than Willard was paying me. But, no complaints, money doesn't go to be fair."

"You're crazy."

"Willard, and I guess his buddies, own you, Nico. Maybe that's not a huge surprise to the world. I don't know. I was surprised, but I'm unfamiliar with the ways of smart people. Hell, left to my own devices, I never would have dreamed the pope owned a bank."

Nico looked around, maybe to see who was listening. It was just Hector and George. Even the marshals were over by the car, maintaining a respectful distance.

Nico said, "Tree, I believe you've been drinking."

"And plan to continue. It's a thing soothing to me."

"You're out of your mind. Just give me the letter, and we'll let this drop."

"Wait, Your Eminence. There's more, it makes me kind of joyful to say. Turns out Big Frankie is frowning serious about all that Jesus talk about the poor. Big Frankie says you've spent your life helping the rich, and OK for that, water under the bridge, forget it. But the big guy wants to see some rulings for regular folk from now on. 'The least of these' is I'm thinking the way he put it."

"You're crazy. Stark..."

"I know, Nico. It feels all the way crazy, don't it? I mean the way I get it is that Big Frankie is almost blackmailing you. A squeeze like. Rule against Willard, and Willard cuts off the money. Rule against Big Frankie, and he lays out the money trail. It's right at really being something."

"Just give me the letter so I can go. There's no telling what it really says."

"That's another thing, Nico. I think the letter's better off with me. Just being careful all the way around. If you doubt my word about what's in the letter, you can just ring up the pope tomorrow. The beauty of being you is that you can call the pope when you take a notion, and he'll take your call. Maybe call him tonight. I can't keep straight on the time difference. But just call him up, and the two of you can have a big laugh over this crazy Alabamian. Be sure he understands it's Alabamian and not Albanian. I don't want to prejudice him against those good Albanian folk. Call Big Frankie. Ask him what the letter really says."

Nico raised his voice to the marshals. "The letter is mine. I want it now."

George seemed stunned again, more so even than with the *Iliad*. Hector was not too stunned to wave off the approaching marshals. "No, I don't think so. I'm having a tough time getting this straight, but so far what I've got is that Tree didn't steal this letter out of a mailbox, something I understand to be a crime. Sandra gave it to him in the creel. The judge would know better than me how all this plays out legally, but for right now nobody is taking any letters at gunpoint. Forget about that." Hector still had his jacket in his lap and his hand under his jacket and maybe had a gun in his hand or maybe was conspicuously horny; we did not know each other well enough for me to fair judge.

Nico left. Just left. He was all done saying stuff, I guess. And he got up like some fleet animal, maybe a gazelle? Seriously fleet—no sarcasm here. An alligator maybe—alligators are a lot fleeter than people give them credit for. Just let one get in behind you.

"They're right," said Hector to me. "Give you a campfire and some whiskey, and you can tell a story."

"I need a little drink, right now, for my throat. It may look easy from where you're sitting, but all that concentration is wearisome. Halfway through, I never know where the ending is."

"So, what just happened here?" asked George.

"There was a campfire. A great big one, thanks to you. Some whiskey. So, I told a story."

"You made that story up?"

"Some of it. To make it better."

"Which parts?"

"I don't want to say that right now. Maybe later."

"I don't quite get it, but you sure got his attention," said George. "Grasso looked like he was ready to kill for that letter. But, hell, maybe that's how he looks all the time."

When I was telling my yarn, I sometimes caught a glimpse of Julie in the fire, and it felt like I was telling my little story for Julie, to Julie, even. That makes no good sense, I know that. I know it. I told the story from love, from rage, from mischief, and some bit from whiskey. I could pick which one if I knew myself better. Truth, I was surprised Nico didn't catch on to the mischief part when I got to that bullshit about the money. What do I know? Maybe he just played along because I tell a hell of a story. I like to think that was it because, you know, it's pretty, pretty to think so.

Chapter 6

Lena was too short to paint. When I pulled into their drive, she started in on Billy that he had promised to paint the living room. He promised! He could go off skylarking in the hills with Tree ("Hi, Tree," motioning me to lean down for a kiss) some other time. Today was painting day, and the living room was going to get painted if Lena had to paint it all by herself, but she was going to need a ladder because she was short and God knows how she was going to tape the ceiling, but she would damn sure find a way.

So, to be plain and clear, no one was planning on painting Lena, not because she was too short to paint, but because no way she'd hold still for it, and, more besides, no one was planning on having Lena even do any painting, since Billy could do this himself, and I was there specifically to lend a hand. Neither of us was going to much need a ladder, especially not Billy. Lena was happy when she found this out and made me lean again for a kiss, and Billy asked where was his kiss, and she said you got yours last night, and then she blushed, honest to St. Moses, and giggled. I lean strong to the notion that Lena invented giggling. No one else should ever giggle without paying Lena rent, which is fair and right, and which would let Lena and Billy buy a fancy new house (freshly painted).

Billy said it was a nice surprise, but there was no need for me to help with the painting, and I agreed there was no need, and we left it there and went to work. It was a blue-sky day and a small living room, so we stored the furniture in the front yard. I brought with me a six of PBR that we stored in the refrigerator. Lena had already shopped for masking tape and drop cloths and brushes and other such truck of the painting trade. And, bless her short bones, she had shopped for paint. Paint chips, in my experience, had no known relationship to the color the paint would be on the wall, or even to the color spectrum that Mr. Isaac Newton fanned out across the world of optics like a card trick. I don't know how Newton thought of that. Could I take plain light and run it through the right kind of prism and see again the colors of Julie, just those colors, the glow of her red hair and the gleam of her liquid blue-green eyes? No. Sorry. No. But I'm not done with my grudge against paint chips because I once personally picked out a classic puke green for the boys' locker room at R.E. Lee High. I stirred the paint for an infinitude of time with the supplied paddle. I stuck one end of the puke green paint chip in the thoroughly paddled paint and left the chip to dry and came back and one end of the chip was still puke green, but the dipped end was a serendipitous slate blue that Coach Randolph liked because he was so sick of puke green he could just...you know.

Billy began taping the edge of the ceiling because the plan was to leave the ceiling white and replace the hue of soft blue wall with what appeared from the paint chip was a rich cream color. I liked them both, but the blue was showing some wear, and a body just gets in the mood for change. Lena came in as Billy was taping; I didn't see it, but she must have frowned because Billy asked, "What?" She said there's dirt in the corner of the wall and the ceiling. I pointed out that this was good vision on Lena's part because she was short, so it took a good eye. I was mistaken to say this because I think Lena didn't care over much for random people going on about her height; and, more, I was also mistaken because I believe that Billy was irritated about scrubbing the dirt out of the corners, but neither was quite aggravated enough to banish me to that circle of Hell reserved for those who speak before thinking things all the way through. Dante Alighieri, a comedian of the old school, would have said Purgatory was the place for me. I took notice and resolved to reform.

I got a saucepan of warm water and a washcloth and began scrubbing the juncture of wall and ceiling. I could reach, barely, but Lena brought me a sort of apple box to stand on, and it was no longer such a stretch. Billy taped along behind me, without benefit of box.

"When did you get your growth?" I asked.

"Born eleven pounds and kept growing. Babies born at this altitude usually run small, about six pounds. Do you think it was destiny that I should be so large?"

"Nope."

"Me, neither. But I have been able to do things, like Samson, that wouldn't have happened if I wasn't so oversized. Pick up tall buildings, stuff like that."

"Pure chance—a roll of the genes."

"OK, I get that. But it takes the mystery out of it. And people love a good mystery."

"Amen, brother. But I disagree that it takes away the mystery. Chance is the mystery."

"Humph, I will think on that. You finish the taping and I'll shake the paint."

Billy did just that. He didn't open the gallon bucket and stir the paint with the paddle. He picked it up with a hand on the bottom and a hand on the top and shook it. The paint store has a nervous, herky-jerky machine for this. I believe that Billy did it better, but maybe not. Unlike the machine, Billy would have tired by and by, but he was a sufficiency for our small purpose. I liked the quick rasping sound the tape made as it came off the roll. I taped doorframes and window frames and tried to tape Lena's hair to hear her giggle. Lena got Billy to scrub a couple places on the walls before he could spread the drop cloths. He tried to drape the plastic sheeting over her, and she left, trailing clouds of giggles. Billy chose a four-inch brush and began spreading paint. We both stepped back and looked after he had a three-foot block filled in. It looked good and, more besides, it looked like the paint chip. Billy shrugged and said Lena had a gift for color. I began painting, and it was nice doing this rhythmic work with a visible result.

"You were born to be a painter," said Billy.

"I believe I was born to be a janitor. I like cleaning things up."

"All the same stuff. Painting is cleaning up. I drive a snowplow in winter, another cleanup job."

"You're right. How much school did you have?"

"Ninth grade. I needed a job and was plenty strong at fifteen. Lena and I married young and had kids. The idea of college never entered my head. I didn't know anybody who went to college except my teachers, and they were just teachers, diagramming sentences and stuff. I never saw anything to make me want to go to college."

"Regrets?"

"Nah. I've had a charmed life. Wife, kids. I'm still living and some of the people in my life aren't. Don't want to be a teacher or a doctor. Sure as hell don't want to be a lawyer or a banker. I like driving a snowplow. Maybe would have been cool to be a biologist for the wildlife department. Maybe George's job—that could be good. But after a bunch of years with the state, they pay me good. I'm not fancy enough to believe that all my dreams should come true."

"But you are an educated guy."

"I guess, some. But, like you, self-educated. Mostly educated by George, who is one smart son of a bitch. Mine was all adult education. George told me what books to read, and I read them. Still reading them. George gave me quizzes in the Moose Jaw, a local bar. If school kids got to study in a bar, maybe they'd do better. That was interesting to me about meeting you. Same deal as me. Was it your wife who told you what books to read?"

"No. I mean, yes, later. But no one person. Librarians, mostly. My mom. I started young."

"Lena picked out a good color. I don't know why she thought I was trying to get out of painting. I like to paint. I just hate all the taping and cleaning. Painting takes no time—it's all the getting ready crap. When I was a kid, I worked one summer on a framing crew and learned the most important lesson of carpentry—the painter will catch it."

"Come again?"

"You make a bad cut and end up with a joint that doesn't fit tight, you can either redo the joint or depend on the painter to slop enough filler and paint in it that it hides the gap in the joint. A painter is an important person to a bad carpenter, and I was a certified bad carpenter. Did you want to be something besides a janitor?"

"Never. And I think I had more encouragement about schooling than you. My mother saw I had potential. Some of my teachers. I started being a reader way before I started school, so I didn't have to wait for George to take me to a bar and give me a reading list. A few teachers noticed. After a while they talked to me about scholarships."

"So why didn't you do something better?"

"There isn't anything better."

"College degrees? The life of the mind? A respectable job? Money? Women? Fast cars?"

"I thought we were talking about the life of the mind."

"Broadly speaking."

"I couldn't stand to hear my teachers talking. When they talked about a book I had read, an idea I knew about, I couldn't stand it. I wanted to run away. And sometimes did. They made me help Clarence Reed, the janitor, as a punishment. Clarence only talked about things he understood, like how much bleach to add to the mop water. And, also, don't drink the bleach. Clarence knew his stuff. I won't say he was all that nice to me, but he let me work for him and got me a little pay and by the time I graduated he told me to apply for his job because he was going to fish for a little while before the cancer took him all the way over. And he did and I did. The school had a decent library, big on the classics. There was a good public library. And no more did I have to listen to teachers saying things about books, things I could not abide. Except, later, for Julie. But that was different altogether. Because she loved the books she talked about, especially she was nuts for that Welty woman. And because I loved Julie, which makes a difference every time."

We finished three walls, so at lunchtime there was a wall to go, a vestibule, a bunch of edge work, and an easy second coat. We ate sandwiches at a picnic table in the shade, satisfied with ourselves and happy that Lena was satisfied with the paint color and the behavior of her tall employees. She brought out chocolate ice cream and an oversized black scrapbook.

"Can I show Tree this?"

Billy was slow in answering but said OK. He abruptly took his ice cream inside, and I was left alone with chocolate ice cream and the restless shade of a small clump of cottonwoods and a scrapbook that contained newspaper articles, some yellowed, written by one William Mapp, a Billy by any other name. He had said George's job could be fun, and I started to get it. I opened in the middle and read a column in George's small, local newspaper. The words were careful and crafted and all of them were about squirrels. I was a fan of squirrels, but I was mistaken to think I had ever seen a squirrel. Billy had bothered to look. I learned that squirrels are quarrelsome out of all proportion to their size. They chatter and menace and complain, but when the chips are down, when the time for posturing is past, they always, always run away. Mostly up a tree, where they use their tails like the long balancing pole of a tightrope artist. When they run across a street, they leap high over nonexistent hurdles in the road. Maybe this works for the forest floor, full of actual hurdles like sticks and stones, but it's a lot of unnecessary up and down for an asphalt street. Squirrels are rats, tree rats, under the protection of the sacred order of cuteness. Billy speculated, reasonably, that if they had hairless tails like their rat cousins, we would shoot them all on sight. I liked his story and was happy to have a whole scrapbook of Billy stories left to go. The only thing missing in his story was flow—he was a careful person, guarding against mistakes, and overly conscious of his duty not to crush the fragile words with his great strength.

I wondered was this enough for Billy. Better said, what is enough to make a body want to notice a squirrel, to seek out life, to seek out another day after this one? Billy had a lively wife, good kids, a job he liked, enough money, and a wonderful moonlighting job carpentering up careful sentences about squirrels. I was jealous of him, maybe, and happy for him, surely. I rejoined Billy for the painting.

"Great."

"Which did you read?"

"The squirrels that we allow to live among us because they have decorative tails. Fine work."

"Thanks."

"George schooled you and then put you to work."

"He did, except he doesn't pay worth a damn."

"And you like doing it?"

"I do. I was always shy, so that was hard. Giants always want not to be noticed. But you'd be amazed at how many people read the column, see the name William Mapp, and still don't connect it with me."

"I looked through some of the other titles. It seemed like all nature, not much people or politics?"

"That's fair."

"Even Thoreau had politics. He beat up politicians with his nature stick."

"True. But I've never been able to do it. You think I should?"

"No idea. I was just curious. I don't read newspapers enough to have an opinion about what they should look like. I liked the squirrels, though. It felt true. It didn't make me want to run away."

"OK. And I'll think about writing some politics because I take what you mean about Thoreau. He's the best. Politics just seems like a dead zone to me. Politicians. Zombies is what my kids would call them. I got a little of that feeling from Grasso. I could be wrong."

"Explain."

"Hell, I don't know. I drive a snowplow..."

"Isn't that great?"

"What?"

"I do the same thing. The snowplow dodge. The janitor dodge. I get backed into a corner and say, I'm just a janitor—what do I know? I already know you drive a snowplow—now tell me why Grasso is a zombie."

"I'm not sure..."

"And don't be so careful."

Billy took a deep breath to shake off his aggravation. "Grasso only lives skin deep. A squirrel is alive all the way through."

"And excuse me, I'm just a janitor, but that also means if you write about politics you run the risk that you might become part of that world, change yourself from a squirrel into a zombie?"

Billy grinned at me, which I took as some reassurance for my physical safety. I had been pushing my luck, but, you know, it's what I do.

Billy said, "I know they can't all be zombies, but they give me the creeps. Grasso does."

"OK. Maybe he's a zombie. Who knows? But take Hector. Don't you elect your sheriffs in Colorado? Hector's a politician, and a squirrel all the way through."

"No, you're right. I never think of Hector as a politician. And I guess that makes your point. But I've known people who were dead inside. Nothing but skin. It's like that thing where when you start freezing to death, all the energy goes away from your skin, to your core, your heart trying to stay alive a little longer. Some people are the opposite—their heart dies, but their skin and muscles keep going."

It was a time for me to be careful, but I did not know what to be careful of except that Billy wasn't just fooling around with this zombie talk. He really knew someone like this, and it disturbed him.

With caution, delicacy, tact, I asked, "What the hell are you talking about?"

He grimaced. "I knew a man like that once. I made a mistake not realizing how bad he was. I didn't really understand how crazy people can get."

"How was he crazy?"

"For him, it was religion. And having sex with children. But I think it could have been anything. It could have been fluoride in the water or Catholics—he just needed something to wrap his crazy around."

"You think you could have helped him?"

"No, but I could have stopped him. I could have done that for damn sure. I could have squeezed his head until it popped. I just didn't know to."

"Stopped him from what?"

"He killed his sister. Megan was her name. I loved her. She was like my own little sister. We all loved her. Especially Ben—they were going to be married."

"What happened to him?"

"Ben?"

"Uh, no. The brother?"

"Larry."

"OK, Larry."

"Iris killed him."

"Wait. Iris? The one I know?"

"The same. Shot him four times. With the muzzle of the gun against his chest until she ran out of bullets. She meant to make sure."

"Iris? The friend of Hector's?"

"Yes."

"Don't you go to jail for that?"

"Not Iris. We couldn't spare her. Anyway, Hector took charge. Ben had knocked Larry down after he shot Megan, and the gun popped loose. Maybe Larry was out cold or maybe he was getting up to shoot some more. Hector decided it was self-defense, a wise call."

"I wonder if Cleopatra ever personally killed someone."

"What?"

"Never mind. Was Iris troubled? Troubled by having to kill this man?"

"I never thought of it. She was troubled by Megan's death. I see what you're asking. If I had to guess, maybe she was troubled because there were only four bullets left in the gun."

"I understand. Does she have a thing with Hector?"

"You're just into everything, aren't you? Like a puppy."

"I wasn't into everything. Wasn't into anything after Julie left. Now, maybe so. Maybe more so, for some reason. Will you tell me?"

"They didn't have a thing when Iris shot Larry. Except they were old friends from forever. Iris's husband had died. Now, we all hope they have a thing. That would be wonderful. It's hard to know with those two."

"Maybe it's hard for them to know, if they've been friends for so long. It looks like they belong together, but what do I know, I'm just…"

"A janitor?"

"No, a romantic."

It was a day I liked. We finished the painting and it looked good and it was a happiness to see Lena happy. It's a gift when you can get others to delight in your happiness. And when you can reward their efforts with a giggle. I suspected, knew, that I did not giggle enough. Lena made me stay to dinner, a roast with carrots and potatoes simmering in a crock pot, so that the work of the afternoon was also the smell of new paint and roast beef, depending on which way you pointed your nose. As we moved the furniture back inside, it included the tangy smell of PBR. The teenage boys, John and Chris, came in from their summer jobs, boisterous, sublimely confident of their days, this day, and the days after. They also did things, I think as lovely ritual, to make their mother giggle, and to make their father survey the table, looking closely at all of them in turn, memorizing them as if they might be squirrels.

I was grateful for it all and especially grateful for the chance to drift back and hover, seeing these, the living, and also Julie, across the table, her chin on her fist, her auburn eyebrows raised, pretending to be angry at me and preparing her decisive refutation of my foolishness. Truth, she approved of me and even approved of my nickname, my treeness, or treehood, or mayhap, treedom. That was it—others might have a kingdom or a fiefdom, but I had a treedom, watched over by Julie. And, I'm just a janitor, but I believed she liked those boys, John and Chris, like the ones she used to teach, and this large Billy and small Lena, and Hector, and Marcos and Maria, and especially Javier. She was, as I believed, reserving judgment on George, and Iris was completely outside of her experience. Julie's feelings about Nico had not changed; when she thought on him, her eyes flashed, and I took note. Mostly, though, she thought I was doing OK, sitting here at this lively table, and of that I also took note.

Chapter 7

My sainted mother said look on the bright side so you don't go dark. I once asked Julie her view on this, what you might call, philosophy of life, and she agreed right on through. So, there is a bright side (sorry, Julie) when your wife passes through the (pearly?) gate that separates those of us in the now from the multitudes that have passed on to the then. The bright side is that you get to zone out at will, and be yet forgiven.

Sometimes folks do get concerned, which I can abide, or they find it "concerning," which I cannot. I digress, but it's what I do, and digressions about "concerning" are a luxury to which you are judged entitled when your wife dies. And dies. So, thanks, Julie, for that bright side. I don't fool myself that this luxury will be limitless; sooner or later, people will tire of my mental absence; they will be as one in finding it concerning; they will want me to get over it because, you know…it's time; I will then have to fake being present, or, more like, just strap my camper to my truck and slip away.

And another thing about absence. One day in high school French class I looked up and paid attention for a second and learned the French word for absence. I loved to pick off these gimme words, words the same in both languages except for the pronunciation. Course, I don't know French in any way that a French person would style as knowing French. And, like Huckleberry, I "dasn't" try to speak even English in cultured places like London or Mobile. But people in the Muscle Shoals tri-county area swore (with conviction) that I had no Southern accent that they could detect. Sometimes, when I had a story going, and the little gang around the campfire in Alabama right with me, I would cunningly throw in the word, *absence*, with its sophisticated French pronunciation, and they would be tickled. Because of how Baroque it all was.

So, when George and Billy came by my camp and wanted me to go on an adventure, I said yes, because I knew I could always just zone out and be forgiven. I didn't much want to go because my plan for the day was to sit in the sun in the morning and the shade in the afternoon. And sun or shade, I could read *The Rider of Lost Creek* by L. L'Amour or *A History of Western Philosophy* by B. Russell, both recently and kindly loaned to me from the library, and both offering consolations to the spirit, each in its separate way. And both writers kindred spirits in the remarkable decisiveness of their visions, stars for wandering barks like Vernon (Tree) Purcell.

George wanted to spy out whether Nico was still in town and thought, wrongly, that I would be myself curious. Billy was guide because he knew his way every which way in the mountains because it was his passion to hike around looking at things (like squirrels). Billy knew a place high on the mountain where the hidden Willard Jordan ranch house could be spied on by intrepid spy people in the secret service of a Richard III or Charles I or other such English royalty. Billy claimed this spy place was on public land, so there would be no trespasses that would cry out for either forgiveness or arrest. When I worked on the ranch, I had lifted mine eyes unto Willard's high mountain, and I had no idea how you would know where Willard's forested private mountainside left off and Billy's forested public land began, but I was one with Mr. Rhett Butler in not giving a damn, Scarlett, frankly.

I also got myself secretly intrigued (some things are best not shared) by this idea of fractional royalty that popped into my head. Mayhap, before Charles I, there was a Charles I/II, then a Charles II/III. This amused me, but I knew it was damned unusual thinking, and I knew that, without vigilance on my part, I might become too peculiar for human companionship. Still...Good King Willard I/II? Half Willard? I liked it passing fine.

I offered to make some sandwiches to take along, and Billy went to the back of his battered Dodge diesel pickup and lifted out his backpack. He took out three brown paper sacks and one was bigger by some and had hearts drawn on it and my name spelled Tre. Billy and George had no comment on Lena's spelling, and I for certain did not, and, more besides, I kind of liked being a Tre. George looked at the hearts and said my, my, how that Lena does love a stray, the more strayed, the more pathetic, the better. Billy let go a shy grin and said yeah, true that, plus she caught him reading on the toilet yesterday and she hates that and is now getting back at him.

"Why does she hate you reading on the toilet?" I asked.

"Because she's not much of a reader. Makes her feel left out."

"She doesn't like reading?"

"Not that. Can't really catch on to it. We've tried. Thing is, when we met in school, we both read about the same. Then later George took over my education, and I leaped ahead. She's proud of me, proud of the articles I write for George, even if I have to read them to her. It's just not what she's good at."

"What's she good at?"

"Pot roast. Raising kids. Making us happy."

"Good things, all. It's interesting to see how people go."

"She got irritated at me for wandering the hills and secret reading and reminded me that if I get too uppity writing a fancy newspaper column that she might just find herself a barely literate, barely bright high school janitor and run off with him."

"Wow. You tell her I'd take her up on that in a flea's half-second. But it's a doomed relationship."

"Why?"

"Sooner or later she'd catch me reading on the toilet, too."

We went to get in the truck, but George tugged at my sleeve as we were behind the truck and nodded to watch Billy getting in. The trucked whimpered, sighed, and sagged deeply left. George and I got in, with George in the middle, but still the truck did not come to level.

"Making fun of the large can be dangerous," growled Billy.

"The kids," said George, "are all about jacking up their cars. Jacking them up or dropping them down. Why don't you just hire one of them to jack up the left side of this old truck?"

"Why," asked Billy, "are we going to spy on this judge? What's he to us?"

"Damned if I know," said George. "For sure, he doesn't want to be anything to us. But here's this other thing. That crazy-ass story that Tree told about the letter and the pope got to him for some reason."

"Maybe," said Billy, "because it was true."

"I'm telling you, I made it up, the interesting parts, anyway."

"Not what I mean," said Billy. "Maybe you made an inspired guess."

"I'm still telling you. Nobody knows what's in the letter except me and the pope. Makes me feel kind of special. And—there's this—Nico has had plenty of time to call the pope and check on my story. So, Nico, if he's so worried about it, he calls Big Frankie..."

Billy: "Big Frankie? Oh, never mind. I got it."

"Stay with me on this," said George. I did some snooping yesterday while you guys were painting Billy's house and Tree was charming Lena. I don't get that, by the way."

"Should I be jealous?" asked Billy.

They both turned and stared at me for a longer time than I thought polite, looking for some feature, anything, that might justify jealousy.

George said, "He reminds her of a drowned puppy, a wet, homely puppy from the Land o' Goshen, which I think is in North Alabama. Can we talk Justice Grasso? He was supposed to give a speech yesterday at a conference in Chicago. The story on the wire is that he couldn't make it because he got sick, caught giardia on a camping trip in Colorado—roughing it and all. Supposed to have gone home to Washington. I'm not buying. I think he's still here."

"Why?" I asked. "And what difference does it make?"

George said, "You've forgotten your own campfire tales..."

"I can't be expected to keep up with all the lies I tell when drinking."

"You told Grasso the pope was unhappy with him, was blackmailing him to stop being an asshole. And you told him to check your story with the pope if he didn't believe you."

"So, Nico checks with Big Frankie, and they both have a laugh at my expense. Actually, I win because I made him check."

"I don't know. Maybe the pope's not taking his calls. Maybe Grasso really wants that letter back because he's not sure what might be in it. Maybe he's a guy with a black heart."

I wondered about that. Not whether Nico had a black heart. But where this black heart thing came from. Did people in Africa (darkest Africa?), black people, speaking their own language, did they refer to the scoundrels in their midst as having white hearts? White carried more plausibility for evil, more colonial weight, than this silliness of the black hearts. I thought to ask George and Billy about the true color of hearts and then thought to keep my mouth shut for just this once. I did that...and was proud.

Billy drove us to a trailhead a few miles south of Half Willard's ranch. Billy handed me a daypack crammed with assorted plastic water bottles, some dented and partly crushed. I wondered how far we were hiking that Billy thought we needed this much water, and, after deep reflection, I decided the situation was concerning. Billy wore the backpack with the sandwiches and I heard the telltale tinkle of beer bottles, as cheerful a sound as ever warmed a wandering heart. I wondered why Billy didn't trust me to carry the pack with the beer, and the question answered itself. I was left to follow the tinkling beer up the trail. George did not carry anything and hiked faster than should have been possible for a short man. In an instant he had crossed a small rise in the trail and disappeared. When it was too late to take a closer look, I wondered if he was one of those short people with long legs, legs out of all proportion to necessity.

"He'll wait for us somewhere up the trail," said Billy. "He likes to go on ahead and stretch out under a tree for a toke."

"Is that what makes him so fast?"

"Damned if I know. I've been watching George hike off and leave me so long, I don't give it any thought."

"Aren't you the one should be fast?"

"I guess. I don't like to go fast. You miss stuff. Every time I catch up to George I ask him did you see this or see that. Nothing.

I think he goes so fast it's all just a blur. I finally figured out the only reason he stops to wait is so he can have an audience for all the ideas he's had on the trail."

"And to have a toke?"

"Well, that. George is also a famous hiker. He hiked the Appalachian Trail before most anybody knew there was one. He wrote a great book about it. But you can tell he got a little obsessed by the mosquitoes. There's a footnote on mosquitoes in his book that goes on for about three pages. You get the idea that a crazed bug doctor pushed George away from the typewriter and started writing a whole different book. It just takes off on mosquitoes in this tiny footnote type with a bunch of scientific terms and you start to think you're going blind and crazy. And then, up in the large type, George the hiker meets a cute, grubby chick on the trail, and you are rescued from the mosquito footnote by trail loneliness and lust. You do come away clear that George hates mosquitoes."

"I didn't know that."

"Which? The mosquitoes?"

"All. The book. Any of it. A three-page footnote?"

"Longest I've ever seen. Interesting, too, but a pain because of the tiny type. Sorta made you wish he had just written a separate book on mosquitoes. It was a little cracked, though, like George was about to go off the deep end."

"The great white mosquito," I said.

"Call me Ishmael," said Billy from ahead of me, proving once for all the value of a liberal, barroom education.

The trail kept side-hilling up and up Storm Peak. Mostly the trail was treebound but sometimes there was an open place to look out and down at the Rolling River and assorted ponds along it and the highway on the other side. We picked up George twice;

each time he was napping beside the trail. He was for sure a roadrunner, but, different from Billy's forecast, he was more inside his own thoughts than talkative when we picked him up. Maybe he was composing a footnote. After the second time we picked him up, he did not go on ahead but dropped in behind Billy.

There was a moment when Billy was on the trail ahead of us and another when he wasn't, which was curious, and I thought to ask George about it, and then he was gone, too. George whistled me up, and it still took a minute to find the two big pines and squeeze between them and follow on the invisible trail that only Billy could see. We dropped into a gully and followed it down until one side of the gully flattened out and we turned right beneath a ridge that kept getting higher. We went for maybe an hour and stopped in a tiny clearing in the trees, and I looked down and saw the ranch house. A buddy of mine in Alabama lived in a cabin in the woods, and his place was not like the palace of Good King Half Willard. When I worked there, I had never seen Willard's house because it was hidden from the ranch buildings by a ridge, with a small road that slipped up and through the trees and over the ridge. That ridge formed one side of a little valley and the ridge behind us at this moment formed the other side, and Willard's house sat between.

There was what I took to be a helicopter pad out away from the house. I can't say I had ever seen a helicopter pad, but I tumbled to this one because there was a large helicopter nesting right in the middle of it. Off to the other side of the house was a largish pond, decorated with three islands, which were decorated with big aspen trees. There was everywhere a lot of brilliant green grass and splashes of color, which had to be cultivated wildflowers, but it was too far to make out what kind.

My eyes seemed to skip away from the house itself because, asking due forgiveness for the commonness of my language, Half Willard's house was fucking obscene. It put me in mind of rotting skunk. It was rotting skunk that went on for maybe miles. I was mostly sure I remembered that Half Willard was married and had two adult children. Maybe some grandchildren. I guess they liked to spread out when they came for Christmas. That was one creepy house. Maybe the house itself was embarrassed to be looked at. I understood common ideas about money—it's yours, do what you want with it. But what rot inside a Half Willard would make him want to do this to good timber? To so much good timber? I swear I couldn't look at it, couldn't keep my eyes on it. It may have been an architectural masterpiece for what I knew— I still couldn't look at that steaming pile of shit. Wait, no, I already said it was a rotting skunk. Could it be both? Yes, and more besides. My final word: It was a half-mile long skunk that took a huge, steaming shit and then curled up in the shit and died. It was odd that the three of us were the only ones who could see it from far enough away to take in the whole thing and decide whether it was an architectural wonder. George was writing notes, but he was a trained journalist, accustomed to viewing the putrefactions of the flesh. Billy was sitting with his back against a big pine, facing away from the house, tossing a peanut to a chipmunk.

"It sucks, huh?" asked George.

I leaned back against a log and drank some of the water Billy made me carry. I passed another bottle to George. "Say again why we're here?"

"I'm trying to get you interested in the Right Honorable Justice Grasso."

"What's interesting about any of that...that shit?" I nodded behind me in the direction of the house. The image that came to me was that Julie would weep, just weep, in the way that Jesus wept.

"What's interesting to Grasso is that this is where his boss lives, one of them. This is the money tree."

"That's what you think?"

"You're the one told the big story about Grasso being on the take."

"I was just telling stories."

"You don't think Grasso is on the take?"

"George, I never gave it any thought until I made that story up. I don't much care for the guy, but lots of people can be jerks. It doesn't signify. People who work in convenience stores can be jerks."

"But you knew that Grasso always rules for the rich."

"I guess. Julie, my wife, sometimes picked up the paper and went on about this guy. This is her thing, not mine."

"What's your thing?"

"Just what you see. I like a job where I'm left alone. I like reading books and talking about stuff, even if it's mostly talking to myself. Sitting around a campfire with some friends."

"And you liked Julie. Enough to make up those big lies you told around the campfire."

"That's fair."

"That was another piece of research I did yesterday while you were flirting with Lena."

Billy chuckled from behind his tree.

"Would you guys give me a break about Lena? What research?"

"Justice Nicholas Grasso makes two hundred and fifty thousand dollars a year, round figures."

"Getting at what?"

"Getting at he's being horribly ripped off. He makes rulings that are worth billions to Willard Jordan and his friends. Literally billions. Grasso makes it all possible and he gets 250k? And keep this in front of you. Grasso thinks he's about the smartest person in America. Not about. He thinks he absolutely is the smartest person in America. 250k? And he comes down here and gets to stare at what a couple of billion looks like. A couple of billion that belongs to one of the dumbest people in America. Even Willard's wranglers think he's dumb as a post. 250k? Let me tell you what else. Grasso went to Harvard. He's got a good Catholic family with about forty-seven kids. None of those kids is applying to the local community college. A Grasso kid goes to Harvard or Princeton. On 250k?"

"If that's what he's about, he could resign and go off on his own. Probably make a ton of money."

"Sure, a few million, easy. But it's still hard to make a billion. And Grasso is worth billions to the rich right where he is. The last thing Willard and his friends want is for Grasso to go into private practice. All Grasso has to do is talk about resigning, or develop an ominous cough, and Willard shits his pants."

"OK, I see the reason for being on the take. But what about getting caught?"

"Maybe. But rich people know how to hide money and how to move money. So...maybe. Hell, I don't know. How's someone like you or me supposed to have a clue about the things that can be done with money? We're lucky to remember whose turn it is to buy the next beer. I'm a bull-shitter just like you. I got no proof. I don't even have a letter from the pope."

I was still trying to decide if any of this made me interested in Nico when the great man himself appeared, together with Half Willard. Or at least that's what George said. All I could see were two small figures beside the pond, one of whom might have been fishing. George claimed it was Nico and Willard, and it wasn't my place to argue since it was George with the binoculars. The stout one of the two began to trot back and forth beside the lake, so, yes, that would be Nico, trying to land one of Willard's fat fish, heavy with only the finest Purina fish chow.

Chapter 8

George snapped a picture of Nico and Willard.

"Do you think that will turn out at this distance?" I asked.

"No fucking clue. Cameras, to me, are like bringing the space shuttle back to earth at the right spot. I understand it can be done—trajectories, gravity, shit like that. So maybe all the detail of Grasso's face is in the camera and can be blown up. Or maybe it will be like those grainy pictures that might be Bigfoot or maybe just a tree with moss on it. If it turns out, though, it would be a sweet picture—Grasso, Jordan, that house. And Grasso's supposed to be giving a speech in Chicago."

"Does that matter to anybody—missing a speech?"

"Not really. It might be a ten-minute story, and then Grasso puts out a statement that he got sick and had to cancel and then he miraculously got well because he's a superior human being, so he went fishing, but the liberal media just can't stop picking on him. Ten minutes, tops."

"So why are you picking on him?"

"Because I'm the liberal media. Picking on Grasso is my job. Because he's an arrogant prick. There's no news in this place except when the married school superintendent gets it on with one of the married school board members. That was a couple years ago, and it was like a hundred-year flood for me. I used to work at a big paper, with real news. Maybe I'm not too old to win a Pulitzer. This stuff with Grasso and the pope intrigues me."

I was too slow to respond, I guess. I was not used to having news crowded up this close against me. History I liked better than journalism. I don't want to exaggerate this, but news for me was mostly how someone's day was, Julie's especially, but also when one of Eunice's kids gained or lost a tooth. I also liked old, dusty stuff, seeing what Mr. Dickens thought about the news of his day. Or Mr. Shakespeare. I knew some about the news of my day, but I was in my feelings distant from it, safely distant is a fair accusation. George was looking a question at me.

"What's good," I asked, "about Grasso? There must be something."

"Your Mama teach you that? Look for the good in everybody?"

"You know, I guess she did."

"Grasso is smart. Supposed to be smarter than Einstein. I guess he is. But here's the thing. I take one look at him and just want to bust him one. Matter of fact, I'd pass on the Pulitzer if I could just take him out back of the Moose Jaw without his bodyguards and bust him good. You trying to say you don't feel that way, after how he's treated you?"

"I don't know. I'm thinking on it." I was thinking about it. But what came to my mind was about killing the kitten; I guess that memory sort of fit what we were talking about although a memory is verily the most vagrant of zephyrs, belonging to its own whims. Memory can be cruel master or kind companion, and the kitten memory was not kind.

I was maybe ten, and my mother loved kittens and stepped on a new one. This one was a soft gray with a sort of banded look. It liked to purr and play and curl up with me and ride around on my shoulder. Regular kitten stuff. In the way of things, my mother let me name it, and I named it Mouse. I was sitting on the floor at one end of the hall, slowly rolling a tennis ball at Mouse, so she could attack it. My mother came down the hall from the other end, carrying with both hands a heavy lamp, and she stepped one way and arrested her foot in the air because Mouse ran under her foot, and my mother did a little bobble, which was kind of fun to watch, and brought her foot down the other direction to avoid Mouse, and Mouse darted this new way, and my mother only had one more bobble in her because she was about to fall over, and at the last tiny instant Mouse darted again, right under her foot, and my mother broke its small back when she landed.

Mouse was silent, but my mother howled in her grief as Mouse slithered on the floor and drooled or maybe it was throwing up. My mother and I sat beside Mouse on the floor and petted it, but my mother said don't pick it up though that's what she was doing as she tried to lift it to a standing position and it slid floppily to the hardwood floor each time. My mother cried and gasped for breath and Mouse and I were silent. Finally, my mother said the kitten needed to be put down, put out of its misery. We did not use veterinarians for mercy killing; at ten, I don't think I knew the word euthanasia. Veterinarians were expensive, and country folk could diagnose a hopeless case and figure out a cure. My mother sent me for help to the closest neighbor, Mr. Benton, who was not to be found. By the time I got home to tell her this, I could hear her wailing in the hall, and I had figured through what had to be done.

I gently picked up the kitten, now lying in a large pool of drool. I kissed the soft fur on the top of Mouse's head and rubbed my cheek against it. My mother did not get up but sat slumped and frozen. I took the kitten to the tool shed because the thing needed to be done, and I did not want my mother to have to do it. I had never killed a cat before or seen it done or had any instruction or specialized training. I knew that Mr. Benton would have done it quickly, mercifully, but I did not know how. It seemed improbable to me that he would use a gun for something so small, and anyway I was too young to own a gun, so said my mother. I set the kitten down in the grass and petted it and fetched a baseball bat from the shed. It seemed to me that one quick swing from the bat would do it.

I say right now to warn you of what you almost certainly don't truly know—cats are hard to kill. I guess more so if you're ten. I didn't know that then. I hit it sort of medium hard because I did not know but what its head might instantly explode. The kitten already couldn't move and still didn't, but it drooled more, and mewed or gasped, and its eyes came wide open and stayed that way. Other than that, there was no change, no change, at least, in the kitten. But I was full of panic and hurried to hit it harder. There was still no change except that its head was sunk deeper in the soft spring earth and some blood seeped out of its mouth and I believe out of its ear, and its front legs scrabbled feebly. Those front legs kept scrabbling while I hit it six more times, while a crack showed in its skull, with gray and red seeping out. At one of these blows, an eye came out and fell on the kitten's cheek. The eye did not roll away like a marble but hung there on a tube of viscous white tissue, snaked through with swollen red veins. I kept hitting it, each blow made harder by my panic, and then harder still until I killed Mouse.

I buried the kitten in a deep hole in the soft, rich dirt, as deep as I could make it. My mother later gave me a hug but did not like to talk about it. I didn't either, and the thing was gone into the past. Part of it gone. Part stayed, because how could it not? I was ten, and this thing went terribly bad on me because I had no idea how to do this thing, this thing to ease the suffering of Mouse, this thing to ease the suffering of my mother. She was wrong to let me do it, but I only came to see that many years later. I remember being sharply surprised as an adult when the realization dawned that she should never have let me pick up that burden. With a family of only two, I naturally reached and picked things up, sometimes things too heavy for the slenderness of a child.

So, I wasn't sure whether I wanted to bust Grasso one, as George did. Country kids grow up rough, and I did, too, and that's OK. We sometimes fought, sometimes mostly for show, sometimes hard, and at rare times dangerously. The soft, gray kitten named Mouse made me hope not to die that slowly. My mother and I were bad luck for Mouse on that day. But I had learned about myself that I could keep hitting living things until they were dead and that made me careful, a good thing. But that was also before Julie died; I didn't know whether I was still careful. You might say that with her death I was reborn, and I was still about learning who this new person was to be. It's wrong to think being born again belongs only to such as Christians or Buddhists, and it's wrong to think we are always reborn by and into the light. The loss of your great love will give you a new birth every time. But with no guarantees about what kind of new life. I did not answer George's question about the busting of Grasso, and he let it drop, I guess in the light that I was off somewhere.

"I'll be damned," said George. He had returned to studying Jordan and Grasso through the binoculars. When I looked over, he was giving the house a friendly wave. "We're busted. I'm staring at them while Al's in the guardhouse staring up at me. Unlike me, it looks like he's got a quality pair of binoculars. He just waved at me and now he's on the phone. Maybe calling in airstrikes. You know, Hector turned me on to those Louis

L'Amour Westerns, and I remember now you're not supposed to look towards the sun with your binoculars because the bad cowboys will see the reflection. I should've paid more attention."

"Let me see," said Billy, from behind his tree, as he started to get up.

"No, stay there. I don't think Al has seen you. Just me and Tree. There's no use you getting arrested, too, if it turns out we're trespassing."

"We're not trespassing," said Billy, defensively. "I know where I am."

"And in the US of A, you only get arrested when you're in the wrong?"

"I've never even been arrested...well, once, maybe. Hector took me in because I was surrounded by motorcycle people. I don't like those machine people."

"You drive a snowplow," said George. "One of the larger machines."

"What happened?" I asked.

"Hector made it look like he was taking me to jail but then just took me home. I told him I hadn't been doing anything but minding my own business, until the machines got so loud I couldn't stand it, and all I wanted to do was have a quiet beer after work at McCourt's. Hector said what I already well knew. Being large is enough by itself to make some people mad." Billy grinned. "That and calling a machine person a loud, ignorant motherfucker."

"They have feelings, too," said George.

I motioned down the hill. "Are they going to climb up after us?"

"No chance," said George. "Not up that hill. But Al can get to the trailhead a lot faster than we can."

Folks said there was a fight at the trailhead. By folks, I mean George and Billy and Nico. What they said mostly fits my flickering memories, flickering because somewhere along in this fight I got a heavy blow to the side of my head, and I recall feeling surprised. I clearly remembered being hit in the nose because getting hit in the nose is a hurtful thing, and I always carried my hands too low to protect my nose and never could learn better. But here's the other part where surprise fits in: I woke up and who was tending my wounds was Nico. He was holding his handkerchief to my nose, which was leaking a right smart of blood. He later told me that he had a passel of his own children who collected scrapes, but none who fought with such abandon (his words). I guess abandon would be right if by that you meant looking for a door to a far room. Nico didn't know that about me, and I don't think ever in his life would have been able to understand it because we were not made the same.

I have a clear memory of getting to the trailhead and walking up a gully to pee, out of some fanciful concern that a car full of nuns, The Little Sisters of Perpetual Purity, might come screeching around the curve. And be embarrassed at me peeing in the road. The nuns, that is, would be embarrassed—OK, also me. After that, I did remember something like what the judge called abandon. I didn't abandon all hope of personal safety. More like, I abandoned the thought of it. I ran down the gully toward the fight. Sometimes in the past I liked fighting, and sometimes I didn't care for it, and sometimes it was pure, uncaring joy. But never as pure and uncaring as running down that gully with the thought of peace at the end, with the prospect of lying in the sun like my mother's dead pig. That's as near as I can think to describe it. Storybooks like to go on about heroes rushing in when all seems lost. But mostly, when all seems lost, that's because all is lost. Julie seemed lost and truly was, no matter what amount of rushing I could think to do. So, you might say I was not rushing so much at a short, sweet fight but away from one that had me in its grip, one that mostly seemed like it was going to be just brutal long. I don't know. I just don't. Because moments came on me that I liked things, liked people, liked living, and then came the other kinds of times. If you could choose your exit, is it better to go out at some sweet moment you long to hold on to, or the other way, when a pig's rest seems all the sweetness left to a body?

I call seeing as I came around the bend of the gully that George and Billy were on the ground, with a couple guys holding George, and more, a big pack, swarming over Billy and some of this pack being tossed out and others diving in. Al was supervising and for some strange reason, maybe show, maybe fear of Billy, had a gun out, so I took a true aim on him. I remember him turning to me and standing straight and holding his pistol out with two hands and moving the bead to follow me in. Then my mind gets some mist on it because I was swarmed by another pack of guys coming up from the side. I was, you might say, unhorsed, like that poor devil the third King Richard. At that moment, I had no kingdom to trade for a horse, but I wanted to get to that gun-toting Al, and for lack of a horse my wish came up short (course Al would have just shot the horse, so no point in getting too fanciful).

I have always had a portion of sympathy for that Richard, even if he was a bad guy, because Mr. Shakespeare snatched from him his soul entire. Richard did not know that he would lose horse and life and kingdom forever to a small, solid army and a boggy field. More besides, he did not know that his soul would be stained forever by a man who told stories for a living. Mr. Shakespeare had a harsh judgment on Richard, and it stuck hard to him. What I took out of it was that it's flattering to the famous to have Mr. Shakespeare write your life if he likes you, but the other way, beware.

After I was swarmed, there was a blur of a struggle. I know I hit some people because there were faces in front of me that popped up and disappeared and I call the feel of my arm and shoulder following through in a sweet line. But others had a sweet line on me, and I never made it through to Al. I pieced together from George and Billy that this was when Nico's Suburban came bouncing up the road with Nico driving by himself and jumping into the swarm and shouting stop. Course they all fell back before Nico because no one was of any mind to hit Nico except for sure George and for unsure me.

But I came to, and there he was kneeling beside me holding a bloody handkerchief to my nose. I struggled up on an elbow, and Nico assisted me to lean back against a nearby boulder, showing some of that strength that he had when he pushed me in the river. By then I was holding the handkerchief to my nose, and in my fog, I wondered if maybe I just slipped down and hit my head on the boulder. The brain just powerfully wants to make sense out of confusion and will make up most any story that acts like it might fit. Then I looked around and saw my audience, all gathered round in half a circle. It turned out that I was the chief casualty, and I guess Al had made up his mind in the direction of not shooting anyone.

Nico bade them go, now, right now, no more fighting, and he was a leader in that moment and could bade folk. He made them believe he was the land's highest law, and no one argued with him. Nico went back to kneeling beside me and tending to my war wounds as the wranglers left. George and Billy stood watching and then Nico said you go, too, I want to talk to Tree, and I'll drive him home, and George looked at me and I surprised myself by nodding, and Billy looked at George and George nodded, too, and there we were, Tree Purcell and the country's own high justice.

"Why don't we be friends?" he asked.

My head was clearer but not so clear for that to make any sense. I grinned, or think I did; I can't promise it wasn't just a pig rictus. "You want to be my friend, or you want that letter?"

Nico seemed to find this an easy one. "Both. You feel like moving? Let's get you in my car."

We had coffee from my speckled coffee pot beside my granite coffee table that was beside my small camper that had a blooming rust splatter on its white propane tank. My theory holds firm that rust is viral and that my rusty truck made my camper sick. The wind must have blown the tiny rust virus back onto my camper whilst traveling, like unto a rusty sneeze. I explained this to Nico over coffee and caused him to scratch his head, a result I found satisfying, and one that made me think I would yet recover from that stone hard blow to the head delivered by one of Jordan's handier wranglers. Though I can't be exactly sure who hit me because I didn't see the blow coming, so it could as well have been delivered by one of the Little Sisters of Perpetual Pugilism. I thought on explaining to Nico about the Little Sisters, but I judged the dose I had given him on the viral rust was strong enough to hold him. Nico was sitting with his coffee in a camp chair he had retrieved from the back of the Suburban, and that gave me something to scratch my own head over and to keep rust from my mind.

"What is it exactly you do for a living?" asked Nico. "I asked Willard what you did for him before I got you fired, and he didn't know. Sometimes I think Willard's not too bright." Nico seemed to be in high spirits about having gotten me fired; as best I could guess, his thinking was that I shouldn't mind my being fired if he didn't, and he had made his peace with my loss.

"Maybe Willard's got other good qualities."

"He does." Nico's face lit up. "A few billion of them." Nico's face shone all over, and my idea was that Nico looked at his own humor with a sense of childlike wonder, a feeling I well knew.

"I was a janitor at the ranch, but I think they called me something else in the computer. Maintenance technician, or something like. I've always been a janitor, starting in high school. At the school, the assistant principal came to me a few years ago and said I wasn't a janitor anymore but was now a Class III Custodial Provider. I asked him if there was more money in it and he said no and I asked him if my work was to change and he said no and I asked him what it meant and he said nothing was what it meant, and I was content because I got to keep being a janitor."

"I love it," said Nico. "You like things to mean exactly what they say. A man after my own heart."

"That's as may be. I expect life will show us."

"You know, I thought we would get along if we just had a chance to talk. I had Willard's people check you out. No criminal record. Not so much as a speeding ticket. No political associations. As a matter of fact, you might as well not exist on the Internet. A simple working man from Alabama. I knew we would get along if we got together and talked. No need to be at cross purposes. If I just took the time to explain some things to you in a way you could understand. You may not know this, but I have always been in my public life a great friend to the working man."

"Yes, I didn't know that."

Nico's face smiled all over. "I wasn't always who I am now. I started out in modest circumstances, the grandson of immigrants. I know what it means to work. I know what the working man wants."

"I wish I knew what this one wants."

"Freedom. Liberty. He doesn't want to be made to join some union. He wants to sell his services on the open market, without government interference. There's dignity in that. He wants to be free to sell his labor to the highest bidder, so employers will have to compete for his services. If he does good work, if he keeps training himself, if he's willing to take on overtime, willing to be valuable to his employer, then his employer will reward value. The working man does not want the government to interfere and tell his employer that he's got to hire a man that's some other color or maybe a woman ahead of him. Because that distorts the market. If the government makes rules for his employer, then the government is making rules for the worker. So, if the government says the employer must provide health insurance or safety helmets, then the employer just takes the money out of the worker's pocket and pays it toward insurance the worker might not want or need. I'm just saying, Tree, in words I hope you can understand, that the worker needs to be left alone to make his own decisions, making his best deal, man to man, with his employer, and free to advance or not. It's all up to him. The American worker stands equal before the government, equal to the richest man and the mightiest corporation. That's what liberty is. The job of government is to stay out of their way and let them manage their own affairs, as becomes equals."

Truth, I was all over amazement. I guess I kind of knew how Nico thought, but it was remarkable to hear him say it out loud and direct to me and with a kind of sublime conviction that just swept him up. I was swept up by him being swept up. It was one of those moments of happiness for me, of renewed curiosity about the world. George had said this man was smarter than Einstein. He was what I understood to be an intellectual, a leading light of society. And it was the written words of some of these people, the cream of civilization you might say, that I liked studying on. So, it came to me that here was one wanting to talk to me, and to be honest I had mostly not encountered this circumstance in Muscle Shoals, so the right and proper thing for me was to listen up.

"Nico, I am all over ears."

Chapter 9

But it turned out I was not all over ears. I maybe had a baby concussion because I got drowsy as Nico talked. When he got wound up, he would go on. Sometimes I fought through the fog on my brain and paid attention, but every time I focused it sounded like Nico was repeating himself, and the difference between what he was saying from my one lucid moment over to the next was too tiny to give notice to. Maybe I had this all the way wrong and just wasn't in my best mind.

I woke up in my camper. Nico was not sitting beside my bed still talking, and, as blessings go, this was big. My head was sore, but when I felt it all over I couldn't find much but the original imperfections. My nose was tender and swollen. To his credit, Nico had warned me not to drink whiskey on top of a blow to the head, which I drank whiskey anyway; I'm not sure how much, possibly a lot; my excuse was that Nico would go on.

My teeth were desperate to be brushed, and I took care of this right off. I scrambled a few eggs to settle my stomach and then brushed my teeth again. My jaw was sore and didn't want to open just right, but I was happy to be brushing my teeth and happy to know that I could come back and do it again at will. This thought cheered me as I sat with my morning coffee beside my granite table. Even though my sins had left me in a ragged state, I still could look up at a beautiful day. I was getting fond of these unnaturally blue Colorado skies and dry air.

Talking to Julie in the morning freshness was nice. She helped me to know my mind. And, also, to know her mind, which I always craved. You might say I married Julie to know her mind. I know. I know. Laugh if you feel that calling. But leave me alone to tell my piece of the truth. I already knew what I thought about things. I didn't need Julie for that. I had years of being alone by a campfire in the woods to listen to my own thoughts. What I craved to know was what Julie thought.

For one, she thought, rightly, that I was too withdrawn from the general run of folks, that I lived too much in books that took me too much into the past. Guilty for all that. I didn't think so much that I liked history for itself but because it rounded up the most interesting things my species had ever been up to. Look, for example, at those cunning Greek tricksters—not just Ulysses, but you might as well say also Plato and Aristotle and the whole like roll call. They played deep, fanciful tricks with Trojan horses, and deep, fanciful tricks with ideas, ideas too deep for me and for most folks. And lots of folks just get mad about it and throw down the book, and I get that. One of Lincoln's many below average generals sat frozen with his troops as General Lee faked left and faked right and then serenely escaped across the river. And this faked-out general most ruefully summed it up by saying it was all too deep for him. Equally, I freely confess it's all too deep for me, but I sorta don't mind because it's a happiness to watch Aristotle and Plato fake left and right. I said before that sometimes I couldn't stand to hear people talk about books I had read. So, it will not surprise you that I skipped out of my high school history classes. This was one they punished me for, and the punishment was that I had to go help the janitor, and little enough did they know. In that way, I was like that crafty Brer Rabbit, who begged Brer Fox to do anything to him but please don't throw him in the briar patch. So that was a true part, but another true part, kept mostly hidden, was just pure, howling rage at these people who did not know me and who would never know me because Hell would freeze over at the exact time I let them into my thoughts.

Julie saw this or some of it and coaxed me more into the world. Course I was shy in no particular with my regular hunting and fishing buddies. Lots of times, their most loving and tender wish for me was that I should only shut the fuck up. And none of this would have worked between Julie and me but that she was also happy to spend time in my world. She liked talking about the old, odd stuff that my mind lived in. And I liked reading the books my own loved English teacher told me to read, or, even better, read to me. Because then I could tell what she thought about what she was reading by the tone of her musical voice and the small frowns or smiles she could not suppress.

Truth, I don't know what to say about what happened next as I sat in my mountain living room. Maybe I should keep it secret, but I will say on anyway and just say I'm sorry if I give offense to delicate spirits. Who knows when to be explicit? I would never be so about sex with Julie. That would be a scalding sacrilege, even if I had the words for the wonder of it. I will say this: I hope that if enough time passes with me still in it that a day will come when I can think on such a thing and smile, the smile I used to have sometimes when Julie was alive and I was alone, working maybe, and the feel of the smile on my face was by some sublime transfiguring the same as the feeling of Julie against me. Getting that smile back, with the pain taken from it, would be a gift worth going on for although of it I despair.

I sat beside my granite coffee table with my blue-speckled coffee cup in the dry mountain air and looked up at the mountains and the absurdly blue Colorado sky and felt the always breeze on my bare arm and thought on Julie reading to me *The Mayor of Casterbridge* and the looks moving over the surface of her liquid face. And mind that I am a big man, tall, lank, rawboned, and strong. And the part I am reluctant to now tell is that my body was wracked. Wracked. Should I say again wracked to help you know it better? I cried, convulsed. I held my knees against my chest to stop the jerking that threatened to pitch me off the planet. I never knew when one of these episodes would come. It was a seizure of loss. I vomited between my knees, and vomit and tears and snot moved across the surface of my plain face. I wiped my face a little on my pants leg, maybe out of some stupid thought that I would not want Julie to see me this way. With my knees braced against my granite coffee table, I howled to the granite hills and to all the world's granite. I suppose this is not polite or pretty to describe and is maybe too shocking to those who have never personally killed a kitten. I am at one about being sorry to show it to you but also thinking you need to know.

In the way of things, this passed. When I could breathe yet again, I slowly cleaned up, moving carefully so as not to break some fragile part of my body, or, for all I knew, not to break the granite coffee table, which, for all I knew, might have become fragile in my presence. It's just what I did for the self-respect of cleanliness. I went inside and cleaned my face. I always had a determination at these times to clean my face, to not be seen, and I thought this a good thing. I brushed my teeth again, and again grateful. I blotted my pants and a place high up on my shirt with a wet washcloth. I found a large piece of bark and scraped the vomit from the sand and pitched it into the trees. I broke off a spruce frond and scrubbed the vomit from the side of my coffee table. My howls, I could not scrub them from the hills.

.....

"Did the judge make you cry?" asked Iris.

I guess my cleanup job on my face was shy of perfect. We were sitting around my coffee table, Iris and Hector and I, and I was so deep happy they were there I felt like crying again but didn't because it wouldn't be proper hospitality. They brought, of all things, two more camp chairs that Iris said were a housewarming gift. And you could fair say that wasn't the biggest deal ever, but yes it was.

"He left sometime last night, I guess. When I heard your car, I was afraid it was him."

"Why?" asked Hector. "Was there trouble between you?"

"Ah, I see what you're saying. No. We sat by the fire. Nico built the fire and by God knew how to build a fire, so figure that one. No trouble like you mean. We talked. Well, Nico talked. I drank some whiskey. I have a headache."

"What did Nico want?" asked Hector.

"The letter, I guess. Though I don't think he ever asked for it. Maybe he didn't get a chance before I nodded off."

"What did he say?"

"He talked on and on."

"And said?" Hector's voice was still patient.

I poured myself another cup of coffee and tried to remember. It was no fun concentrating.

"He said that 'the law, in its majestic equality, forbids the rich as well as the poor to sleep under bridges, to beg in the streets, and to steal bread.'" The words I used belonged to a fellow named Anatole, a cool name, but the ability to see them on the long-ago page, every comma in its place, belonged to me. For a brief while in the long past this ability made me feel special and then it just made me feel different, and different is a way of separate, and separate is a way of alone.

"He said that?"

"Not in those words, which properly belong to someone else. But that's what he said. He kept saying it over for a couple hours, or years as may be. My idea is that he thought he was saying different things. But he wasn't. I confess that made me angry."

"Who cares about this guy, anyway?" asked Iris. "He's no friend of mine and not likely to be."

Hector said, "No, you're right. I only care because it's my people sleeping under the bridges. I don't trust him."

Iris reached over and took his hand. "We're all your people, love."

"Love? Hah! Love?" I said. "I knew it all along, and I may have told you so, not sure about that."

Hector said, "Pay no attention to him. He's from Alabama. It's how they are."

"Ben," said Iris, "is from the South. He's kind of weird, too."

"Where in the South?"

"South Carolina."

"I'd be out on a skinny limb if I called a South Carolinian normal. Where is he? I'd like to meet a fellow refugee. He could give me advice on getting along with mountain folk."

"Ben's a teacher. He bums around in the summer."

"The thing is, does he know about you two?"

"Of course. He's family."

Hector said, "It's a small place. Everybody knows, or thinks they do. They're just cooler about it than you. What is that with you?"

"I know. You're right. Sorry. I don't all the way know."

Iris said, "It's just two old people finding love. It happens."

"I know," I said. "I don't get out much, don't always know how to act."

Hector said, "Speak for yourself, Iris. I'm not that old. Word gets out I'm old, they'll make me retire, and Al will get my job."

"Hector and I have known each other since we were kids. Heck got divorced. I got widowed. It was a long road. Here we are."

"OK, so maybe I'm happy because I like you guys. And I grab onto it because I get some hope from it."

"Of course," said Iris. "Any fool…"

"Any fool what?" asked Hector.

"Gets that."

"OK, but I can still celebrate. Hector can't step on my neck and arrest me for that."

"Tree," said Iris, "you're earning your way in," and I was happy to have her approval, whether she was a murderer or no.

Hector said, "This is still new to us, too, being officially in love, or something. We don't know how to act, either."

"Were you always in love a little bit?"

"Not always. When we were kids, Iris was out of my league. Her family had money. And was Anglo—that was more of a thing then. Not with Iris—but just sort of who was in your league."

Iris said, "So instead the rich girl ends up marrying Buster, a guy who drove a delivery truck."

"Buster, what a fun guy. Everybody loved Buster. If Iris hadn't married him, I might've married him myself. Buster taught me to ski—thing is he didn't know shit, either. We came barreling down the mountain, two big guys, whooping and hollering, one of them wearing a gun, and the tourists were terrified. I had to quit skiing because my boss got complaints."

"Buster and I," said Iris, "were too wild. People thought of us as crazy, but mostly we were crazy in love. We had a daughter, a good family. People didn't see that part of it so much. The truth is it was mostly me that gave us a bad reputation. I had a temper.

I was the one who liked to fight in bars. Buster was just a sweet hippie with a pony tail. But then he's the one who didn't survive."

"What happened?"

"Hector busted him for drunk driving. We were going through a tough time. Buster was drinking too much. He was in danger of losing his job. I told him to hell with the job, I've got enough money we can live on forever. Not the right thing to say. But he was still a sweet guy. He didn't want to disappoint me or even disappoint Hector. So, he started riding his bike in the dead of winter. He drank some beer and rode his bike down a steep, icy hill to the store for more beer and collided with a car."

"Sorry, Iris."

"My world closed, like yours closed on you."

"I know. I know I'm not the only one. In one way. But I am in another. You're the only one who lost Buster. I'm the only one who lost Julie."

"OK," said Iris, "I get that."

And I told them a story, as I do.

"Here's a story that might be about social class, like you were talking about with Buster. Julie and I were not exactly from the same background, either. A time that comes into my mind is when Julie took me to her faculty party when we were dating. There were only half a dozen English teachers, so it wasn't large; I was grateful for that. Christmas party. Eggnog. The chairman's house. These folks didn't really know we'd been dating. They only knew in the way that Julie had told them she'd been dating a man named Vernon Purcell, and it's getting serious, and they're all excited cause Julie was kind of their pet, as such things happen. But they only knew me as Tree, the janitor. They knew me pleasantly enough, I suppose, those who had paid any attention at all."

Hector and Iris sat still for my story and by doing this made me happy.

"The faculty folk and their husbands and wives, who all loved Julie, who all gathered at the chairman's house for Christmas, who were all atwitter to meet Julie's new beau, well, they were some surprised. For that, I hold no blame against them. Their brains had trouble catching up to their eyes. One recognized me and came over and asked Julie if she had had car trouble, and I thought this a quick and excellent guess. I think it safe to say that Julie was some too naive about Southerners and class boundaries. The faculty and I pressed on out of our shared love for Julie, and, though I am shy, my eventual amusement was a help. We stumbled onto the topic of cleaning products, a fine idea, full credit to Mrs. Rather, who was schooled in the good art of finding something in common with everybody. She would have gamely talked with Hitler about his dog, and I mean that to be nothing but compliment. Bleach came up, and there was not one among us who was not a fan. There was spirit in the discussion of how much to dilute it for which purpose, and I learned some things useful for my work, things I would not automatically have expected to learn from such a group of scholars. Julie, I could see reclined on a sofa across the way, simultaneously holding her shaking sides and pressing a pillow to her face. It pleased me that we were making her laugh, and it pleased me that these good people were doing their heroic best, realizing that this heretofore almost invisible man knew some useful tricks about bleach and ammonia, not to mention dust, that creeping scourge of civilization. I lack proof, but it is my idea that igloos in the Arctic gather dust inside them. Later, Julie tried to turn the conversation to books, and they were shocked at her thoughtless expectation that I might have read a book; as one, they began talking of sports, even old Mrs. Scott, the widow, who confused American football with soccer but gamely carried on, secure in the knowledge that she was doing her duty by Julie, and who was I to say her nay?"

"I guess social class is even bigger in the South than here," said Hector.

"That's not what the story's about," said Iris. "It's about that little peek of Julie laughing in the background, covering her face with the pillow. And it's about everybody loving Julie. Yes, Tree?"

"You're earning your way in."

"Can I see a picture of her?" asked Iris.

"Forgive me. Not now."

Chapter 10

Nico came back, alone, and some too soon for the perfection of my happiness. He started in about my mother, which I saw coming in no way. My belief was that Nico had a hangover based on his bloodshot eyes, as squinted at through my bloodshot eyes. We had both been drinking immoderately when last my memory served. Nico did not look healthy was my expert opinion, bearing fully in mind that I am only a high school graduate from Muscle Shoals, Alabama, and closer to the bottom of my class than the top (but Eunice still proud the same). But even I could see what was plain, that Nico was old and fat and drank too much. He still had lively eyebrows, though, eyebrows right onto being ebullient. He could still do an altar boy grin, and that, together with the ebullient eyebrows, could distract you from the blotched skin, the yellowed teeth, and hard to guess what of the altar boy remained. Not much was my thought.

"Tell me, Tree, about your parents."

We were drinking coffee in the afternoon sun beside my coffee table, and now, thanks to the gift of Iris and Hector, Nico did not have to bring out his own camp chair.

"Deceased—my mother. I never knew my father." I had some edginess because I leapt to the unreasonable idea that he was about to say some transgressive thing about my mom that would require me to kick his ass and what a recipe for trouble that would top to bottom be.

"Did she bring you up?"

"She did indeed until she told me the Lord was calling her home. I was thirteen."

"Ah. She was a believer. A Catholic?"

"She followed John the Baptist right into the deep end of the pool."

"Still. A believer. I might have been a Baptist in a different home."

"Or a Buddhist, maybe?" Nico didn't like this and it made his eyebrows veer around some.

Last night he tried to be friends based on our shared politics, and he just assumed it worked because, well, he was Nico. I envied him his ability to utterly persuade himself; with this ability, he was never lost—lacking it, I wandered. Today, Nico, sober and confident, was going to persuade me that we were brothers in Christ, and I, *mirabile dictu*, would fork over his papal letter, and all's well that ends well, and Nico off to Washington to stop rich people from sleeping under bridges. Like as not Nico would be getting to Washington on Half Willard's private jet. Truth, my feelings were wounded that he thought it was all going to be this simple.

"I confess to you, Tree, my faith has been everything to me. That's why I was upset that you made out that Pope Francis was mad at me."

"He is mad at you, as you'd know if you called him like I told you."

"I don't need to call to know you were lying. I'm a judge, for God's sake."

"And you think that means you can tell a lie from the truth?"

"That's what I get paid for."

"I guess that settles it, then."

It clearly did for Nico, and he gave his eyebrows a rest and told me more about his faith, faith that he had always shared with his children to their everlasting uplift, and he hoped my mother had done the same for me.

I was uneasy and irritated at Nico for dragging my mother into this as it did not seem fitting; he had a way of pissing me off, and, actually, he may have been aware of this. The truth is that I sort of turned down Nico's volume at this point and let him run with it. And run he did. I listened for a while because I did have a bitty interest to see if he had some original-like thoughts on religion. But he didn't. He and my mother sang from the same hymnal, and both could run on like that little artesian well on the south side of our property when I was a kid. It flowed without ceasing from a pipe buried in a clay bank; it flowed, always, with no spicket (as we pronounced the word) to turn the water on and off. (My Southern people turned spigot into spicket, which I liked. Could we turn bigot, of which we have a few, into bicket? I'd hazard that we have near as many bickets as spickets. Just a thought—I feel some better for having said it.) As a small boy, I sat sometimes before our flowing artesian water and enjoyed the sound of it but could make no sense of its everlastingness. If my mother got to Heaven, as she confidently expected, it's a place where she could keep on, as she had on earth, about her faith, and that would strike lots of folk as a beautiful thing, and I don't argue. I hope she was right and is at this moment flowing on, taking as her text the glory hallelujah of the faithful.

But I could not hear ever in Nico's tone anything that captured my mother's heart on religion. I allowed that religion has more than one purpose. For my mother, the purpose was to stop once for all the separations. What's a heaven for if not to stop the separateness that makes us alone? There was no tone in Nico's voice that captured her fear of loss. Without that fear, I suspicion she wouldn't have needed John the Baptist. This renegade John brought to her a cure for separation and loss. Like most cures it wasn't free, but that's a different song, one that I sang one way and my mother another. She thought the cure was free—grace. I thought there was a price, and a spendy price it was. There was no knowledge of loss carried on Nico's tone, and I was confused by this. My mother knew loss, as did I. At his advanced age, Nico must have also known loss, but none of that made it into his talk on religion. I don't know why. The best I could make of it is that there are divers people in this world, and they naturally create the gods that make them feel most to home. My guess was that Nico's god would throw you right down if you got out of line, and his god did not countenance being sassed, which, you know, sassing is a thing I have deep studied.

It was in my mind that Nico's god made us separate, created distance between us, and between us and him. So, OK. If you fail your math test or fail your life, then you think you knew separation before, well, watch this, because I'll separate you from Me, from God, and I have all the supply of love in the universe, so you'll be separated forever from love (God said, lovingly), and that will be such a deal you might as well be burning in Hell, so here's your ticket to ride. I rebelled against these notions at an early age because, well, I was rebellious, and it's troublous to change a thing that's well begun.

I can't say clear why I rebelled so young, even before I was thirteen and sitting there beside my passing mom. I don't say I was as quick about it as young Bertrand Russell, turning over in his curious mind the first cause argument for god. Russell claimed that as a young child he asked himself, well then, if God made everything, didn't somebody have to make God and what about that? At that age, he probably even understood the idea of an infinite causal series, which I had gotten to be thirty-two and still fuzzy on it. I was rebellious, but that Russell, well, that has always been some finely tuned Russell. Russell's parents died when he was very young, and one of my wonderings about him is did his grandfather, once Queen Victoria's prime minister, bounce him on his knee and sing him a song and call him Bertie? A gift, you know, for a small boy's heart. I hope so, because boys don't live by genius alone.

"Please, Tree," my mother had said many times before, and again as she lay sick, "please come to Jesus."

"I can't, Mom."

"Do you love me? If you love me, believe. Accept this grace that God freely gives."

I did and do love her. She was my whole family, excepting Eunice. Mom was suspicious of Eunice on religion, so I guess like every family there were eddies and crosscurrents and sometimes right on up to savage riptides. My mom never had much flesh to her, and then her face hollowed out with sickness and beads of sweat were there, always, high on her forehead, like maybe they had freely dripped from her thinning brown hair. Why did that have to happen? Was it necessary to take away the beautiful thickness of her hair? I thought in my childish way then and still think the same now that the dying, the parting, should have been pain enough, without losing the pride of her hair. When Eunice gave her a bath, my mom smelled good, but only for a brief while, and I hoped she did not know that.

"I can't do that, Mom."

"Then if you don't do it before I die, do it before you die. I will pray for that. Because I will be in Heaven waiting and please God you must come. You have to come."

And even then, the stubbornness in my mind went to the idea that if Heaven brought peace and joy, then she shouldn't be sitting up there fretting at the Heavenly kitchen table, the table covered with our same brown oilcloth with a field of yellow daisies, and she shouldn't be twisting a strand of thick, gorgeous, brunette hair (she at least got her hair back in Heaven), and still worrying like on earth. Worrying was I going to repent. Worrying that I was late getting home from the library, and worrying that I had no friends and likewise the opposite worry that I had bad friends leading me to badness. I did not like this idea of Heaven. On the other hand, if I go to Hell, as may be, it will be because I was too stubborn to comfort her, to lie to her and say that, yes, I believe, I surely believe, Mom, and will join you in a little twinkling of the eternal eye. I could not tell that lie even though I have told so many others, forgive me. For sure my mother understood the problem of separation. As one now singeing my own eyelashes in the hell of separation, I also knew the problem.

Nico had no way of knowing about how my mother's hair got thin and had no chance of me ever telling him. The same, I had no way of knowing what he knew of suffering, me knowing that if he told a story of tribulation from his own life I would scarce believe it, because of my special feelings for Nico. And more, I had to be careful not to make a romance of suffering because Southerners are prone that way. I could not presume to know his heart although I could not escape the suspicion that the arrogant bastard presumed to know mine.

"Your mother," said Nico, "wanted a life of faith for you. I helped my children to understand that their work, whether it was teaching college or being a doctor, their work was to do God's work. Your mother was no different. I didn't know her or anything about her, but I know that to be true. You probably don't know this, Tree, but I have said publicly and I'm saying the same to you that I want more religion in the public square of our country. Do you know this idea of the public square, Tree?"

"I do. Thank you."

"Contrary to what you might think, I don't intend to condescend. I ask because I want us to understand each other. My ancestors in the Old Country, like you, did not have much education, but they worked to better themselves as best they could. I want you to see that helping me is the same thing as helping your mother. I don't know what the good Pope Francis, who means well, said in that letter, but I can guess some of it. Don't be frightened, Tree, of what the pope might say. As you know, especially you, being a Baptist, Francis is a man and not a god. He is the temporary occupant of Peter's Chair. Peter, in our faith, he was…"

"I understand, Nico, what you mean by the Chair of St. Peter. But thank you, sincerely, for being willing to explain." It was also interesting that he assumed I was a Baptist. He was, I think, a man who could only see Christians, which was the natural myopia of his eyes.

"Don't be fooled, Tree, when you hear this talk from Francis of helping the poor. It is romantic foolishness that appeals to the young and naïve. I am not being condescending when I say that I worry it may appeal to you on this account. It does seem beautiful. But when you're older, you see something better and stronger—the power of the institution, which is itself the moving shadow of God. It is the Church that must be preserved, defended against dissolution—almost literally, Tree, against being dissolved, like sugar in sweet tea."

Nico laughed and enjoyed showing off this sweet tea nugget about the South, and I grinned because I did appreciate that it was quick and apt. I also appreciated that he could move so quickly between Plato's moving shadow of God on the cave and Tree's sweet tea. I liked this nimbleness and guessed that as a younger man his mind was more often nimble and less often numbingly ponderous.

"Your mother, Tree, I think would understand about preserving the institution. All the institutions could dissolve. The unbelievers would like that, and our job is to stop it if we can."

"Is this the kind of thing my mother meant when she said the poor will always be with you?" I was baiting him, but it just added to the list of sins for which I was not in any measure sorry.

"It is, Tree. I'm happy you understand what I'm trying to say. And I'll tell you another thing that you may or may not understand. Francis likes to talk about doing the work of Jesus, and that's fine, but I am talking about doing the work of God."

"I'm not sure I get that."

"I know. That's a hard one." On this idea, there really was no condescension in his voice. There was in this a little moment for Nico of genuine mystery and uncertainty. Course, it was his own fault for subscribing to the Trinitarian silliness of three gods. What a load!

Separation, loss, they scratched at my mother like mean briars. When I was seven, she told me of my father. She said I was not to forget because she would not tell it again, ever. I had best remember the story of what happened to my father, or it would be gone forever. I sat before this story, rapt and afraid. There was no chance of me forgetting her words. Looking back, it appeared that my father's character could not be separated from his chosen profession, so I will say first, as she did, that he was a surgeon.

My father, the doctor. He came to town and healed the sick and married Corrine Rankin and left my mom and me to be called

Purcell. She did not say this, but it must have been something, really something, for Corrine Rankin, a housekeeper at a motel, to marry a doctor. Vernon senior stayed at the Red Rose Inn when he came to town to take the local hospital and my mother for a dance. You can see that, traveling into the past, I am embellishing and cannot help it. My mother's account, to the contrary, was teeth-gritting terse.

In later years, I got a little more of the story from Eunice although she was young enough at the time not to know a lot. And there wasn't much to know. I always thought of it as a kind of Gothic Southern tale, but that's not all fair to the South because peculiar things happen also in Cedar Rapids and Brooklyn. The interesting thing is that I eventually went into the family business—Corrine, my own mom, was a motel janitor, and my place was in her path. I did not feel called to take up doctoring, doubtless noble work, except when practiced by the gleaming Dr. Vernon Purcell, Sr.

He was a quicksilver quacksalver. He flowed fast and shifted his shape and shone silver, but he was a through and through medical quack, even though he favored a scalpel cure over a salve cure. Fake Dr. Purcell, with no medical training, must have had a cool head and steady hands. Not to mention my quick reading skills, or I guess that should be that I have his quick reading skills. I have from Eunice that in emergencies he told the nurses he had to be alone to pray and in his medical bag he carried a basic surgery textbook and maybe he carried a Testament, too, for the effect of it. The nurses thought of him as saintly and that's as may be, but he must have been talented because he bluffed it through long enough to marry my mother and conceive of me and buy a new car, which he used to make his escape. Such escapes are required to be in the dead of night and just ahead of the posse, and his apparently met those dramatic requirements.

Also, there was the nurse, Edith Stillwell, he took with him, surely to roll bandages in his next hospital job. My mother told me he had a previous wife (only one?) somewhere that he had been too hurried to divorce. My mother was too kindhearted to explicitly tell me I was a bastard, even at those aggravating times when I surely was. My origins, it seems, they are shady, shady enough to please a rascal spirit. Except that the son of a bitch broke my mother's heart. He probably broke Edith Stillwell's heart, too, but I did not love her.

My mother, always afterwards Corrine Purcell, just wanted him to stay. Just don't leave me. Please don't leave me. As surely as I wanted Julie to stay. Please, Julie, stop dying. My mother never said this to me, but I knew her heart, knew what she would say to fake Dr. Vernon Purcell. Don't leave. Stay. Stay. And they never do, do they, Mom?

There is a branch of theology, which in my understanding is called apologetics, devoted to saying to man why God does what he does, and well-named it is. My belief is that it never occurred to Nico that God needed to apologize for anything, and that's how people are different because I surely had a bone to pick with God. A right big bone, like unto the jawbone of an ass, a big-ass ass, elephantine even. It was Nico's god as chose loss, certainly not me. His god created the loss and made everything separate. God even divided himself into thirds, a neat trick unless you find you're divided against yourself. And why three gods and not two or five or twenty-seven? Does it ever happen that God and Jesus and the Holy Spirit have a falling out over the question of oatmeal for breakfast? (Oatmeal? Again?) Do God and the Holy Spirit, when they hit their thumbs with a hammer, say <u>Jesus H. Christ</u>?

119

Does the Holy Spirit get pissed every time he thinks of God you might as well say personally nailing Jesus to the cross? Has Jesus forgiven God? I wouldn't. The only part of this separation business I am grateful for, humbly grateful, is the part that separates me from Nico—with that I can surely live.

Nico sort of implied earlier that he was doing God's work and Pope Francis was doing the work of Jesus. Nico didn't think I got it, but I did. The apologists, of course, never really apologize. They defend. And I get that. But they should. Apologize. For all this silly shit. For fake Dr. Vernon Purcell. He quacked beautifully, the little quacker. He left my mother, and she cried. This cries out for apology. Every kind of apology. God should have had the simple decency to say, "It makes no sense, Corrine, even to me, especially to me. I can't explain it. I'm sorry, Corrine. So sorry."

Maybe those with the kindest hearts could offer God forgiveness. Julie had such a heart. Maybe she would forgive Him. Me, I'm not so sure. The Christians say that I choose to separate myself from God, but no such thing. It was God was in the separation business. God separated himself into parts and the rest of us, living and dead, are just all over scattered about.

My mom was desperate for me to accept all this freely given grace, so we could be together, a damn good purpose, and a better theology than Nico's. She didn't have the book learning, but she had a good intuitive understanding of that famous wager of Pascal. Pascal was a Frenchman, one of those Christian apologists, who liked math and who liked to think about the odds of things. My mother had some of these same thoughts although she was no kind of math student. My mother thought I was being contrary and foolish about religion because she figured, along with Pascal, that the smart bet was on the side of Christian belief. Once you choose belief, you have Heaven to gain and not much to lose. OK, in theory you might lose out on some shapely and fetching sinning partner along the way. But even here there was a promising escape hatch. I personally liked the odds of sinning now and repenting later, as, mayhap, you are trudging up the steps of the gallows. That always seemed to me the kind of loophole made for rascals.

Unfortunately for the peace of my mother's mind, I stumbled my way to the view that Pascal should have stuck with math and left religion alone, to keep himself from saying silly stuff. Pascal said that your smartest wager is to be a Christian (and tell your mother this to save her some worry, because she's the only mother you've got, you ungrateful wretch). Pascal and Nico, howsomever, could see only Christians, which made them silly and made this argument spin around in circles. I am no kind of philosopher, like that good Mr. Russell, but even I can see that, if you can think of a religion, any religion, you can, by God or by no God, also think of its opposite. So, for example, in "opposite world," Noah's boat sank in the flood with the tragic loss of all hands (and hooves) because Noah's God was not the real one. The real God, AKA Harold Proxmire, having foreseen the flood, kept man and other animals going in a distant place called High Groundistan, whose inhabitants held Noah's intelligence in low regard. Pascal thought I'd best get in church because I had everything to gain and not much to lose. But an opposite religion, with just as much evidence (that is, none), reverses the rules and says by believing I have everything to lose and nothing to gain because the Good God Harold Proxmire doesn't hold with idiots. I guess that silliness was OK for Pascal; we are all, me especially, entitled to turn out to be the fools of our own lives. But Mom was scared and lonely and just wanted some company in Heaven's strange land. I couldn't bring my mind to believe Pascal did my mother any kindness, but neither did I, so a pox on us both.

Chapter 11

Nico had a much simpler reason for wanting me to believe in his god, and it was not because, like my mom, he wanted us to spend eternity together. Truth, we both thought we had already done that, only subtracting out the heavenly bliss. I think Nico, with his arrogance, felt this way about me but could never have conceived of the vice versa. He pretty much just wanted the letter that was rightfully his. And my only claim to it was having been conscripted into Supreme Court Swim Class.

"Nico."

It happened that Nico was too busy at that moment to bring me into focus. He was waxing on about church-state relations in the sixth century and, by me at least, doing a damn fine job of it. That Nico for sure could organize an argument. He went on, and I could always see where the paragraphs stopped and then began anew, with one of those oversized capital letters, with flourishes dangling like earrings off any part of the letter strong enough to hold one. A letter had to have a stout back to get hired on by Nico. It was breathtaking in its way because nobody with this skill, this word mastery, had ever talked to me (with Nico, I was spared the burden of thinking of things to say back, for which both of us grateful). Maybe this word skill was common in New York City, I don't know, but for sure rare in Muscle Shoals.

"Nico."

His eyebrows clanged together and apart, and one eyebrow elevated in a way that struck me powerfully like unto a symphony conductor's baton, and I don't know why exactly, because I had never been to a symphony, but Julie, my cultural lodestar, sometimes tuned one in on the public television station, which we both watched for a full thirty seconds and then ignored because of the things we were desperate to get said to each other. You might reckon that we somehow knew time was running out for us, but, truth, we didn't. That was the last of our thoughts. We were just in love, and it made every word between us make haste unto the telling.

"Yes, what?" He dragged himself by his eyebrows out of the sixth century, the first time, to my rustic knowledge, that this had ever been done.

"You can't have the letter."

"That's my..."

"Your letter. Your private letter, direct from Peter's Chair. It belongs to you, no question."

"So, give it..."

"When Hell freezes over, solid, so you can skate between the red, frozen flames."

"Hell! Hell is exactly what I'm talking about, Tree. We are believers, both of us. Catholic and Baptist, no matter. Alabama and New York, the same, all Americans. God wants us to work together. Thanks to Him, I've been given earthly power. You, Tree, can help me use it for good."

"Nope."

Nico struggled, as I had seen him do before, like that delightful time when Hector refused to buy into Nico's unabridged bullshit. Nico probably had some real worry that the letter might be damaging to him, but my thought was that mostly he hated,

hated, and hated some more not getting his way. I wondered what always getting your way would be like, and I was never to know in any imaginable future. I got things to go all my way that one time but never thought of it as getting my way but just this one miracle that happened that night Julie wandered into the gym and heard me reading Mr. Dickens aloud. To this day, I think she truly fell in love with Mr. Dickens's great heart. Later, she said not and said things about my own heart I cannot repeat because they would make me cry although maybe that's not so bad because if you are under the benevolent protection of Mr. Dickens, crying is permitted.

"What do you want, Tree? Money? You stole my letter and now it's blackmail? How much do you hope to extort, my young fool?"

"Why would you pay anything when you say the contents are harmless to you? I don't get that."

"Tree, there's so much you don't get. You're a janitor. From Alabama. And you don't get it? There's a shocker. There's something Tree doesn't get! He's a graduate of Redneck High, in High Cotton, Alabama, and he doesn't get it! I tried to be nice to you, Tree. Tried to persuade you what was right."

Not for the first time, I sensed that Nico was unhappy with me. Not only was his face richly red, but it had yellow streaks mixed in with the red, which set me to wondering if you could have gangrene in your face and did that call for amputating the offending appendage to prevent the infection from spreading to a vital organ? I didn't want to say this aloud at that moment because Nico might have the stroke that it looked like he had been working up to for the last thirty years, but the truth was I still didn't get whatever was up with the letter. I knew what was in the letter. Nico for sure knew what I told him was in the letter, which was some part truth and some part whoppers for seasoning. What I didn't know was whether Nico had done the obvious thing I had told him to do. Call the pope, Nico. For crying out loud. Make the call. He'll tell you what's in the letter, with the added advantage that he won't mix in a bunch of lies like Vernon (Tree) Purcell, Jr. is prone to. It was looking like Nico didn't want to call Big Frankie or Big Frankie wouldn't take his calls or some such that I couldn't know about. Cause the thing is the letter wasn't that bad so far as I could figure it. I mean it was mostly just Big Frankie reminding Nico of his duty to be as kind as possible to the poor, with, granted, some undertow of chicanery sliding beneath the surface. If George published the letter in the paper, Nico might be embarrassed or Big Frankie might be embarrassed, but I couldn't see how it was the end of the world. Unless my great big lies about Nico being on the take were closer to the truth than Nico felt comfortable with. I guess that could be funny in its way or dangerous in its way, but I cared more about a good laugh than danger because the danger just seemed sometimes as welcoming to me as the good laugh.

Nico slid a hundred-dollar bill from his shirt pocket, and it seemed odd to me to carry a bill this size in your shirt unless you had an idea that this is where the conversation would be heading. I would not have guessed that, but an associate justice of the Supreme Court had just held forth on all the things I didn't get (plenty). Nico exposed just enough of the bill that I could see the three numbers and then he placed it palm down on my coffee table (that table was proving itself useful for so many things since it bobbed to the surface of the earth those millions of years ago). Nico pushed the bill, covered by his hand, over in my direction. He did this casual-like, all the while staring off into the distance, like his mind was perfectly on the pileated woodpecker fussing over the soft bark of an aspen tree on the other side of the gully, and like even Nico would have been surprised at what his hand was doing with the largish bill. When he got the bill over to my part of the granite table, his arm was far extended, to the point that if enough time passed this could be uncomfortable. To ward off this unhappy prospect, Nico signaled me with his eyebrows to, goddamn it, take the money, which I pretended not to understand, though, truth, never were eyebrows more eloquent. I confess I took some sport from jerking Nico around, and, in this moment, I couldn't figure out what spy movie we were in, with the money and the woodpecker and the sliding of the money from one miscreant to another. I can say that Nico was getting tired of making a perfect arrow with his eyebrows.

The arrow was getting twitchy, so I picked up the bill and held it up to the light to see was it counterfeit. I spat on it and rubbed the spit in hard with my thumb; this is something I did for no reason at all. Nico and I now knew each other so well that he did not even need to say aloud that, of all the stupid Alabamians on the planet, I was, past all doubt, the stupidest. I reached into my own shirt pocket and took out a kitchen match, which I fired, in the way of country folk, on my thumbnail, and then fired the bill. I eventually had to drop the burning bill on my coffee table, which did not mind the heat. My coffee table, made to my order, was igneous rock, fired in the deep earth's coffee table pottery barn, so what kind of shit did it give about the heat from a burning hundred-dollar bill?

With the same smooth motion, befitting a Don Corleone, my own Don Nico fished forth another hundred. And another. And another. A handful of hundreds, which he tossed carelessly on the coffee table. This began to deeply amuse me, and I was intrigued by my own jumbled moods. A few moments before, I was thinking I could as soon embrace death, relieved of life's wearisome load. And then a couple minutes further into this burdensome life, I was all in a stitch over Nico's pocket-sized US Treasury printing press. I am large and contain contradictions in multitudes though not as large as that good Mr. Walt Whitman, with his generous spirit.

"I don't have that many matches left, Nico. How about I just give you the matches and you can burn the money as you see fit? Better still, let me rustle up some firewood, and we'll get a jump on tonight's fire. I am storing up some beautiful memories to take back to Alabama with me. This one stars me and Mr. Justice Grasso using large bills for kindling. The thing is, I can't really guess whether anyone would believe that story. What do you think, Your Eminence?"

I got up and went to the ragtag woodpile and came back with a bunch of small sticks. I began making a loose pyramidal structure, and Nico was, praise Jesus, speechless. I gathered up the bills, including a couple the wind had skittered off the table. Crumpling the money, I stuffed it under the peak of the firewood pyramid, where it would do the most good. I didn't count just exact, but it looked like Nico was prepared to pay me a thousand dollars for the letter. I scratched another match under my thumbnail and it flared nicely and I might have looked like the fearsome Don Tree. I once tried to light a kitchen match this way to impress Nellie Hopkins and the sulfur caught fire but broke off and lodged under my thumbnail as it burned. Nellie and I were both fifteen and impressionable and to my best knowledge she has never married.

It was stubborn as did it. Nico's stubbornness almost entirely. OK, maybe some mine. Nico came to me with a thousand dollars to buy that letter and thinking most like that surely a hundred would do the job. I could sort of see him saying to Half Willard that no way did he need any money because he and Tree were becoming good buddies. Good old boy buddies and the day he couldn't snooker a son of the South would be one of those chilly days in Hell we keep hearing so much about. And Willard saying, I know, I know, but take the money anyway because it's more cash than a janitor sees regular. And about that my former employer would have been right. I had no doubt as to what I was up to as I kneeled over with the match. I glanced at Nico to see if he had a doubt, but he didn't, and only later did it come into my mind that Nico didn't care about the money burning up because, don't you just see, it was Willard's money. So, I burned the money and it made a nice little blaze. It was a lark for me, seeing that much money go up, but what you might call a mixed lark. I could have danced around the flames, in the ways of old, but there were people in my mind who could have used the thousand and what would they think of my dancing, and I was damned if knew, except that I hoped they would understand the dance to be bittersweet, as most dances grow, with time, to be.

For sure, Nico wasted no time mourning this money that Marcos could have used to buy a good floor machine for our dreamed-of janitorial business. Nico did seem a little reflective as he watched the bills curl and blacken, but, then again, I'm not sure it quite does to call Nico reflective, but let it be, let it be.

"So, what's next?" asked Nico.

"Next is you getting gone. Right soon. I believe I could hit a Supreme Court justice but sorry to say not an old one."

"Don't let my age stop you."

"I will let it stop me. I'm stronger than you. And it's right to be stopped by that. But there's a thing I wish you could keep in your mind. Every day, weak people and strong people come before you, and you raise your mighty fist and bring it down on the heads of the weak. I wish for you to stay your hand."

Nico slapped his fat belly and laughed and farted, and he did not know that he was having a near death experience at that moment.

"What," asked Nico, "are you and George going to do with the letter?"

"George?"

"I did a little research on George. He's got some brains. A fiery, liberal, newspaper type. He accomplished a few things before he moved to this small town. I've got this one figured. George talks, you move your lips. I do give you some credit, Tree. You're a little bit shrewd sometimes in a primitive kind of way. More than I expected. So, what does George plan to do with my letter? Or has he told you yet?"

I did not answer, could not answer, and Nico left. I sat there in front of a cheery, crackling little fire, lit with hundred-dollar bills, and the heat did not reach me. Julie was not in the fire and of course never was in the fire and could not be in the fire. Nico was in the world, and no longer the smallest part entertaining to me. I didn't see or hear him leave, but he remained in the world, and I guess you could say was the world. Explain that, you who can.

Half Willard? A man with an adequately large house, a roof over his head, shelter from the storm. Let's hear the explanation for him. The people kept coming at me as I sat alone by the fire. The assistant principal who hated, hated to see me reading a book. My father, the doctor, the quacksalver. He could have been a janitor and taken me and my mom fishing so she could have had that memory in the nick of her time. My kingdom, my treedom, I would surely give for that memory for that woman.

But instead we got Dr. Purcell, who was an uncannily quick reader. I know it's wrong to give you my burdens. I wouldn't if I knew what else to do.

You see there is a man named William Martin, who, by the calendar in my camper, has ten years and three months and seventeen days to live. If he's marking off his release date in prison, he has a calendar companion he does not know about. Ten years and change is how much life he has left in him. About the end of his life, there is no ambiguity. I will break his body when he walks out of prison to board that freedom train.

Mr. Martin had some drinks and a fast, new car and did not see Julie's red hair until after he ran over her. He specifically recalled that he noticed red hair as she lay twisted against the curb, and he thought she might have been a hot chick, but he couldn't get a good look. She lived for a little while in the hospital but not long. Long enough to make me promise not to kill Mr. Martin. And, you know, think on this one: I would not lie to my mother on her deathbed, but I lied to Julie on hers. I don't get it.

The fire built on Nico's money crackled, but the flames did not warm me—me, the master of warming myself before fires in a dark wood. The uncommon idea came to me that maybe Hell operated on the principle of the heat pump, which device cleverly cools a room not by pumping cool air in but by pumping the heat out (and stacking it neatly in the side yard). I moved closer to the fire and still cold. There's no shortage of engravings, paintings of naked multitudes dancing in agony in the flames of Hell, these same flames towering frightfully above them. Maybe the Devil took a community college HVAC course (heating, ventilation, and air conditioning) and made some alterations to his system; maybe those leaping flames are, contrary to regular thought, sucking the warmth from the gathered sinners and

131

transferring it into the soaring vaults of Hell. Those miserable sinners are writhing and dancing to stay warm, not the other way. Because they are freezing.

I was cold.

Chapter 12

I was studying a dark helicopter, tipped onto one rotor. A crash landing? Hard to tell in the dim light. Perhaps it was Willard's helicopter from the ranch. Maybe the thought of Half Willard was causing my head to hurt. The helicopter seemed close enough to touch, but I pushed hard on my sluggish brain and decided that it had to be at a far distance to look that small. I was lost between these possibilities until in a magical instant it came to me that it was Javier's toy helicopter. It was then plain that the copter was lying, tilted, on a blanket and the blanket was on my chest in a bed in a dim room that contained Javier's helicopter and contained Javier on top of the covers beside me, eyes wide and studying me silently.

"I'll be damned...Javier. I'm happy to see you."

"*Tio* Tree. Are you OK?"

"I don't know. Is this your bedroom?"

"Papa brought you here. I'm watching you. Do you want me to go get Mama?"

I could hear adult murmurs slipping through the door. "Not yet. I'm...not yet."

"OK. I gave you my helicopter to play with."

"Thanks. Is it dark outside?"

"Yes, a little."

"I slept a lot?"

"Yes."

"How did I get here?"

"Mama sent Papa…"

"Oh, you already said that. OK. Just let me rest and wake up for a minute. I need to wake up."

"Are you going back to sleep?"

"I don't think so."

"Are you going to play with the helicopter? I left it there for you."

"Not right now."

"Then can I play with it?"

"Of course." I patted Javier on the back as he sat up and sent the helicopter in circles. I moved my pillow so I could sit up in bed and continued to fight off sleep or paralysis or whatever it was. Javier reached back and felt my forehead, maybe to see if I had a fever. I loved that kid. I wanted a cup of coffee but was not ready to talk to Maria.

The memory came to me of talking with Nico, which made me shiver, and I began to understand. I had frozen up. It had happened before sometimes at Eunice's house. I remembered waking up there and Eunice's little daughter, Edna, my second cousin, coloring in bed beside me. At that moment I missed Edna, my loyal friend. Missed her brother, Ethan, too, the hyper one. I missed Eunice, who knew to keep a child, a child's voice, nearby when I froze up. Even in the icy mists on my brain, I saw the power of it.

I remembered, sort of, Marcos coming to get me. I knew I was in my camp chair when I froze up, but I must have tried to get up because I was face down on the ground beside my great granite table when Marcos pulled on my shoulder and rolled me over. When I was on my back there was a small rock under my shoulder that hurt and I asked Marcos was he trying to kill me. I saw so clearly that I smiled at Marcos, meaning this as a joke, but what I thought was a smile was most likely a pig rictus to Marcos. I had a memory of Marcos lifting under my shoulders and telling me that he couldn't lift me alone and I would have to help and I did because who would not want to help Marcos? Although I don't remember feeling any other reason to get up besides helping my friend.

"*Tio*, are you sick?"

"No."

"What's wrong with you?"

"Maybe it's nothing."

"Mama says you're depressed. Is depressed sick?"

"Yes...no."

"Mama says yes. But what is it?" Javier felt my forehead again. "You don't feel hot. I had the flu once."

There was a dim lamp on top of the chest of drawers. There were toys, maybe some clothes, stacked along the base of the wall. I saw a baseball mitt and the excellent thought came to me that Javier might drop all this if I took him outside to play catch.

"Are you sick?"

"When you had the flu, Javier, you didn't feel like doing anything. I was like that. I didn't feel like doing anything. I just sat in my chair."

"But..."

"And then maybe I fell down. I was just resting when your papa found me."

"*Tio*, you threw up on yourself. Mama had to clean you up."

"Oh...I'm sorry she had to do that."

"If you have the flu, OK, but if you don't, you should feel like doing stuff. I always feel like doing stuff. I feel like doing stuff with you. You should have played with me and not be depressed."

He was all the way right. That's an easy one if you're strong enough to live for others. If you're strong enough to take arms against your own sea of pain and fight it off. I knew that were I to kill myself, or let myself die somehow, as I was surely thinking on, that I would be passing my pain to others, the folks I left behind. But, hell's tolling bells, that's just the sadder because it says that folks are busy playing hot potato with pain and hoping it won't be their hands the potato is scalding when the tolling music stops. Please, potato, don't toll for me. And that sucks and makes it seem this world is not all that much worth living in anyway, and we should all hurry up and shuffle off this mortal coil for a penny or a nickel, plus whatever relief is in it. I always liked that Christian notion that said you can cure pain by dumping it off on Jesus, the pain-catcher in the rye. That's a big job for Jesus and mighty handy for us regular folk if there were the slightest reason to think it might be true.

It does make me smile to think there might have been a real guy named Jesus who saw this problem and convinced himself that maybe he was just the guy to step up and take on the sins, the pain, of all the world. I tip my hat. But even if Jesus had wanted to do this, I say respectfully he would not have had the strength. No one would. But here is a happy part. Because there are people in the world who would be happy to try to do something, some small or large something. The damnedest thing is they would suffer for others, or try to, and they do it all the time. My mother, for me. Maria, who washed the vomit off me (I rubbed my face and it felt clean). Marcos dragged me from the wilderness. Javier, for the sake of his great love, gave me his helicopter. OK, only a loan, but still counts. These were things I should make myself memorize.

"Mama says you're sad. She says she has never seen anyone so sad. Even when you're laughing all the time. I don't get it. Is that still depressed when you laugh? Is that why you don't want to do things?"

I believe it may not be possible (and for sure not desirable) to try to justify a death wish (a peace wish?) to a child. We hope devoutly their minds don't work that way. I don't know, don't know. Maybe such death as I had been thinking on is for truth justifiable. Just not to a child? Damned if I know. It's something I wish I could talk to Julie about and maybe I will. Whether it's possible to justify such a wish for death to such a child as Javier, I didn't know that, but I knew I was not going to be about the business of trying. Besides, I was waking up and taking an interest in the idea of food because at Maria's house that was always an interesting thing. I knew, also, that I was not depressed despite the excellent judgments of Maria and Javier.

I don't think I have ever been depressed any day of my life. I have been sad and mad and deliriously happy and deliriously grieving, but never, never depressed. Call semantics on me if you like, but I believe that I have ever, ever been deeply in touch, directly in touch, with the actual vagaries of life, not all of them kind. Once, as I sat in Eunice's yard, studying her deep green magnolia leaves, I overheard a neighbor ask her was I clinically depressed. If Eunice answered the question, I didn't hear, but the words, clinically depressed, stayed in my head. I have seen these words on a page, but I have never seen the words, clinically happy, so until I do I will do what kindness requires and pay no attention to the sluggishness such words bring to the world.

"Javier, I do want to do things. I want to have fun with you."

Javier let go of the strain of being solemn and we were both happy to be shed of solemn. Solemn is nobody's friend.

"A fort, Javier. I believe we need to fort up against what dreams may come."

"What?"

"A fort. Let's build a fort in here. We can use that chair and these blankets."

"Yes. Cool. A fort."

"But soft. So your parents don't hear."

We worked in whispers like the night. Javier wanted to build too small because he saw himself as the measure of all things. Fair enough, but some intense whispering convinced him to build big, or at least big enough to accommodate the likes of me. I moved a chair from the wall to the foot of the bed, so we had two bedposts and the chair as a frame. Javier liked the grandeur of it all and so did I. I took the blanket off the bed and draped it over the frame and there we were. Javier tugged on the blanket so that we had a door at one end. I moved the lamp from the chest to the inside of the fort. We both crawled in and sat with our backs to the bed. The lamp was too bright, but when I turned it off it was too spooky for Javier. I made a fold in the draped blanket and slid the lamp inside it to get to the Goldilockean happiness of just right. There were shadows and nice dark corners where stuff could lurk. Javier got out and pulled up one side of the blanket for light so he could find provisions. He brought in a cunning Nerf sword and some stuffed animals that turned out to be supplies like food and water. (I think Javier was getting hungry.) He parked the helicopter on the roof for air defense. We rearranged the lamp and the blanket and sat with our knees up. We whispered and then were quiet as we strained to hear what Marcos and Maria might be saying. I thought they were discussing dinner, but Javier said, no, no, no, they were plotting an invasion of our fort. We fought off this imaginary invasion by throwing stuffed animals out of the fort, which exploded as if they were grenades and the concussion knocked Javier over against me and me over against the bed. When we won this battle, Javier wanted a ghost story, and I could not think of one so I told him the startling story of Moby Dick, which served.

When Maria did come in, we were caught completely off guard. She promised us tacos if only we would surrender, forfeiting our lives, fortunes, and sacred honor. This was an easy call, and we went to dinner.

Maria took my hand and then felt my forehead and then gave me a hug and a look that kept searching around in the shadowed alleys of my heart. I wished she would quit and she did and went about the business of dinner. Marcos was quiet and inscrutable, but there could only be one reason for the inscrutability, so despite his best efforts he was entirely scrutable to me, and I was sorry for what I knew was coming. We ate tacos and I had an appetite that seemed not to fit with the doings of my day, but I was big and strong and for better or worse had to feed the whirring engine of my life. We friends only talked about how the tacos were good and how Javier and I built the best fort ever. I said we should name it Fort *Felicidad* and Maria rolled her eyes and Javier didn't care what we called it so long as he could talk on and on about it, and he could because the grownups couldn't open their minds to each other until Javier was in bed. Javier gave me a kiss and Maria and Marcos tucked him smoothly into bed and then came out so the music, a dirge was my guess, could be faced.

Maria gave me another kiss as I sat at the kitchen table and she said, "You built him a fort...only Tree would do this."

"Us. I built us a fort. It's mine, too. Fort *Felicidad*."

"Tree, I don't ask you if you're OK. You're not. And I don't know how to help." She shook her head and her black hair flowed.

"Marcos?" I asked. I had expected the fiery Maria to light me up, but she did not, and I understood what was coming from Marcos, the entirely scrutable.

"You have been having some type of disagreement with Associate Justice of the Supreme Court of the United States Nicholas Grasso. I studied up on who he is at the library. He is dangerous to my family. Maybe you can understand why. I can't be around you anymore. I can't risk that for my family. You are my friend. Do you understand this thing?"

Maria was crying and was pale at the mention of Grasso's powerful name. "We love you, Tree. Javier loves you. Maybe someday we can come back together and you and Marcos can start that business. But we don't know about the future. Don't know where we will be."

"I understand." I wanted to point out that Maria should not have sent Marcos to check on me, wanted to say that it was not me who had contacted them, but this was just me being small-minded and defensive, and fortunately I stopped before it could get said. I could not imagine how they were in any danger but also could not argue with them. They knew their own fears best, as I knew mine. My thought was that Nico troubled himself with the pope or the president but not with such small fish as were friends of mine.

"A beer," I said. "A farewell beer among friends? I'm sorry to have brought you worry." Marcos got up to get the beers. "Give Javier a kiss whenever you get the notion and tell him it is from Tree."

"*Tio* Tree," said Maria. "You will always be *Tio* Tree. You will have children, too. You need to have children. Why not?"

I evaded by taking a long drink, made longer by the mention of having children. The world was fill of grippy stuff. As should be no surprise, Julie and I had been gripped by the idea of children, and the plan between the two of us was that they would have her red hair, her blue-green eyes, her smile, her ringing, singing voice, and some quality of mine to be named later.

"Some of your features are attractive," Julie had said.

"Name two—quickly."

"This is not a quiz show. But I love you—that should be enough."

My feelings were beginning to be hurt. "That's not an answer."

"You have many features, and I love them all."

"You love everything about me? That's absurd."

"You're right. It is absurd. You have the ugliest knees in Alabama. But I still want to have your baby."

"Now. Now. We should do that now."

"Have sex now?"

"Make a baby now."

"Sex, yes. The baby has to wait."

So, we waited and life took one turn instead of another, and that's OK. Who can know the consequences of such decisions? I could have been bouncing a baby (baby Vern?), and Julie could have been knitting a pair of those silly baby shoes and thereby she would have magically acquired a new skill (knitting) and magically missed her collision with the car that broke her and us apart. Stuff like that is not much worth thinking about. You get carried away with trying to make sense of this hypothetical stuff and first thing you know you've invented God or, alternatively, the chaotic notion that a butterfly taking flight in Japan ignites a causal chain, so that the butterfly is the first and incredibly intricate cause of the gas I just passed. I do shine to the idea of blaming all my gas on Japanese butterflies because it makes farting poetical.

Maria wanted me to live happily and have a child. Maybe she wanted me to marry Irina, Marcos's sister, but I had the idea she wasn't that crazy about Irina. And truth, I wasn't that crazy about Irina, either, though I was happy to notice that she was a voluptuous woman with full lips. She might use those lips to sweet purpose, but I don't think she had any notion of using them to read aloud either Chuckie Dickens or Mikey Cervantes. Somehow, I, a high school janitor, had found a woman who had an interest in kissing me and also in reading Mr. Dickens and Sr. Cervantes, and how about that? And, when I worried about it, Julie said I would be a good father despite the father I had but never had. She believed that Vernon Purcell, senior, was a jerk of his own creation, and I was in no way in danger from his genes. And the thing is I just straight on believed her about this deep fear.

"*Hola*, Tree," said Maria. "Are you there?"

"You told me to think of having children. That's what I was doing."

"And?"

"Why should I have children when I can build a fort with yours? A toast to my friends." We touched our bottles. "Who will I speak Spanish with?" I asked.

"Tree, your Spanish is imaginary. So, you require only an imaginary friend to talk to."

There was a knock on the door, and I expected it to be Irina, but it was Iris, and I saw once again that what I knew had not kept pace with what everyone else knew. As, for example, I had not realized that my Spanish was imaginary.

Iris kissed Maria on the cheek and bumped fists with Marcos, which I thought was kind of cool. She did not kiss me or bump my fist but rather crooked her finger for me to follow her. I thought this was presumptuous, but I had never been Cleopatra and had never yet personally killed anyone, so I followed. But not immediately. I demonstrated my independence by first hugging my friends and wiping a real, not imaginary, tear from Maria's right eye.

As we walked to the parking lot, I thought I saw Al, Willard's foreman, leaning against a building in the shadows. But it was dark and I couldn't be sure and couldn't figure out why his presence might matter even if he had once aimed a pistol at my chest. Maybe he had a secret girlfriend who lived in the apartments.

When Iris and I got in the car, I asked her if she was going to take me back to my camper. As before, I couldn't quite catch up to what was going on.

"Your camper is gone."

"Gone? Where?"

"Burned up. Hector says it's still smoldering. The fire department hosed it down. I'm sorry, Tree."

I tried to think if I had left something on to start a fire. One of the gas burners? Maybe the fire pit outside threw an ember into the camper? And then I thought on stuff, possessions. What about my stuff? I tried to remember what I had in the camper. All I could think on was a picture of Julie that I ritually said good morning to. I couldn't think whether there was another copy of this picture somewhere. I sat silently in the car beside Iris trying to recall this. I expect she was waiting for me to say something or ask something, but nothing came to me.

"My truck. Did my truck burn up?"

"No, it's fine."

"What happened? It makes no sense."

"Sense or no. You're burned out. You're staying with us."

"Who's us?"

"Me and Hector. Hector's house. Not mine. He was too proud to move in with me. Maybe I'll put you in one of my houses, but for now you're with us."

"One of your houses?"

"I'm rich, Tree. Rich people own stuff."

"Is there something I should be doing?"

"Like what?"

"I don't know. My camper. I don't know. Tell me again why I'm staying with you."

"We like you, Tree. Who knows? We might end up loving you."

"OK, but what would I do about that?"

"Also, Hector wants me to keep an eye on you. He thinks, we think, that you're kind of simple."

"'Tis a gift."

Chapter 13

I pressed the button that made my watch glow in the dark, and it was 3:15. I believed that this button also made my watch glow in the daytime, but try as I might I could never be sure. I had come awake in the wee time because it came to me in my restless sleep that Eunice had a copy in Alabama of the picture of Julie that likely burned up with my camper. I liked saying good morning to that picture and was relieved to know that I could perhaps do so again.

In the picture, Julie has a shit-eating grin as she balances a brim-full wineglass on her head; she wears a pale blue towel over her shoulders, anticipating the failure that came when I gave her left shoulder a loving nudge. Maybe I could call Eunice and ask her to send me a copy.

Eunice would do that and do it promptly and would not say yes and then forget. Eunice was as reliable as my mother. When she promised something, she marked it and some part of her was not at rest until the promise was redeemed. She was a redeemer, as was my mother, and I loved them for it. It's a good world in many parts, but one of the poor parts is that most folks tell a lot of small, ridiculous lies; they lie and say they'll do stuff and then lie again and say they forgot, on which I politely call bullshit. This lying is just a way of small talk, and I'll say straight out that I never liked it. Words should not be mocked. Mark it. Do not mock the words. I don't know what I would have done if Julie was this way, but happily she was not.

Julie and I were compatible on main things, despite our differences in social class. Julie's mother was a pediatrician, and her father had a sort of proper, lackadaisical real estate business. Julie grew up around refined things, and she never had to kill a kitten. I'm just going to outright guess and say that most folks fall in love before they find out if they're compatible. Julie and I had an argument on this, and she said girls were practical-minded and boys were romantic (It's in my mind that she may have used the word horny.). I named bullshit also on this and luckily could throw down to her an example from the very before week, when I was virtuously building her a wooden lap desk in the garage, and she came out and admired the desk and then set to pulling off my clothes, only pausing to pull off her own, and anyone could have walked in the side garage door, including the head of her own English Department, and how was this supposed to be practical-minded? When I reminded her of this incident, she promised to never do it again, and for one shining, deeply foolish moment I thought I had won the argument.

I turned on the bedside lamp and looked around Hector's guest room. I guess it was Iris's guest room, too, but she had said that Hector made her move in with him because of his pride, and that must have meant that she set her own pride aside. I made a note to try to find out about this, if I could do it without being accurately reckoned a jerk. I was just naturally snoopy about how people advanced love's gears, and I always thought of gears, once meshed, as slow, stately, and inexorable. I pictured the gears I liked as being about five feet tall, like wagon wheels, and fitted with wooden teeth. Hector's guest room was not as cluttered as Javier's room. It seemed comfortable in the dim light but not the kind of room where you would think to build a fort. I wondered if Javier had ever gotten to look at Hector's pistol, and, of a sudden, I missed Javier sharply.

Iris had brought me home and tucked me in only a few hours before. I was surprised because in my thinking about Cleopatra there were armies of the Nile (charging and retreating under boiling clouds of dust), pyramidal architecture, and some sort of boats that I thought of fuzzily as barges. But there were no thoughts about tucking in. Iris gave me a pair of Hector's pajamas and hung my clothes in the closet and took my elbow and guided me into bed and pulled the covers up to my chin. And then she honest to God kissed me on the forehead, and then maybe she had a second of asking herself, did I just do that? Or maybe she didn't because I never heard of a Cleopatra with doubts. When you are Queen of the Nile, you just act, and leave it to others to figure you out if once they can.

In the muted light of the bedside lamp, at 3:18, I could see a picture, unframed, maybe painted on something like smooth slate, of a fisherman on a large bay. The full moon in the picture was low in the sky, just clearing a black ridge of land and throwing wavering light on the copper bay and the black boat and the fisherman as these things took station between me and that white moon. I started worrying that picture like a hound with a borrowed bone. The boat was like a pirogue, with the man standing up in it and holding for some odd reason a huge spear at the ready. Big, big spear, that big as would make an elephant veer off, and why was this man spearing elephants in a Cajun pirogue in a great moonlit bay? Was he about putting the slain elephant in the boat? If so, he was headed towards nautical disaster. The boat and the man threw down quavering black shadows on the coppery water, but the huge spear must have

147

been a ghost vampire spear because the artist gave it no shadow on the water, which, by itself, likely scared off the elephants because there was nary pachyderm in sight. After a while I let up on the picture and went to sleep, not without being grateful for the distraction.

I found the kitchen in the morning, but Hector and Iris had found it first and they were sitting at the table smooching like a couple of slobbery puppies and I could not think what good manners required, so I said, "Nice kissing," which made them stop. Only Iris had the composure to thank me for the compliment.

"Sorry for your camper," said Hector. And, "Welcome to my home."

Which he changed with speed when Iris corrected him. "Our home." I formed the idea from this that he was capable of learning, which would naturally have been a requirement around Iris.

"Thanks. Is there any chance that a picture of my wife could have survived? It was taped to a cabinet."

"No. Even your dishes melted. Iris and I can help you with some supplies. We've both been collecting stuff for years, so we have two or three of just about everything."

"Thanks. I was uneasy that I ought to go out there last night, just to look, but Iris said no."

"There's nothing I can think of you might want to see. Just burned and charred and melted stuff. Everything, even metal, curls up in a hot fire."

"How did it start? Did I leave the propane on? Even so, I can't see how that started a fire."

"Gasoline is what it looked like to the fire crew."

"Gas? I had some gas for the generator, but it was in a plastic container, off by itself. How?"

"You pour it over everything and toss a match on it. It's not that hard."

"Somebody burned me out? Why?"

"I think Justice Grasso is unhappy with you."

"Nico? No chance. He's unhappy with me, but no arsonist."

"I'm sure you're right. Neither is Willard Jordan. But Al? Al is Mr. Fix-It. He wouldn't even have to be told. He's good at guessing what the boss wants. Stuff in the camper was kind of scattered around when it burned. Did you leave it messy?"

"Not too. There may have been a coffee cup on the table. A book."

"Was the mattress from the bed pulled over onto the sofa?"

"No, nothing like that. I see what you mean. Can you arrest somebody?"

"Almost surely not. It's one of those deals where, if I've got no evidence, then that makes it more likely it was Al. Al would enjoy that. The lack of a mark is his mark."

Iris got up abruptly and muttered she was late. I asked for what and she pointed to her running shoes. I asked Hector if he was going to run with her, and he snorted and said no one can run with Iris, and that made sense because she was slim and straight and strong. I never heard of Cleopatra running, but I could easy make an argument that she would have if she lived in this century and was now Iris. I know—this whole Cleopatra thing is peculiar, but it interests me.

"How bad is your loss, besides the picture of Julie?" asked Hector. He remembered her name as he had promised he would. Another redeemer.

"Not much. The picture. Some library books. Clothes."

"What else?"

I was stumped. "Pots and pans. A fishing pole. Oh, did my generator burn up?"

"A nice Honda 2000. Gone. What else did you lose? Letters from Julie?"

"You know, no. There were some, but I left them with Eunice. I was afraid I would read them."

"What else? Other letters? Documents?"

"Ah. You're being the sheriff. You're asking after the letter from the pope."

"Yes."

"No. I didn't lose that in the fire. I mean, I took account that somebody might one day come looking for it. I didn't think they'd burn me out, though. I still don't get it. The letter's not that big a deal."

"What if it's a big deal in ways you don't understand?"

"Maybe. Or maybe it's still not a big deal, but some people just find me aggravating. As surely I can be."

"OK. Could be. Do you want to tell me where the letter is?"

"No."

"Do you want breakfast?"

"Yes."

Hector fried bacon and scrambled eggs while I located dishes and set the table and mixed orange juice from a can of concentrate. I found a jar of chunky salsa for the eggs. Once more, I was hungry. I ate a lot and Hector ate more. He was a big man and at the age to put on weight, but then sheriffs are supposed to look prosperous, hefty, and forbidding. Then all they really need do to make an arrest is threaten to topple over on top of you. At my urging, Hector sat and drank coffee as I washed the dishes.

"Why did you want to be sheriff?"

"*Por qué no?*"

"Well, there must be big loads of aggravation, for one thing. Having to deal with people like Tree Purcell. Nico Grasso. It's not like you're all the time rescuing grateful little old ladies from the Hell's Angels."

"I still rescue people sometimes. Lots of cops, most of them, want to be the cavalry, riding to the rescue. That was me. Still is, but now it's mostly paperwork and bidding on new police cruisers. I get tired of the crap sometimes and think I should just retire and go fishing, which would be perfect if I liked to fish."

"*Por qué no, mi amigo?* Fishing can be a happy thing."

Hector gave me a look to see if I was being a jerk with what Maria called my imaginary Spanish. He decided I was not, and I was relieved because I saw him as living inside a genuine force field. After so many years, I guessed that he looked at situations and thought about what force needed to be applied along which vectors, in the same way that I surveyed a gym floor and thought about how to arrange the disparate waves of dust and litter and the tear-stained, shredded notes from discarded teenage hearts. These, I did not mind pushing with my broom. Once I tried piecing back together shards of love confetti, so I could read them, but I saw it was a wrong thing and stopped.

"When did you start?" I asked. "Forty years ago?" I meant only to be aggravating with this guess but turned out prescient.

"Close."

"You grew up here. So, this was your first job?"

"Yes."

"And you were the only Hispanic deputy? Maybe the first?"

Hector gave me another look, but he let me skate merrily along on my fragile ice and then he grinned at me, permitting my bold curiosity, and I was going to be OK.

"And now you're the Hispanic sheriff, and it's not like this is a hugely Hispanic county, so you made it across the tightropes?"

"Yes."

"You did it for your peeps?"

"You could say that. But all the peeps. Even the Alabamian peeps."

"I get that a little bit. And I think it must be wonderful when all that comes together, the Hispanic peeps and the Alabamian peeps and even the Willard Jordan peeps. We're all blind puppies, wishing for a growling presence to keep us safe. Maybe a warm meal like the eggs and bacon you just served me."

"Tree, you are one long stretch. I enjoy, we all do, that you're a little bit the poet. You like your fairy tales, your stories of Hector fighting Achilles. A dreamer."

"Guilty."

"Well, you and your dreams are welcome in my home."

"Your home and Iris's home?"

"Roger that."

I finished the dishes and found a broom in the pantry and swept the kitchen floor, making Hector lift his feet. He told me I did not need to do that, but he was wrong. After this small chore, I poured myself a cup of coffee.

"I was married for like three seconds and my wife died. We spoke of this at the party."

"Yes. But I don't know how she died. She was young."

"An accident. A kind of accident. She was walking. Hit by a drunk driver. Julie lived a little while. We got to say goodbye. Do you think I should be grateful for that?"

"I'm sorry?"

"Should I be grateful that we got to say goodbye?"

"I don't know. Yes. Yes. I think so. My friend Ben got a moment to say goodbye to Megan. I believe he was glad of that."

"Ben?"

"Someone you will meet if you stay here. He's…"

"I remember. A schoolteacher."

"Yes."

"Megan was his wife."

"Engaged, but yeah."

"Do I have it right that she was shot? By her brother?"

"Yes. Larry was her brother."

"And then Larry was shot?"

"Ben knocked Larry's gun loose. Iris shot him. Iris loved Megan and Ben and Sarah."

"Sarah?"

"Ben's daughter."

"You weren't there?"

"I should have been. I'm the cavalry. I didn't get there in time."

"You make it sound like it was a close thing. Like you almost made it. I didn't know that."

"I would have saved everybody everything if I had done my job right. I knew Larry might bond out of jail. I told the jail deputies not to release him without first letting me know. They followed orders. They called my home and left a message with Rose. I didn't think to tell them to talk to me directly. Such a small thing."

"Rose?"

"My wife. At the time. She was jealous of anything to do with Iris."

"Wow."

"Who knows? Maybe she really did forget. She couldn't have known, anyway, about what was at stake, because we were at a pass where I no longer told her much about my work. Doesn't matter. I should have made it clear to my deputies to contact me directly. Even so, I was first on the scene. Megan was dead. Larry was dead. After Larry shot Megan, Ben tackled him and knocked his head against the doorjamb. Larry was out of it and Iris picked up the gun and shot him. I wrote it up to say Larry could have been trying to get the gun when Iris shot him in self-defense."

"And that worked? You got away with it."

"I guess you could say it worked. I've never made any special secret of what I did. The peeps, my peeps, they trust me to take charge. To do what's right even if it's not perfect. The only one who argued with me was Iris. She worried that I might get into trouble, but the DA signed off on it. Iris didn't give a shit about any report, so long as Larry was dead. That's why she shot him so thoroughly. To make sure. It's a small place we live in. People loved Megan and loved Iris and had no use for Larry. If all the evidence didn't line up just perfect, well, the truth and the facts aren't always the same thing."

"But that left you and Rose?"

"It left a lot of things. Iris. Ben, without his girl, like you. Things changed for a lot of people."

"And you and Rose? That's a beautiful name, by the way, as is Iris. What is it with you and flowers?"

"I wondered about that, but neither of the women in question has ever mentioned it. Maybe flowers don't know they're flowers."

"Granted, but what about Rose?"

"It's an odd thing, but we had a kind of happy divorce, a relieved one. Rose could never forgive me for anything until Megan got killed. And then she forgave and let me go. We're pleasant now."

"But not before?"

"We were OK until I ran for sheriff. When I was a deputy, then a sergeant, it was OK. When I was elected, I then had this big family. My deputies...my peeps. The whole county was officially my family. I had twenty thousand children to look after, and Rose and I couldn't have children. She would have been the best mother ever. Bad luck. The good luck from Megan dying is how that somehow evened up me and Rose, lifted the curse. We got divorced and Rose moved in with her sister's family and turned to church work. Now, she has a family she can be happy with."

"And you have Iris. Your family."

"My family is a lot bigger than Iris. But yes, now she is the center."

"Are you lucky?"

"How? Lucky?"

"You said that good luck came from Megan dying."

"I didn't mean that I was happy about Megan dying."

"I know that. Of course not. Just that some good thing can sometimes come from bad. In the old times in Europe, the Black Death carried off tons of folks; and, every single one of them decided to leave their extra clothes behind. So, rag paper, made from cloth, was cheap, and the printing press came along at the right time to put to lucky use all this paper. I'm just asking what you think. Do you think something lucky came your way because of Megan's death?"

"OK. I guess so. Not something I expected or hoped for."

"Understood. I guess I think that's the nature of actual luck. That something good happened you never saw coming. It almost has to be a surprise—to be real luck."

"And are you waiting on a surprise? From Julie's death?"

"Maybe. I don't know. But maybe yes."

Hector shrugged and put his hand on my shoulder and got up to rinse the coffee cups.

Chapter 14

"Are you sure they have a buffing machine?" I asked.

"I don't know why they wouldn't," said Iris.

"Are you sure you know what a buffing machine is?"

"I keep one on my night stand for my fingernails." Iris curled her fingers and inspected them thoughtfully. "Couldn't live without it." From this, I learned that Iris took no crap from Alabama farm boys, perhaps not even from farm boys of other states.

Iris and I were parked across the highway from Summit High School. It was about the same size as the high school in Muscle Shoals.

"Maybe you could get a job there. Are you sure you want to be a janitor?"

"I'm not sure I want to stick around at all. But if I do, I want to be a janitor."

"You could be something else."

"It's honest work." I did not also say that it was where Julie found me, where she would always know to find me.

"Nothing against the work. Don't know that it fits you."

"Not high-toned enough?"

"Hush, Tree." My mother used to use the same tone with me in the same circumstance, meaning, when I was being a jerk. "Maybe that's the right job for you, I don't know. If I can help, I know people with the schools."

"Thanks."

"What did Julie make of you?"

"Right next to everything."

Iris leaned across the seat and patted my shoulder. She had, of course, meant to ask what Julie thought of me and my work, and I had answered a different question and that was not all the way fair. I was darkly suspicious of my own motives because I had no straight answer to give to Iris or to me. It bid fair that Julie and I had not finished working out who we were going to be to each other when the clock ticked but did not tock.

"Julie used to tell me this story of what she made of me, a story that explained to her satisfaction the two of us. An old Buddhist chestnut of a story."

"Tell me."

"Once upon a time, long ago and far away, there was an emperor who was partial to fine horses and could afford them without a payday loan. The emperor lived west of here, in the Far East. Julie knew this emperor's name in the story, but I can't call it. It's for sure the name was not RJ Billy Ray, so that's what we'll call him. When Emperor RJ began to pine for a new horse, he always sent his chief factotum to hunt up a poor farmer name of JR Ray Billy, and it was Farmer JR's job to go search out the best horse in the kingdom. Farmer JR, you see, had some talents as a horse spotter. So, this time, like others, Farmer JR left his six wives, one child, and thirty-two grandchildren in charge of the farm and went looking. On this trip, he was gone for months. He never said much on where he had been, but no one in his travels ever suspected he was working for the emperor because on the one hand Farmer JR was old and stooped and dressed in rags and then on the extra hand Farmer JR's name was so completely different from Emperor RJ's name that no one the wiser. When

Farmer JR returned, he sent word to the factotum where the best horse in the kingdom could be found. Later, the factotum went to Emperor RJ and told him he had the horse. Emperor RJ studied the horse and saw for true that it was the finest of all horses and expressed his delight at the work of Farmer JR. Easy for you to say, said the faithful factotum, but you should know that Farmer JR caused me no end of problems in getting this horse, and I believe his mind is slipping. Why speaketh ye thus, asked Emperor RJ? Because, said the factotum, Farmer JR told me where to find the horse and the landowner's name. But Farmer JR told me the horse was a black mare. After much confusion, it turned out that this landowner only had one horse, and it was a gray stallion, the horse you see before you. Emperor RJ clapped his hands in delight. Is Farmer JR really that good? He no longer notices the external appearance of the horse. He sees only the inner horse and is blind to all else."

"I've got this one," said Iris, "You're the gray."

"That's who Julie thought I was. And that left her to be Farmer JR, seeing essence, blind to appearance."

"Good story. Julie loved the real you. She didn't care what you looked like or what work you did."

"Julie treasured that story."

"Wait. You don't?"

"I treasure it because she did. Because it's a lovely, mystical piece of the truth. But there were other pieces to the truth. I may have been a janitor, and no movie star, but I wasn't the worst looking guy in Alabama, either. Some people, even people unrelated to me, have said I have a good if lopsided smile, and I like it when they say that. I am big and strong and useful around the house. I can rebuild rotting stairs and replace flooded sheetrock in the basement. I can square up the corners of a new deck with a piece of string. English teachers especially are impressed by these skills. From me, Julie learned to love big, fat carpenter pencils. She took to taking one to class and marking papers with it. The pencil was too big for the pencil sharpener, but she sweet-talked the principal into letting her keep a tiny penknife in her locked desk for this purpose. She loved pulling the round metal trashcan in front of her chair and pushing up her sleeves and bending over to put a point on her carpenter pencil."

Iris nodded to me in that way she had that implied she was giving me permission to keep talking, or perhaps provisional permission to keep living.

"When Julie married me, she drew to her the attention of her mostly indifferent parents. Her parents were minor local nobility, so she had the luxury of being able to marry up, down, or sideways. They neither opposed me nor approved of me. Julie's mother gave it out to her that she expected this marriage not to last, but on the plus side she thought Julie would eventually find the right marriage for her. This is where I was backward because I did not know this way of looking at the world. I was a romantic like Julie; also, I was, am, a rube. In the way of such things, her parents' attention to our marriage or to us did not last long, and this gave Julie the tiny beginning of some lines of care, vertical lines scratched between her eyes."

"The royalty part, with Julie's parents," said Iris. "That was a little bit like me with my parents."

"Unlike Julie, I didn't have living parents when we married (don't know about my father). I don't know what my mother would have thought of Julie with her free spirit and dazzling hair. I think my younger mother might have liked Julie but not my older mother. My mother the elder would have said no good can come of such dazzle. For my mother, in her later years, she got mean in a way she couldn't all the way help. She was apt to rhyme the words flash and trash, and it's how she saw things and most like how she came to see my dazzling dad. And in the part I could make sense of, it was just how you naturally get to thinking when you've been thrown down too many times. My mother would never own up to her anger because she reckoned God disapproved of it. I didn't make good sense of this, either—I mean, was it only God who was allowed the wrath of God? She acted like she had never read the Old Testament, but the truth is I had personally seen her read it, her eyes and lips and frowning concentration moving right along with the words on the page. So, she could let herself be a little snippy mad and mutter about flash and trash, but she could never allow herself a scorched-earth Old Testament rampage. Worse, so much worse, she couldn't decide when a rampage was justified because her Bible has always confused everyone but fools, and the fools, well, they have a serenity unmolested by good sense. Love and forgive your neighbor? Or demand the one eye for the other? Which is it? Make up your mind, Bible."

I paused to draw breath and to see how much I was aggravating Iris. She made no move to strangle me, so I took this as permission to go on.

"Jesus famously came to earth to join the common folk, to show them how to live. Good for him. But maybe also the fools did some teaching to him—because even Jesus, in a petulant fit, cursed a fig tree for having no winter fruit. A fig tree? For crying out loud, if you can't love a fig tree, can't love a fig, can't love fig preserves on hot biscuits, you've tumped the wagon into the ditch. Yo, Jesus, you expect the tree to rain figs for your convenience in winter? Like you're God or something? Give me a break. Not even the Emperor RJ Billy Ray would have demanded a fig tree produce fruit out of season. If you can't do as well as Farmer JR and Emperor RJ, who respected the essential nature of things, their truest heart, you should get out of the business, which Jesus, abruptly, did. Because, I guess, he found it was all just too damn much, and I for sure get that part."

Iris patted me on the shoulder and got out of the car and walked around it twice and then walked over and stared into a little brook that cut through the meadow. When she got back in the car she held one hand up, an invitation, as I earnestly believed, for me to shut up.

"Did Julie ever say to you that you should try being something besides a janitor?"

"No, but maybe she would have, given time. I hope not."

"She certainly saw your abilities. Because I do, and I'm no Farmer JR."

"But Julie was no Cleopatra." This Cleopatra stuff irritated Iris, so I pushed on to change the subject. "Of course, we used to talk about what we might do. Truth, most of this was a spotlight on Julie. Could she get her Eudora Welty book published and maybe go on to teach at a college? Neither of us could get straight in our minds what I might do because I was too much the riddle for good planning. Sometimes Julie, more than I, tried to dream up how things might have been under different stars. The thing is, we were mostly content as things were. We found each other under stars that put us both in the gym of Muscle Shoals High of a fall night with crisp air. Crisp so that Julie had pulled from her oak drawer (that held sweet-smelling cypress shavings) an emerald green sweater that set off her dazzling red hair. And she told me later that she had a twinge that morning because the sweater was almost too tight to be worn in the presence of high school boys (or high school janitors), but she wore it anyway, and there must have been dozens of us that fell in love that day, that night, under a beguilement of stars."

"You," said Iris, "and your beguilement."

"Now you. Tell me about being a princess of Summit County."

Iris leaned her head back against the headrest. "Buster, my husband, was beneath me, in the social class way you're talking about. I was once the richest women in the valley and, like Julie, I could marry any way I wanted because my parents were rancher royalty. Buster drove a delivery truck, among other jobs, and liked to ski and drink and hang out with his pals. When I was young, my parents and I were trying to sell off some of our land to Denver developers. One of this developer bunch was about the prettiest three-piece suit you ever saw. Stewart was smooth, sophisticated—I was a little taken. We had meetings that I didn't invite Buster to because none of it was any interest to him. Once, after a meeting, I took Stewart out to a bar for a celebration drink. Buster happened in, delivering, of all things, a load of toilet paper, and I mostly ignored him. But that was the first and last time ever I ignored him because when Buster was on the way out with his dolly I caught a quick glimpse of my reflection in Buster's eyes. I stared at my reflection the rest of that night and right on up through today. God, he was a sweet man, a big, rough, sweet man who never owned a three-piece suit. Stewart came around one more time, and I told him OK but not again or I would break the bridge of his perfect nose with the bottom edge of a beer bottle."

"See, that's what I'm talking about. That's Cleopatra talking."

"Cleopatra was a queen. Me, I just got in fights in bars and embarrassed my parents. And I let my spirit wander from the sweetest man I knew."

"I didn't know Buster, but Hector's pretty up there."

"He is. As a matter of fact, Buster and Hector were best friends, and Buster used to describe Hector as a sweet man—those exact words. With Buster, he and I were just young. Like you and Julie. Where the world is full of smooth temptations, like Stewart. And everything is a test of who you are."

"I have to take a break," I told Iris. She nodded and continued to lean back against the headrest, now with her eyes closed. I got out and found the path down to the sliver of stream and followed along it into the tall, nodding meadow grass. I lay down in the grass with my chin resting on the edge of the bank and my eyes tugged always to the right by the purling water.

Reality right then was slippery as fish guts for me. Maybe Iris was reading my heart, calling it forth, calling me to talk about my own temptation story. Maybe Iris understood that everyone has one. Or maybe she was just going on, the way creatures on this earth do. As is not impossible to guess, Julie had a Stewart, too. A young professor from the U of A, come to talk with the high school English Department about curriculum planning and such. Julie's color that day was high. Her blood was up. General Longstreet, another faithful factotum, said of Lee at Gettysburg that Lee's blood was up, else Lee would not have ordered Pickett's hopeless charge, a charge that Longstreet despised as charnel.

Julie had her Stewart to our house for dinner—it is a comfort not to have to use his actual name (thanks, Iris). Julie wore the emerald sweater, and I believe she did this outside of her own comprehension. Just as Lee attacked straight ahead on the third day because it was outside his comprehension of himself to move sideways, to wait, to let the world see him hesitating.

I believe that Julie had this learned professor of education from the prestigious University of Alabama to dinner in part so she could show off (or try out?) her oddly learned janitor. I was prepared to show off because all this was new to me, and to Julie, and I was starting to see a need to find my place in the goings-on of Julie's life. She liked spending a night in the woods with me and my friends and the dogs, but not to the exclusion of all other varieties of human experience.

So, turnabout, I needed to sit by her campfire and please (if it were in me) her friends. I was learning to do this some small bit, at dinners and such, where I was getting more comfortable talking with my betters in a little bit of a natural way. Sometimes I liked it, but I had some ways to go before I stopped feeling like a performing monkey. Grind the organ and see the untutored janitor display a completely unexpected knowledge of King Lear's disappearing Fool. I was odd, and I understood Julie's wish to find and fix a place for me in her life, and I wished I could be of more help. It likely didn't help much the times I told her friends that my dream job was to be Lear's Fool, or to be any King's Fool. I wanted to speak jokes to power as power spoke jokes to me.

I don't all the way know what Julie was thinking with her professor. I recall she thought she could prompt me into repeating some smart talk on the essays of this deeply clever Frenchman, Michel Montaigne, a task within my reach. (It was a pure relief to me that I could read those essays in English without having to rely on the French that my teacher, Miss French, failed to teach me, with no fault on her for not trying.) I was at the time much fetched by Montaigne's handiness at turning the digression into the story, and I had been going on to Julie about this. What you first thought were only digressions was Montaigne opening a window to his own heart. So, Montaigne liked a story and didn't mind wandering around some on the way to the point; he was a rambling Frenchman, not as purely wild as his poetic countryman, Francois Villon, but still. That Villon was a bad man and a criminal, but he cared about where the snows of yesteryear had gotten gone to, except he phrased it considerable better, so much better that it made me think he had known Julie in a previous life and lost her, the poor bastard.

All this could have worked with Professor Stewart if Julie had not worn the emerald jewel of a sweater, which once stole my heart and now my tongue. I was not school trained, so I did not know how to rein in unseemly exuberance in the small, smart, before-dinner conversation. What I needed was this ironic detachment thing, but I was never trained up to it in janitor school. This kind of talk sounded to me like my hated high school teachers, who droned into wilting somnolence the spryest ideas of the very cream of the species. The sound I wanted, needed, was fresh, alive, and alert in every cell. M. Montaigne refreshed this way, as did Mr. Shakespeare, as did also that cunning biologist of a later time, Sir Peter Brian Medawar, who thought hard about how to transplant organs from one body to another, and who might have, if kindly asked, figured out how to transplant into me the essential heart of Julie—so to never be without.

I tried to talk to Professor Stewart but was strangled by fear of the sweater and couldn't do it. The one idea as came to me, not a good one, was that Julie married a janitor, so by God I would be a janitor, a sullen one, with a chip, and a hokey way about me. Julie stewed, and I got off one to Professor Stewart about how he would like her stewed tomatoes and then I went on to explain the joke, just to flesh out my role as *l'idiot du village*.

Professor Stewart was patronizing, I guess. But, fair, he could have said the merest hello and I would have found it patronizing. I had a bulldog grip on wrong, and wrong tasted like my own blood in a losing fight. It was a dinner that could not be made to be over with. The only one having a fine time was Professor Stewart. He got to admire Julie's sweater and feel superior, and feeling superior was only a notch down from feeling Julie's sweater. She walked him to the door, kissed him on the mouth as she closed the door, gave me the finger, and went to bed.

I still don't know what to make of it. I was wrong and deserved to be punched in the mouth and to have a split lip to taste. Julie had a fiery temper and other days I would not have been all the way surprised if she hauled off and busted my lip. But this day she chose to kiss Professor Stewart, and it was the meanest thing she had ever done to me and will ever do to me in this world that we know.

Fair to say, other people, in the history of all those who have come before, have done meaner things. Fair to say that in ten more twisty years, maybe I would have done something like this same meanness to Julie; forgive me, my love. But this was Julie doing the meanness. Julie. We had said vows to each other. Mostly, though, it broke the promises I had made to myself.

I have come to think that marriage in some small or large part is a bargain you strike with yourself. If I love this person, then this is the thing that I promise myself will be. The other person may agree or disagree or know nothing of this deal I have made with myself. And she the same, with the bargains of her own heart. I promised myself that Julie would not break my heart. Did she promise me the same? It's a blur, but I guess. And I don't know all the promises she made to herself. Did she promise herself that I would never act like a hayseed in front of Professor Stewart?

Julie and I skidded into the ditch and then used a come-along to winch our marriage back out, and I got better at fitting in with Julie's friends and she better at protecting my hayseed heart. But

I did not want Professor Stewart in my memory of Julie, which was a shrine.

And, hell, I knew that shrines were dangerous for the living but could not make myself stop building one. Julie died, and long before, that good poet John Keats had also managed to die. And as I get the story, Mr. Keats had died on ahead of his poetry pal, Percy Bysshe Shelley, and was sore missed. I like to think that the two of them may have shared a bottle and a campfire and the fine sound of hounds away in the dark. Shelley, in building his shrine to Keats, said that his friend had gone on to that place "where all things wise and fair descend." And those are words—they are such words. And Julie, I could put her there, also, in that place of the words, maybe with her showing Mr. Keats the cunning uses of a carpenter pencil. But only a fool (me) would think she was (completely) wise and fair. I knew she could be a jerk; she knew that, as did all sentient. But here's a thing: I conceived it was still my job to build a shrine. That's not something Professor Stewart would now be doing, if even he knew that she had descended. And it came to me then—a miracle, a miracle thought—that I could build any shrine as pleased me (and square up the corners with a stretched piece of twine).

I was free, free to leave out the professor, as Julie would have left him out because she would not want to be remembered for Professor Stewart. On the other hand, she might want to be remembered for the time she showed off in her class by hefting a heavy stack of books but then lurched and caught herself, at the price of farting sharply. In her telling of this story, her chief amusement was that the books were all copies of *Sense and Sensibility*. She thought that was funny—me, too.

I liked this idea that I could build any shrine to Julie I wanted. I had been thinking the replica of her life needed to be a faithful representation, and it was good to get shed of such silliness.

On the ceiling of the Sistine Chapel, God reaches his omnipotent finger to spark life into Adam. No art is exactly representational, though, nor any life, nor love, nor memory. And for proof is the fact that Michelangelo chose to leave out the immediately coming-before scene, in which God was verily picking his nose with that gnarled right index finger, curled perfectly for clearing out divine boogers.

I think we are required to build a shrine to our beloved dead, to those who have been "startled awake from the dream of life." (Thanks, again, Percy Bysshe Shelley. But Percy, what the hell kind of name is Bysshe? I bet you seventeen cents that no living soul in Alabama has a given name of Bysshe.) Like Montaigne, I digress, and there's no sense pretending I'm sorry.

Old Bysshe, clever fellow, thought life was the (confused) dream from which death awakens us. Old Bysshe sort of flipped things over from, say, Mr. Shakespeare's Hamlet. Me, I like Old Bysshe's way. Hamlet worried about what dreams may come after we die, and Old Bysshe said, forget that, you'd best worry, you chucklehead, about the silly dreams you're living in. I must say that all this Old Bysshe talk makes me want to name a hound dog Old Bysshe. Or name a son that—is that a thing that could be?

So, Old Bysshe Shelley, and Old Will Shakespeare, there's no reason to think either of you knows the great unknowable, that either of you is any less full of it than anybody else, but thanks for the oddball digressions because, ask my friend, Montaigne, the digressions, little glimpses of a beating heart, are the sweetness of the story, a sweetness that eases my way.

Even though we are required to build a shrine, it doesn't mean that one wing of the shrine can't be the Fart Wing. And I can move in or out of the shrine at will. Because I was a janitor in Julie Time did not mean I had to be a janitor for All Time because all the time did not, and does not, belong to her, to Julie, my great love.

Chapter 15

Hector was home for lunch, and I refused to let him cook. And for sure not Iris. Neither was going to cook while I was happy. Happy because now I was no longer required to be a janitor. I could be anything there was in the world to be. My heart sang because of that quirky bit of freedom, and also because, just between us, a small, crafty corner of my mind did not overlook the idea that being free, free to be anything there was to be, did not rule out using a trusty tennis ball on a stick to lift scuff marks from a gym floor, did not rule out restoring a shine to the floor with the almost silent hiss of a dust mop. Other career opportunities might fetch me, and good for that, but I did not forget the joys of a quiet and alone job, where I could hear myself think. And sometimes hear in that quietness the thoughts of others dear to me.

I got Iris to drag lunch fixings from the refrigerator and put them on the counter. I found two beers and two tall glasses and set them on the kitchen table in front of Iris and Hector. I poured off the beers all flourish-like, the way Julie had taught me.

Iris and Hector were casually holding hands at the table, without paying much attention to each other, and I liked that and found that I liked the memory of Julie teaching me to drink beer from a chilly glass rather than a can. I wanted at this moment to feel my hands doing simple things, to sink my thoughts into plain life.

Iris had provided a slab of great, thick bacon, the slices peeling heavy and clean. Even Julie, a princess of Alabama, did not splurge thus on bacon. But I liked it when her mischievous face described bacon as nature's perfect food, and on many mornings I had cooked us bacon and scrambled eggs and blue cheese grits and steaming biscuits with fig preserves (because who cannot love a fig?).

In those mornings Julie and I shamed the appetite of Falstaff and then did eventide penance with a ruby grapefruit, smeared with amber honey. We lived large and were saved from the plague of Alabama obesity by youth and hard hikes in green woods and the partial penance of the grapefruit. (Also by the caloric bonfires of love.)

It's a sadness that Southerners run to fat in the way they seem to be fattening themselves for their own slaughter. But that's the way of it, and, fair goes to fair, a morning in a life is always less fretful after a rich breakfast of bacon and its dear food friends. Philosophers will have to talk among themselves about whether a short, happy, and fat life is a more devoutly wished consummation than a long life that is skinny and full of the twitchy frets.

I set the thick, fatty bacon to frying and washed the crisp, svelte lettuce, serving shamelessly my contradictory food masters. I was having fun and served us up three BLT's, with a bowl of earthy potatoes that had wriggled from the brown, dirty cocoon of their humble origins and, transcendent, taken winged life as golden potato chips. Of the three of us, Iris was the only one with potato chip immunity because if she pigged out she would just run nine miles instead of six. I brought myself a beer from the refrigerator and drank it from the brown bottle because

I was too lazy to get up and get a glass and suddenly too eager for the taste.

"What did you think of the high school?" asked Hector.

"They have a buffing machine." Hector raised a quizzical eyebrow at me and Iris raised a languid, ignore-Tree finger.

"You think you might stay here?" asked Hector.

"I don't know. I started thinking about the people here and the people in Alabama. It came as kind of a shock to me how many there are that I like here. I always thought of myself as kind of an alone person but maybe not."

"Or maybe everybody thinks they're alone," said Hector.

"Some, maybe," said Iris. "But Tree is alone, in his head. More than most because he has a rare head. It gives me a headache sometimes to listen to what he's thinking about. And that's only what he tells me about, the tip, I guess, of the iceberg. Did you used to tell Julie everything you were thinking about?"

I laughed. "Sometimes I got wound up and did until she curled up on the couch with a pillow over her head. What I learned was that women don't all the way mean it when they say they want more communication."

"Oh, we mean it," said Iris. "What we mean is that we want to be listened to more. But the other way around, there are limits. Me, I want Hector to talk more and you to talk less."

"One of us," said Hector to me, "is being insulted."

"Both of you."

"Billy is coming up the walk," I said. "He will defend me. Hector is on his own."

I could not read Billy's round face, but I was glad to see him. He filled the paved walkway to Hector's (and Iris's) door. I tried to think if I had ever seen Billy and Lena walking such a path together. Even as small as Lena was, it wouldn't work. Lena would have to walk in front or behind. They were forever prevented from holding hands on sidewalks. They could, in the pursuit of this simple pleasure, walk down the middle of the street, bringing large dump trucks to a wary halt. I saw why Billy liked driving the snowplow. It was a big machine, Herculean, Samsonian, Billean. Hector got up to let Billy in.

"Marcos is gone." Billy said this and looked too long at me as he delivered the news, and with the news the rightful blame.

"Gone where?" asked Iris.

"We had a little side job splitting firewood today for John Mathis. Marcos didn't show. John sent me to look for him. They've moved out. People in the apartments are acting like they never heard of him."

"Where to?" repeated Iris.

"His sister, Irina, finally talked to me. She wouldn't say where. Marcos got wind the feds were after him."

"Maria, Javier…gone too?" I asked, stupidly. Billy did not bother to answer. The feds. Even I could figure out that this meant some ugly stuff like Nico and Half Willard and pistol-pointing Al. And that meant me and my silly stubbornness about the letter from the pope. I just never thought such a stupid thing could end in such a stupid thing. It was, I had told myself, a lark, a kind of present for Julie. It was still no kind of deal that I could fathom except that Javier was gone and taken Marcos and Maria with him, and what I wanted to do that minute was build a fort with Javier and guard it against that bastard, Nico.

"What?" Iris demanded of Hector. "What do we do? Did the feds pick them up?"

"Doesn't sound like it. I got no courtesy call from any of my friends at immigration. The neighbors say they pulled out, and that's probably what they did. I wish Marcos had called me."

"What would that have helped?" I asked.

"He probably didn't need to run. I wish he had trusted me more. After I first met him, I checked the records. I couldn't find anything on him. Commit a crime, he gets deported. Otherwise he's just one of the eleven million. The feds don't have enough Chevy Suburbans to squeeze eleven million people into."

"So, what happened?"

"A guess? Al cooked up a way to scare him. Wouldn't be hard. Marcos is in no man's land. It's not like Marcos can call his congressman and demand justice. Someone like Al or Willard Jordan, Justice Grasso, they think like, you're illegal, and so from the get-go you got nothing coming to you because you should have stayed home. Stay home—don't come here and steal my job. Hell, I get that. Lots of people think that's technically right."

"Technically!" said Iris. "Technically?" She was the Queen of the Nile and her nostrils flared.

"These are technical people," said Hector.

"Pharisees and Scribes," said Billy.

"OK, sure," said Hector. "The thing is, they are the people who can do it to you. There's always a factory in a company town, a *jefe*, a plantation master, someone who can do it to you. Hell, sometimes it's a sheriff. They genuflect to the law and think about how to make it technically right, and once that's solved then they don't think about it anymore. All the thinking's done and then they just do it to you. They find a river and sell you down it, but only if that's what will make their lives nicer."

Iris said nothing but slammed her hard fist against the table. Hector shrugged and continued. "The people who make things technically right, the big thinkers like Grasso, are very valuable. That's why Willard Jordan treats him so well. Grasso makes everything so Willard doesn't have to think about it anymore, so his life is nice."

"How do we get Marcos back?" I asked. "And Maria, and Javier."

"Sooner or later, I can get a message to him," said Hector. "His parents are here, his sister. He has friends here."

"Can you get a message to him from me?" I asked.

"A message to come back to Summit County? Sure, eventually. But he may decide he's better off elsewhere. Unusually smart guy. Hard working. Gets people on his crew to work without ever seeming to give an order. Marcos may get somewhere else and find he's better off without being hounded by a Supreme Court justice."

"That I brought down on him."

Hector ran his hands through his hair. "Maybe, without meaning to. Someone noticed you were close. Al, probably. It was an easy play for Al, with no down side. He doesn't care what happens to Marcos. Al is no rocket scientist. He always goes for the easy move, and the thing is that the easy move is usually what works. You get too fancy, who knows what will happen?"

"And I got too fancy. Why didn't I just give Grasso his letter? I wanted to jerk him around, and I didn't care what happened because what could he do to me that I care about? Because if you lose your wife and don't care whether you live or die, then you can just say, fuck you, to everybody. Unless you care more than you know. Unless the joke is on you."

"I still don't get why Grasso wants the letter so much," said Hector.

"You think he believed me when I told him the pope was blackmailing him?"

"*Quién sabe*? Who really knows? He'd have to be pretty stupid to believe that. You don't put blackmail in writing. And sign your name to it?"

"My story was that lame? That hurts my feelings. I thought it was pretty clever."

"It was kind of fun. You tell an interesting story, Tree. You get points for that. Hell, I don't know. Maybe even the judge believed it. Lots of judges don't know shit about how the world works. Any more than janitors. Course, to be fair, popes lead a pretty sheltered life, too."

"Is that why you never pushed me to see the letter?"

"Mostly. But I wonder now if you shouldn't give it back."

"OK, you're right. For some reason, Grasso wants it enough to cause trouble. If I give it back, maybe he'll stop."

"Let's hope."

.....

"Tell me," I said to Iris, "about the man you killed." We were sitting, the two of us, on the back deck in the sunshine and there was a scraggly rose bush with one pink blossom, but the rose bush was not taken care of by anyone with time to love it.

"What?"

"I have a reason for wanting to know."

"What?"

"OK, wait, I'm messing this up."

"You are if you think you're talking to me."

"I'm sorry. Sorry. Can I explain?"

"You'd better. Wait. You idiot. You're not thinking of killing Grasso?"

"Is that not allowed?"

177

Iris stared. I had her attention, more than I wholly wanted. "I'd like to kill him for Marcos. But no. If I killed Grasso, I wouldn't be around to kill the man who needs it."

"What? What? What are you talking about?"

"Julie was a pedestrian and killed by a drunk driver named Bill Martin. He's in prison, but one day he will get out. Julie was broken on the sidewalk. Bleeding. Bill Martin got out of his car and his only comment was, too bad, because she's a hot chick. A hot chick is what he said. One day he will get out of prison."

"Oh, Tree."

"That's why I want to know about killing."

"Oh, God." Iris crossed her arms over her chest and shuddered. I was still so buffaloed by her presence, by the Cleopatra that was in her, that I did not expect to see her shudder. But that was just another piece of my foolishness. Who knows? The original Cleopatra maybe shuddered at the assassination of Julius Caesar, at the suicide of Mark Antony, at the sudden, irrevocable reality of the asp fangs, buried in her breast.

Iris went on: "You've been sitting on this plan since Julie died? To kill this guy that killed her? And you think I can help you? How? What are you talking about?"

"I don't know. You've killed someone, and I haven't. Most people don't get to know someone who has killed someone. Those people are out there. Soldiers. Sheriffs. Has Hector killed anyone in the line of duty? I should ask him."

"No. He hasn't. Don't ask him."

"It's not the only plan I've been sitting on. One version of my future had me killing myself and letting Bill Martin live. As Hector would say, *quién sabe*? Maybe I kept myself alive so I could kill Bill Martin."

178

"Or maybe so you could just live. Consider that, you idiot."

"OK. I will. I will. I am."

"You're too kindhearted to kill anybody. Either yourself or this Bill Martin."

"Is that it? Is that what you think? Does that hold up? That says you're not kindhearted because you killed this man, Larry. I don't know that I believe that. Look at you this moment, being kind to me."

"You don't understand. It's different."

"Then explain. I want to understand. That's why I'm asking. Tell me about killing Larry. You're the only person I know who's killed someone. Except for Bill Martin. He killed someone. Maybe I will ask him."

"It was different. Different. I was at Ben's house, next door to mine. Ben and Megan had just decided to get married. It was a dream of mine. Ben and Megan were like my children. Family. When Megan was a teenager, she hit her father over the head with a hammer, killed him, and pushed him into an old mine. No one ever knew about it except Larry, her brother. Their father had abused them...horribly. Years later, she fell in love with Ben. She found out that Larry was sexually abusing his own son. She turned Larry in. Larry was in jail. He got out on bail and Hector found out too late. Ben and Megan and I were sitting at the kitchen table having coffee. I loved having coffee with Ben and Megan. I loved them. Still love Ben, still my family. Larry walked in with a gun and Megan rushed at him and he shot her in the chest. Ben knocked Larry down. Larry was unconscious on the floor while Ben and I tried to take care of Megan. She died quickly. I got up and found Larry's gun on the floor. I shot him until the gun was empty. Hector wrote it up as self-defense, and I'm OK with that now. Then...I didn't care. Buster had died years before. Megan gone. It was all just loss. I was a spider who dropped onto a candle; I just curled up. Hector was the only one who could think, so he thought for all of us. But no way was it self-defense like in the movies. Larry was breathing harsh and was twitchy but out cold and I shot him with every bullet I had. I was so sad when I ran out of bullets, like then there was nothing else to be done. What could I possibly think to do next in my life? Hector got there right after and started straightening out what was left of our lives. Ben still lives in that house that was full of blood and memories of Megan. He rented a sander and got out the blood and patched up some bullet holes, and he won't leave that house. I don't think ever."

"I'm sorry, Iris."

"For what?"

"For making you talk about it."

"Tree, you can't make me do anything." She was Cleopatra, still, and I guess always.

"OK. Can I keep going? Do you want me to shut up?"

"Keep going until you're done."

"Did you listen to yourself? You didn't make much of a case for me to leave Bill Martin alone. I was kind of hoping you would."

"I know. I meant to. I thought when I started it was going to be about my hot revenge and your cold revenge. And that's part of it. Part of the difference between Megan and Julie. You have time to talk to your better angels."

"That's what I'm doing now."

"I'm nobody's better angel." Iris held my eyes. "I'm the killer here."

"With, I think, no regrets."

She shrugged. "The truth is I never even thought about having regrets until you brought it up. All my life, I just do things. I regret losing Buster. And Megan. But I don't think you should wait around a bunch of years and then go be a killer. That's not how it works…how it should work. Would Julie want that?"

"Not a chance."

"Doesn't that answer your question?"

"Maybe. But it doesn't answer my need—my need is different from Julie's. I need to take Bill Martin's throat in my hands. I would not lack for strength. I can feel that grip and do often feel it, my thumbs pressing farther in and down. I can feel at this moment the blood rushing to my hands, giving me strength. I would not want a gun. I would not lack for strength."

"You imagine that this need will still be there in ten years. I don't know. Maybe. But I don't think so. You weren't there on the street when Julie was hit and Bill Martin was standing over her. You didn't catch the act in the heat like I did."

"You think there was a flood tide, and I missed it?"

"I do. You missed it, and now, or after ten years, it's something else."

"No longer Hector's self-defense. Now murder?"

"Maybe murder…I don't know. But maybe fate is the thing I'm after. I had my fate. It's not yours. Your fate turns on something else. *Quién sabe?* Maybe to get pushed in the river by a Supreme Court justice while wearing a letter from the pope around your neck. Your fate is still unfolding, but I don't think killing Bill Martin is a part of it. Your life will take a different turn."

She had, I think, a piece of the truth. I'm not saying I was crazy about this notion of fate. It was all kind of sketchy superstitious post hoc goulash to me. Sometimes your daring ship takes the tide at the flood and it leads on to fortune, and sometimes a storm sneaks in over the low horizon and sinks your impetuous ass and the ship it rode in on. But if Iris meant that you play the cards you've got, which I believe is what she meant, then I understood that, and there is in some cards the merriest of luck and in others, the abyss.

.....

Hector came into the living room to join Billy and me. "It's the damnedest thing. Grasso wants to get the letter from Tree."

"Isn't that why we're here?" asked Billy. "What's the deal?"

Hector ran his hands again through his thinning hair, and I started to think that his hair was thinning because of all this harrowing with his fingers. Or, hell, maybe he was just going bald. "No, I mean he wants to get the letter directly from Tree. I offered to just drop it off, but nothing doing. Tree, are you OK to meet with the judge?"

"Yeah, OK."

"No, Tree, I mean can I trust you not to do something dumb? You don't have to be his best friend, but nothing physical. Say that after me."

"What?"

"Nothing physical, no matter how much he pisses you off, which could be a lot. He has a talent."

"I got it. Nothing physical. The Sheriff of Summit County, Hector Morales, says don't hurt Supreme Court justices—I got it."

"OK. But what I'm also saying is don't hurt old people in my county. The judge is old."

"You know, you're right. All that power he has. It's easy to lose sight. I promise. Do I take the letter to Willard's ranch?"

"I don't get that, either. The judge wants to meet at the campsite. Where the remains of your camper still sit until we get a tow truck out there. You meet tonight at six. I'm guessing you need to get out there a little early to retrieve the letter from wherever you hid it."

"That's easy."

"And here's more. The judge wants a fire. Camp chairs. Beer. Just like old times. You know, I think he enjoyed himself out there. Mixing with the riffraff. Unless I'm confused, he thinks of himself as one of the common people."

"Really?"

"Really. It's a thing with the elite. Be one with the riffs...and the raffs."

"Cool. I'll try to be both a riff and a raff. Just to make the justice feel to home."

"Just a riff will do. Billy will be the raff."

"Billy?"

"Is your protection."

"Why do I need protection from an old man?"

"The judge is bringing Al. I don't really worry because Al will be on good behavior when he's with the judge. But I told Al that Billy would make a nice foursome, and Al had to see the logic. He and Billy aren't lovebirds, but they know each other, and they get along OK."

"Wait. Al is there for something, I guess to protect the judge from me. Billy is there to protect me from Al. Is this a gangster movie?"

"It started out to be a comedy. You get pushed in the river by a bigtime judge. Without knowing it, he's just given you a letter from the pope. You're dogpaddling down the Rolling River with a papal pronouncement around your neck. What I don't get is why you didn't just climb on top of the water and walk."

"That would've been fun."

"It was all pretty fun for a while," said Hector. "It was good fun with you telling the judge campfire yarns. It was even good, clean fun with you guys having a brawl at the trailhead. That's especially the kind of local color the judge would appreciate, the kind he could tell stories about. Then the fun kind of tailed off when your camper got burned and then it went right into the shitter when Marcos had to run. I'm not having fun anymore, and I want it to stop."

"So why don't you come out to the campsite and personally sheriff everything up? Why Al and Billy? And God help us...why me?"

"The judge won't have it. No cops. *Quién sabe?*"

I turned to Billy. "You're OK with this? Babysitting me? Even after I brought all this stuff down on us? On Marcos?"

"Tree, you jerked the judge's chain. I don't know why exactly. Maybe to have fun. Or to let some demons out. I guess the judge deserved it, maybe because he's a jerk, maybe because of his politics; I don't know because the only politics I follow are Thoreau's. Just like Thoreau, I'm a foursquare, rock-solid abolitionist. And like Thoreau, I don't want my taxes to go for war. The country's gotten rid of slavery but no change on military taxes. I don't know where your judge stands on Thoreau's politics. I don't even know where Thoreau would stand since it took a war tax to get him his abolition; I'm still thinking on that one. When I get the politics of Thoreau's time figured out, then maybe I'll push on to the twentieth century. But nobody should hold their breath—I'm not a fast study. Tree, it looks like it was dumb to jerk the judge's chain, but here's a thing I know without even having to think on it, the same way Lena knows things. You're my friend, just like George and Hector and Ben are my friends. Al, Willard Jordan, Grasso, they're nobody to me; and the other way around, they will never care what happens to me, to Lena, to my boys. Like Hector says, I'm just riff to them, or raff, I forget which.

"Raff," said Hector, quietly.

Billy nodded. "I also get the feeling that there's a new kind of Underground Railroad since Thoreau's time. But this one Willard Jordan and his pals built especially for us. They want us to ride the rails, all of us, all the riffs and raffs. We can travel around on the Underground Railroad all day long, anywhere we want to go, and they won't see us. Because the railroad makes us invisible to them—they're smart that way. Tree, sometimes you're a strange guy, but Lena says you can't help it, and she sees who people are better than me. She says we've got to figure out how to get Marcos back. In the meantime, I'll keep an eye on Al while you talk to the judge. And if Al gets out of line, I'll pick him up by his ankles and stand him upright on his thick head. The judge, I leave to you."

Later, Hector had one more talk with me, private. He was in his force field, concentrating, moving things around in his mind. And I was one of the moving things. He told me to talk a lot to Nico and to go ahead and be as aggravating as pleased me (but still no hitting). This encouragement to be aggravating was backwards to my entire experience of others telling me how to act, but I did not question it because he was concentrating on being what he was, the high sheriff of his peeps.

Chapter 16

"My letter," said Nico.

I opened a beer for him. When I reached it to him, he would not lift his hairy hand to take it, so I put it in the drink holder on his camp chair.

"My letter," he iterated. I began to think that he was not going to open himself to the joy of camaraderie until he had in his hand...

"My letter," he reiterated.

I put down my own beer and got out of my chair and walked around to his side of the granite coffee table. I did like that table. I thought Julie would like it, too. It would have been a fine rock on which to build a home, with the coffee table square in the middle of the living room. I wondered if Julie would be proud of me for hanging in there and having a beer with Nico, assuming he ever unbent enough to take an actual sip of his beer.

I retrieved a small pair of needle-nosed pliers from my pocket and went down on one knee beside the table. I scraped some carefully encrusted dirt and dried moss from low on the side of my table, and, lo, there was a horizontal crack in the granite, barely big enough to insert the tip of the pliers into, and, lo again, the pliers backed out with the edge of a letter in their serrated pincers. I dropped the letter on the table, so His Eminence would have to lean forward to get it, perhaps in so doing making him slightly modify the position of his most arrogant ass.

He put on his glasses and studied the short letter on its rich paper. "Well, I'll be damned. It is from Jorge, and it's pretty much what you described, except for the bullshit you added about me taking bribes." I watched his face closely as he said this to see if it revealed some dark guilty stain, which I was dumb to do because this was Nico. What? His face was going to crumple like a guilty schoolboy?

"Jorge?" I asked.

"The pope. Pope Francis to you."

"Ah. But not to you?"

"Never to me. Jorge to me. Should never have even made cardinal. I guess he's bright enough to be a bishop, a South American bishop. Socialist. Liberation theology. The Church has had bad popes before—it will survive. Jorge's no pope of mine."

"Ah, you never called him, did you? I told you to just call him to see what was in the letter. The only victory I was hoping for was to make you call good old Jorge. Kind of like that kids' game where you say, 'Made you look.' I wanted to be able to say, 'Made you call.' You got me, Nico. I couldn't make you call."

Nico laughed. "Never."

"I didn't know you hated the pope so much. He maybe doesn't even know that part himself. Or why bother writing you a letter? I had some hope for that part, too. That me and the pope could get you to sometimes reach a hand to the poor…but to do that you would have to let go of Willard Jordan's hand."

Nico snorted. "The poor. The poor. They have the same opportunity as Willard Jordan did, as I did; we just made better use of it. I grant you the poor may not have been born with as much smarts. But that's on God, not me."

I was mindful that Nico reveled in being a flamboyant jerk, and folks, eager to think goodness on the powerful, thought he must be all teddy bear inside, and I grant he had the winsome grin. Make a big show of having a cold heart and then give them the grin, and they'll think that deep inside it's a hidden heart of gold. Except, in Nico's case, deep inside was an even colder heart than dreamed of in anyone's philosophy. Did I mention cold? I mayhap needed to get better myself at letting go of grudges, but this was the guy who pushed me in the fast, icy Rolling River without asking first to see my swimming license. And here's another thing (because where I'm concerned there's always another thing), and this other thing is that here I was worried about carrying a grudge for too long, and Nico, well, he wasn't worried about anything except his melancholy that Tree Purcell was here before him this minute, and nary a river in sight to drown him in.

Nico was that satisfied with the shape of current events that he shared with me the winning grin. "Tree, you got some brass taking me on. Who do you think you are?"

"I'm a janitor. Or was until you got me fired. But no offense taken on that. I'm young and strong and can buff a floor without missing any part because there's nothing worse than standing back from a newly glowing floor and seeing some dull streak that got missed. I don't like careless work, or careless words for that matter. I don't mind work and don't even so much mind low pay. Those qualities put me first in line for another job, but, in the truth of it, I just haven't looked yet. I've got to see to my camper first."

We studied the burned, drooping shell of my camper. Where the aluminum had softened in the heat, it had shifted downward its shape, like the ancient molten version of my igneous coffee table. Truth, I liked imagining the sooty Vulcan who manufactured my table, a smithy, miles below, eons ago, a smithy who fired and shaped and cooled my granite table. And this same smithy, still working, firing, hammering, arcing sparks across the earth's great belly, and no sign of even a tremor up here, on this home, this earth, this silvered isle, adrift in space.

"What happened to your camper?" asked Nico. He looked at the camper with a bit of dawn about him like he had just noticed something was wrong. When Billy and I had gotten there, Al was poking about things, over things, under things, looking. When we unloaded the camp chairs, they each went through Al's prying, searching fingers. I guess they passed muster because he let us sit in them. (He might have had a tough go not letting Nico sit in his.)

I looked up the hill to where Al and Billy now leaned against a boulder the size of a Chevy Suburban, which similarity in size may be what attracted Al to it. Billy was attracted, in turn, to Al's right thigh, because on it was strapped Al's favorite pistol. In the perfection of truth, I can no way know for sure it was his favorite, but it stood to reason. It was the pistol he pointed patiently at me as I ran down the gully to join the fight at the trailhead. I could testify that he was a skilled aimer as the gun had no waver to it, and I could testify on top that I was now glad he didn't pull the trigger although then I neglected to care.

My thought was that the pistol was decoration, like fanned peacock feathers. A group of peacocks, perhaps on promenade, perhaps out to pick up cute peahens, this group is officially known as an ostentation of peacocks, and it makes me happy to know that, and happy to know the ironical part that me showing off this knowledge is also ostentation, call it an ostentation of Tree's. Billy was here snugged against Al's right side, casual-like, so to keep that favorite pistol in reach if Al the gunslinger grabbed for it, which, fair again, Al showed no sign of doing.

But Billy was here snugged, and, forgive me, I know this is another long stretch, but have you noticed how many times Lincoln used the word, here, at Gettysburg? Eight. Eight times, in a short, staccato speech of less than three hundred words, he used the word, here, and he was not even staking out tomato plants. He was just digging into the Gettysburg dirt, here, here, here, here, here, here, here, and spare us, here again.

Billy had said nothing as he got on Al's right flank, but I marked it, and Al marked it, and Al was most like satisfied because his gun had created a problem, which for Al was always its own reward.

"Why did you even want the letter back, Nico? You don't care what the pope thinks. Why bother on it? And just because I gave you the letter doesn't mean I couldn't have made a copy. Doesn't mean I couldn't give the copy to the press, to my friend George, who all by himself is the local press."

"Sure, you could do that. But there's nothing in it that really hurts me. Which, by the way, I couldn't be sure of until you gave it to me, so thanks for that. Maybe the liberal press could get excited about it for a couple days because Jorge hints I'm on the take. But a hint is not proof. So what do I care? It doesn't get me impeached."

"OK. That's the more reason not to care whether you got the letter back."

Nico again pinched his dense eyebrows together and studied me. "You're partly right, Tree. I started to just let it go. I couldn't let you win, though. Wouldn't have been right."

I gestured to the remainders of my camper. "Does it look like I won?" Nico looked blankly at my camper, and I could see him coming up empty on why anyone would care about this pile of drooping junk. "Why wouldn't it have been OK to let the janitor win one? I remember being grateful to Mr. Jefferson for saying we're all created equal."

"Tree, in some Jeffersonian dream world, you and I may have been created equal. But we haven't been remotely equal since that moment of egalitarian creation. Since then, the cream rises and the sludge sinks. I'll let you win the prize for guessing which one of those you are."

Recalling someone more over the top than Nico did not fly fast to memory. Sometimes...me. Sometimes I was more over the top, but Nico did not quite know that yet. Maybe he would find out although I was still afraid of him in the same way I had been afraid of Julie's professor. I messed that one up by being a bumpkin, and I had the idea that now was the time to try for better if I wanted Julie's approval, much too late, or maybe my own approval, maybe not too late for that.

"Did I piss you off, Nico, from the start? Or after you came here to the party with my friends?"

"From the moment you laughed at me for falling in the river. There was no way I was going to let you get the better of me. But then you did it again at the party. You and your friend, Hector. I promise you he's going to have a well-funded opponent at the next election."

"Good luck on that. Hector is loved in this county. Because he turns on his flashing lights and swerves his patrol car to the curb and rushes out to help folks stack their firewood. Has nothing to do with his politics."

"Willard will still fund Al to run against him, but I take your point about Hector. Me, I don't have any politics, either. I'm a justice of the Supreme Court of the United States of America."

We let that thought grow between us, like a time-lapse movie of a puppy-sized shoat blossoming into a five-foot sow. We had time for a couple sips of beer before the hilarity was too much to bear. Nico broke first, which was proper, and I was glad I controlled myself, out of respect for the office. When he broke, there was beer coming out of his mouth and nose and he almost rolled out of his chair. We laughed, long and satisfying, another moment when I saw Nico's irascible charm.

"Why don't you give it up?" I asked.

"What?"

"The politics."

"Tree, you're a janitor. You don't know shit."

"I know the pope is not a socialist."

Go for it was my thought. I had to quit fretting about getting above my raising. There's an old bluegrass tune by Lester Flatt and Earl Scruggs (fine names, fully lived in) in which they caution a woman not to get all uppity and above her raising, but, of course, country singers drop their ending g's, raising becoming raisin', so the image to my mind was always of a woman, tragical, towering over her poor, purple raisin, lying shriveled in the sun, that same sun being the one this prideful woman had flown too close to.

I had no way of sure knowing whether I was myself a kind of learned fraud, but I knew my father, Dr. Quacksalver, was, and it made me fearful of getting above my own raisin. Truth, I never thought of myself as anything but a country bumpkin with a book; for sure, I never thought about whether I was fit to match wits with such a one as Nico. I never had much practice at wit-matching, except for Julie, and regular talks with the listening hounds beneath the scudding moon.

I had this one pet bloodhound called Pharaoh who liked to pretend to be Socrates. All he had to do was listen to me put up some earnest argument and then wrinkle the cascading skin on his forehead in a way of skeptical questioning. Pharaoh was born to the Socratic method, but he was not as scary to me as Nico was (but scarier than Nico to a waddling raccoon).

"Tree, you seriously say Jorge's not a socialist? Jorge, liberation theologian and close personal fanboy of Che Guevara? That Jorge?"

"That Jorge."

"Capitalism, Tree, has done more to raise living standards everywhere than Che and Jorge ever dreamed of. The poor in this country have microwave ovens. Marie Antoinette, hanging around the palace, would have killed for a microwave. Capitalism."

"As best I understand, Nico, that's a good deal right about capitalism. Economics is for sure a dismal thing, but I get that money is a useful idea. But that's not what I'm talking about. Socialism is some good and some bad and capitalism the same, which I guess is why all the countries in all the world have some of both. Even those communists in China have taken to dosing themselves with capitalism to ward off lethargy. And in this USA, the capital of capitalism, the state sometimes goes socialist and owns all to itself the means of production. Take, for example, the US Army, the means of warfare production, wholly owned by the government. Never mind those other scary socialist schemes like roads, public schools, and those handy potty stations at every trailhead in this bit of socialized, nationalized forest. I just can't understand why this is Armageddon to anybody. Grownups can rightly disagree over the best mix of socialism and capitalism, but to act like it's a question of one or the other is childish, not even an interesting question for those yet sentient."

Nico grunted and most like he was only half listening. "Why am I having a conversation about socialism with a barely literate janitor?"

"And for me the same." I was starting, like Pharaoh, to find the scent.

"The same what?"

"Why am I having a conversation about socialism with a semi-literate supreme court justice? Subtract out the robes and you have as remainder only a tax accountant for the rich. A justice who doesn't know what socialism is. Can you really not know that? What does it mean, Nuncle, when you say Jorge is a socialist? Has he recommended the nationalization of the push broom industry?" I was under orders from Hector to be aggravating, a fish commanded to swim.

This was enough to encourage Nico to take a sip of his beer. Two sips. And what might have been called a gulp. Enough to where he wiped his mouth with the back of his hand and quit looking at Jorge, who had been in his mind's eye, and looked at me. "Nuncle...did you say nuncle?"

"I guess I did."

"Are you trying to call me your uncle? Where have I heard that? Nuncle...nuncle."

"I guess it's kind of a Southernism for uncle, a sign of respect. No offense meant." Huckleberry Finn pretended to believe that lies smoothed the way of things, and, when needful, I pretended to believe this, also.

"What the hell can you know, Tree, about complicated ideas like socialism? And nuncle, a rare word...I feel like I should place that. You graduated high school?" Nico was like a near-sighted bear on its hind legs, sniffing the air and not liking that he was blind to everything downwind of him.

"Muscle Shoals High. It's in Alabama."

"Alabama…you told me that. And after high school?"

"I went straight on to being a janitor. At that same high school. I had been kind of an apprentice janitor even while I was in school."

"College?"

"No. I liked being a janitor. It suited."

"How do you know anything about socialism?"

"Are there rules about what a janitor can know?" Thank you, Pharaoh, and you, too, Socrates, for giving me that good question.

"Tree, I jumped to the wrong conclusion about you because I assumed you had some Alabama good sense. It looks like you and Jorge are both socialists."

"Nico, I use to go to Alabama holiday dinners with my Julie's family, leastways until Julie wore out our welcome by having contrary opinions. Me, I knew my role, which, in the presence of in-laws, was to smack my lips over nothing but the food. Turkey, dressing, gravy. Sometimes an auburn ham. Sweet potatoes. Always pecan pie, which I loved, and which helped to make bearable those freighted family visits. Julie's family was well-off. You would have liked those meals with Julie's parents and their sundry relatives. After the grace, after the meal, after the pecan pie, during the witching hour of the coffee, there came the shouts and murmurs about the dreaded socialism. And about moochers of every variety but most generally black ones. I have reason to believe that this conversation was not just for holidays but was daily ritual with these folks, like bedtime prayers. Julie's relatives sang a song of food stamps for folks, who, if not given the mooch, would lie in the sun and starve rather than get up and open their own State Farm insurance agency. Lazy folks who couldn't be bothered even to buy a convenience store. Sooner starve than work. Only kept alive by the mooch and the powerful urge to get drunk and laid. That was for the lazy black folks, mind you. The grievance on the brown folks was that they worked unnaturally hard and took jobs from deserving white folks. This Thanksgiving conversation was I believe the most satisfying part of the holidays for Julie's relatives. And the horror, the horror when they talked on the public housing, where the government lavished the moochers with monthly subsidies so they could repose in sumptuous cribs and dine on food stamp prime rib. And every one of Julie's relatives, good Christians all, faithfully collecting their own government subsidy in the form of mortgage loan deductions for their pretty houses in the suburbs. And if you gave every one of these relatives a hundred years of deepest thought, they would never, ever, ever have arrived at the idea that they were themselves living in subsidized housing. And Julie's father, making tidy money on his subsidized real estate business. It's what old white folks do is talk about strapping young bucks and welfare Cadillacs, as these same white folks cash their farm subsidy checks for not raising cotton. And just assume, as a class project, that we want to reason out the question of whether racism is good or bad, using no tool but the unaided reason. If we were able to give these folks world enough and time, these prosperous Alabama folks, to solve this vexing question, they would be yet flummoxed a thousand years hence, still trying to reason it all out, and still scratching their asses to relieve the strain of such bulging thought."

Nico laughed, enjoying himself more that I would have most liked, finding me more entertaining than aggravating. I would have to improve.

"Your relations are the salt of the Alabama earth," said Nico. "Where Tree sees vice in his Alabama people, God sees virtue. I join in God's opinion."

I was impressed by Nico's audacity. I had a father who was known some for audacity. All I could think on was how much Vernon Purcell, Sr. would have loved Nico's boldness, maybe my father yet alive and yet loving it.

"Nico, don't you need me?"

"I need you to get me another beer."

I handed it over, and he grunted, possibly in gratitude. "You need me, people like me, to sweep the floors. By my reckoning, I'm still sweeping the floor, and you're still winning. Why, then, waste so much hatred on the likes of me?"

"You laughed at me when I fell in the river."

"I'm sorry. I was wrong to do that."

"You bet you were wrong. Brave but wrong. How'd you get the nerve to laugh at me? You didn't know who you were dealing with. I'm the leading jurist in the country. Read the papers. I am Nicholas Grasso, the living legacy of our brilliant founders."

"And you are brilliant. The line of brilliance remains unbroken."

Nico nodded and looked to Heaven where Little Jemmy Madison looked back with love and then Nico's eyebrows pinched and stuttered when he caught on that he was again on his back in the river, with me laughing at him, and once more I could not keep myself from laughing, forgive me my trespasses.

Nico adapted, because he was Nico, resilient. "Who was this Julie that you talked about, Tree? Your girlfriend? Your sister? Both? It is Alabama, after all."

And, you know, he was decent smart, as I believe. Maybe not smart enough to raise a pack of hounds in Alabama, but decent smart. He was, too, a snarling mean son of a bitch, a scoundrel, and maybe both Iris and Cleopatra would think it was my destiny to laugh at him.

"Julie was someone I loved, my wife. And I guess now it doesn't matter whether she was my wife or my sister, or both as you say. Julie was someone I washed windows with. It was the same springtime for everyone in, at least, the Northern Hemisphere, but we were in love so it felt to us like it was all ours and everyone else was just using our spring leftovers. You may have looked at the cherry blossoms in Washington that spring and not known that Julie and I left those for you, just because we did not have time to get around to all the world's spring at once. One reason we didn't have time is that Julie declared we should wash our windows. One, me, on the outside, on a ladder, Julie on a chair on the inside of the same window. Always the same window at the same time. We mimed and argued over whether a smudge was on the outside or the inside of the glass. Mostly, of course, the smudge was on the outside. But sometimes not. Sometimes Julie missed a spot that I pointed to gleefully, and for reasons unknown this made her smile. Extravagantly. Radiantly. And the glass finally so clear we could see each other perfectly as we paused our labors and looked and looked through the glass that separated us. As still we do."

"I have a Julie, too," said Nico, surprising me. "One of my daughters. Julie and I used to wash the car together. She would sneak up behind me and wash my bald spot. Four girls. Three boys. A Catholic family. My wife, Annie. They are everything to me. All my kids were achievers. Ivy League schools. But Julie, my Julie, she remembers. She's the one calls me on my birthday. She nags at me to tone it down. Tells me to quit showing off. She's right, but I don't care. I don't care. I should have been chief justice. It should have been the Grasso Court. A lesser man got the job. Politics. Now I don't care. I may as well carve them up when they disagree. I'm the one the world will remember. It really will be the Grasso Court. Maybe it will be the Grasso Era, and if it is I will look down from Heaven and be humbly grateful."

Resilient, adaptable, relentless Nico.

Chapter 17

Nico dozed. He was old and it was pleasant in the evening sun and we had tasted some beer. He snored lightly, not unpleasantly. I was surprised that he went down for his nap so abruptly, but good for him. I didn't know many people who napped, but those I did know were better for it. Eunice's little ones, my second cousins, woke up from a nap and rubbed their eyes and for some while were peaceful and snug. And I did not personally know anyone, child or adult, who had bad dreams while napping.

I entertained the idea that Nico might wake up a nicer person, and I marveled at what, on just a Minuteman's notice, a damn fool I could be to expect a different Nico. And truth, even I could see it was more than me expecting it, it was me willing it, the kind of blind, ferocious willing a preternaturally smart boy does when he awakens in the wee hours with questions too hard for his own loved mother, questions for a preternaturally smart father, bestower of two-hearted blessings. In the meantime, or the kind time, as I better liked the sound of, I enjoyed the light, the quiet, and the peace, which peace was rare around Nico. I had this notion that his Julie, his daughter, was happy to wash the car with him but also perhaps relieved to see him fall into a nap in some deep chair such as a patriarch is bound to have.

Nico slipped smoothly awake and smoothly back into our conversation. I wondered if he napped in court, perhaps on the reasonable theory of why the hell not?

"You keep defending Jorge," said Nico. "But I don't think you are one of his flock?"

"Nope."

"What kind of Christian are you?"

"No kind."

"Jewish? I don't think so. My guess is one of those smug atheists. Fits with the socialism."

"Not completely smug although, unlike you, I do know what socialism is. Not completely atheist. But completely, all the way, not Catholic."

"So why defend Jorge?"

"Because he's a guy trying to be kind as best he knows, even though heavy burdened with silliness. So, also, did my mother have silly ideas. It's hard to know what to do about that."

"Do about what?"

"Good people becoming Christian."

"Well, you ignorant hick. I'm one of those Christians."

"But I've never argued, Nico, that you are a good person. I know my mother was. Probably Jorge. I do understand that you're a Christian. You can't be on the Supreme Court unless you're a Christian. Or a Jew."

"The Constitution, as you may not know, forbids a religious test for public office."

"A rule, as it applies to the Supreme Court, honored only in the breach."

"Tree, who the hell are you?"

"A janitor...a good one. And grateful there is no religious test for my trade. For yours, I think the religious test is strict. No atheists in Supreme Court foxholes. No Muslims, Buddhists, astrologers, atheists. all the other things as may be. Only Christians and Jews, believers, like you, in the burning bush."

Nico grinned. "Very nice, Tree. An advantage for God. I'll take it." He finished his beer and tossed the empty onto the ground and requested another, which I did as asked. Nico was bad about a litter of beer cans, but I did not climb up on any high horse about it because it was about the generations. All things equal, younger folks were more like to tune into the earth. Better to be happy about that than mad at old people. I could pick up the campsite later. Thinking of burning bushes pushed me out of my chair, and I stirred myself to get a fire going against the evening chill. Nico scooted his chair closer to the fire and nodded approval at the flames.

"Here's a thing, Nico, that is interesting to me. Jefferson said things, pretty things, and you wonder was there any way he believed them himself. It's an intrigue to me. I believe you must have studied on this, and I would admire to know what you think."

"Specifically."

"Did he have by any stretch a straight face when he said that about all created equal? Surely not. Here's a guy, of course, who owned slaves, including sex slaves. Say he's sitting around a campfire with regular folks, folks who know him, and he said that about everybody equal, wouldn't they be rolling around laughing and near to burning themselves in the hot coals?"

Nico tried to answer, but I decided I wasn't finished. I wished that I could have better found this strong voice with Julie's professor; maybe she wouldn't, then, have kissed him.

"I know, Nico. You can't see into someone's heart to know if they believe their own bullshit. It would be a thing to learn from if Jefferson ever called bullshit on himself, but I don't think he did—that's hard for big thinkers once they've become, like you, all the way famous. My thought, he just had a blind spot in both eyes the size of this granite coffee table that is kindly holding up my beer. And then, on this separation of church and state business, that was just some bullshit he wrote to the Baptists, who maybe feared the whooping Anglicans more than they feared the whooping Indians. Separation of church and state? Jefferson just meant, as nearly as I make it, that the official state religion would be what it now is—Christians and maybe a couple nice Jews for the spice of it. No followers of Mohammed, with scary scimitars flashing, need apply. Or Buddhists or atheists or any other such. Jefferson was saying on black and white being equal, wink, wink, and on separating religion and state, wink again. The state shouldn't take sides in arguments between white men, and it shouldn't take sides in arguments between Catholics and Baptists. But the state most surely will take sides in arguments between white and black and between Baptists and Muslims, scimitars or no."

"Tree, that's it. By God, you're only half as dumb as you look. We are a Judeo-Christian country. So, let me correct the record. Because when I first saw you I was thinking you had the IQ of a houseplant. I mean here to pay you a real compliment. You're like a precocious, beginning chess player. You make interesting, unorthodox moves because you don't know any better."

"From Nico, a compliment. I would be touched did I like you in even the least part. You want this to be a Judeo-Christian country so we can pray to the burning bush at high school football games and praise God that we're not miserable sinners like the other team."

Nico allowed himself his winsome grin because he was after enjoying himself. I noticed that up on the hill Al and Billy had their own fire going. I was sorry Billy did not have a camp chair and happy Al did not have one. Nico, as I believed, was sort of letting me talk for the entertainment in it.

"Tree, where did you learn about the First Amendment?"

"As is fit, the high school library had a copy. Not just of the First Amendment, but in truth the whole Constitution. But I don't mean to puff myself up. I also had a friend we called Pharaoh who seemed to think deeply about such things. I used to talk with him late into the night. I freely credit Pharaoh with what learning I have."

"So, what did this Pharaoh teach you about the Constitution?"

"He thought that Jemmy Madison, smart man as he was, made a little mistake with his Constitution. Pharaoh's thought on this was that Jemmy should have gone right on and said things exactly, but he didn't. And that leaves you, Nico, in a tickle spot. You want Jemmy to have meant the Christian religion, and hell, he likely did mean the Christian religion, but no matter how many times you read it over, the word Christian is not in there. Bad luck for you, Nico. Because by just saying about free exercise of religion, and not being specific, it's in my mind that Jemmy planted a seed for chaos. He left the door open for all manner of religious stuff that good Christians like yourself wouldn't want."

"Not sure what you mean by this chaos idea, but never mind, I'm going to hire you to be my law clerk."

"I don't think so."

"Because?"

"Because I would be a trained monkey to you and yours. An entertainer. A court jester."

"Nuncle!" Nico exploded out of his chair and walked around the coffee table and walked a circle around his chair and sat back down. "I've got it. I knew it was a rare word. I didn't know how rare. You've read *King Lear*! God help us. How can that be? Lear is hard, Tree. I played in a Lear production at Princeton. I was the Earl of Kent. I got great reviews, beautiful reviews."

"That Kent is a hoot. He gets a haircut and a change of clothes, something like that, and is suddenly, for Shakespeare's purposes, totally unrecognizable to the King he has served all his life. That Shakespeare didn't mind taking liberties when needful."

"OK. Kind of a stretch. But Kent, the quintessence of loyalty, the way I am loyal to my friends. And you, with this Nuncle business, you fancy yourself the King's Fool. And if I am Nuncle, then you are trying to make me King Lear, the real fool of the play, and you, topsy-turvy, award yourself the role of the King's Fool, and therefore the actual shrewd one."

"I'm all the way satisfied with those roles, Nico."

Chapter 18

In the fullness of time, it became proper for us to wander a little way from the glowing fire to pee. I went first to show the way because it was dark and the unsteady light from the fire wavered over the uneven ground. I did not want Nico to trip or, mindful of the Rolling River, to get close enough to trip me. He was being friendly, but so was he friendly on the river, and my thought was that there were many good places for Nico to be, but one of them was not behind me.

"Nico, you want more religion in the public square. You like what a Judeo-Christian country looks like. Some of the founders, Jefferson, Washington, were maybe not so orthodox, but...my guess...it would have been hard for them to conceive of anything other than a Christian country on account of it's all they knew. But here's the trickiness as troubles me. Protecting the free exercise of religion in the Constitution. I don't get that. Chaos. Next door to dumb."

Nico might have sputtered here, like my mother's lawn mower, but he was mellow with the beer and the campfire and the entertainment of his Fool.

"Why dumb? Why chaos? If you're going to make an argument, be clear."

"William of Occam, as well you know, liked to keep things simple, so simple that even janitors could grab hold. Not just Occam, also my sainted grandmother, she was always going on about how the unnecessary is father to the unintended...she said that...I heard her. The free exercise rule is unnecessary— 'Congress shall make no law prohibiting the free exercise of religion.' You've already got in the Constitution free speech and free association. So freely associate with your pals at your church and say your free speech about a three-part god, or a six-part god, or whatever number best gladdens your heart."

"Tree. I'm trying to be patient. People came to this country to escape persecution for exercising their religion."

"Well, no, mostly they were persecuted for religious speech and hanging out with those of like mind. You Catholics believe in three gods, so if you say you believe in only one god or believe in 2.3 gods, you might get your head chopped off. Mostly it was about saying the wrong thing, not doing the wrong thing. Not always, but mostly. So, set all the religions free to say their piece. And the state not thumbing the scale to favor the papists over the protestors or vice versa. And all the mean things that could be done to a religious group—head-chopping, assault, arson, and such like—all already against the law."

"Naïve, Tree. OK as far as it goes, but naïve."

"Maybe naïve. I don't know. But I have given thought to my own amendment to Jemmy Madison's Constitution. Why don't we borrow his quill pen and change only one of his words. 'Congress shall make no law prohibiting the free exercise of science.' How does that work for you?"

"The offer to be my clerk still stands, Tree."

"You could endorse that amendment?"

"Of course not. But I like your style."

"So, no chance for my amendment?"

"Not in a million years. My people would go crazy. The free exercise of biology? Evolution? Birth control? Abortion? Climate science? The free exercise of science is a recipe for liberal mischief."

"And the free exercise of religion not a recipe for conservative mischief?"

"Of course, it is. But it's my mischief. A built-in advantage to religion in general and Christianity in particular. That's what makes this a Judeo-Christian country. Let's leave it like it is."

"So, we reserve a constitutional advantage for snake handlers, for astrologers, for the unremitting religious study of the unknowable?"

"Only unknowable by you, Tree. You complained about the janitor not being able to win one. Well, this one's yours. And I'll even help you with your argument. Free exercise can be more than just a sermon or a prayer; it can be doing things. So, of course, the state prohibits some misguided exercises of religion. We do it all the time. Bigamy. No matter what your god says, you can't have two wives in this country. Sorry, Mormons. You can't pray over children with appendicitis instead of giving them medical care. Sorry, Christian healers. Sorry, no, you can't do that...I could go on."

"Nico, you have a couple tiny mentions of religion in the Constitution. But you and Jemmy Madison don't know what religion is—you can't define it, so how the hell do you know when free exercise of religion is happening? It's the chaos I was talking about. You can't tell free exercise of religion from free exercise of a redbone hound. The Constitution doesn't tell us what religion is, and neither does anyone else have a scrutable thought on it. So, you can't tell whether I'm freely exercising my religion, or freely exercising the sacred code of conduct of my hunting dog club. Anything I do, I can claim I am just freely exercising my religion. Taken all around, it's shoal water in every direction."

"Not so hard as that, Tree. Religion involves a belief in a deity. It has elaborate moral rules. It involves people working in groups. People who make sacrifices for their beliefs. Stuff like that. Scholars have been all over this. At those colleges you've never seen the inside of."

"Likewise, my dog trainer's club, it has all that stuff you said."

"A belief in God?"

"Trust me. A wrathful deity is often invoked. Especially if you're trying to train up a stubborn goddamn Walker hound."

"You're making a mockery."

"If there's a mockery here, it's yours. The founders didn't bother to define religion because they blindly thought they knew exactly what it was, something that looked a lot like Christianity. Jemmy Madison just said 'religion,' in the supreme faith that he and all the other good ole boys knew what it was, which was not true by any stretch."

"And my answer to that is, so what? Believers gets a break...always a good thing."

"I grant you, Nico, that most religions involve a belief in a deity. And people believe that god is God because it has been revealed to them by miraculous hearsay. So that's what religion is. It's something somebody said that can't be falsified, except by an opposite and equally unfalsifiable revelation. Whether that somebody saying stuff is Joseph Smith or Moses or Jesus or your friend Jorge. And if we've learned anything from the history of religion it is that if Pastor Bob says one thing then Pastor Bill will come right along and say the opposite. Knowledge by revelation. So many revelations. So little time. That God is one busy guy, whispering the absolute, eternal and opposite truth in so many ears. You'd think God would learn to keep his story straight. One wife...six wives...make up your mind, God, for God's sake. And

Christianity. How many true and everlasting versions are there? And how many yet to come? And when Martin Luther set free the genie that every Christian can be his own priest, then there are as many ultimate truths as there are Christians. You have no clue, Nico, what a religion is. No clue what a Christian is. Because it is literally anything some damn fool says it is, and there is no shortage of damn fools in this world. It is any damn fool that comes before your court demanding that he be allowed free expression of the ultimate truth that was revealed to him just after he had the bacon for breakfast that once again had a miraculous (thank God) effect on his bowels. And the next guy up before your court demands the free expression of his exactly opposite revelation. And it's a fine mess you've made, listening to all these messengers of God."

Nico studied me and studied his beer and gave scrutiny to his own (surprising) thoughts. "There was a time, Tree, when I used to think something along those lines. I even wrote about it. You could be quoting me. There is a chaos when each conscience is its own law."

I was some surprised. "Then we agree?"

"About?"

"The chaos of free exercise. That it sets loose three hundred million individual and contradictory religions on this land?"

"We used to agree. I changed my mind."

"Because?"

"Didn't like the outcome. Sometimes you have to start with the right outcome and reason backward. It's not pretty, but it happens."

This time Nico wandered into the darkness by himself, which I should not have let him, but he had left me with lots to think on. I had expected more from him, but he had expected less from me, so maybe that left us some kind of even up. Even up at least until he pitched down the bank of the gully in the dark.

I hauled him out, and his breathing was harsh. Between every harsh breath, he said, "Goddamn it." He kept saying this, with the harsh breathing, as I got him settled back into his chair and began to inspect him for damages. His face was OK, but his palms were scraped. I got him a fresh bottle of beer to cool his injured hands.

"It's nothing serious," I said.

Nico exploded. "What the hell do you mean it's nothing serious? I fell down."

I didn't get the fullness of what he was saying, but at least his breathing was better.

"Old. Fucking old. God damn getting old. You fall down in the river because you're clumsy. You start the day and don't feel like you're clumsy. You wade around in the river and it feels like everything is fine and then your feet slip and you never saw it coming. You don't even know why it happened. All you know is that it wouldn't have happened thirty years ago. You're on your back in the water and you look up on the bank and there's some young, drooling moron from Alabama smirking at you. Some moron that a young woman like Sandra will always prefer to me. No matter how much Sandra kisses up to me, she will always prefer the moron. And then another cruelty...the moron turns out not to be such a moron. The way you think, Tree, has a power to it, the kind of power that takes you off in new and unexpected directions. I used to have that kind of power. I still have the power to steamroll people. But I'm steamrolling them with the same arguments from years ago. I don't have any new arguments."

So, this was my personal blind spot, one of many. Nico pushed me in the river because he was old and I was young. He was tasting the bile of an "old-life" crisis. He found his own ideas to be no longer original. And while I might flippantly argue that his ideas were never that original, even I could see that was not the thing here. The thing here was that golden dawn goes down, always, to the day's gray ashes. A kind person would say that attention, attention must be paid to this old man. I tried, tried to pay this attention but could not do it, for reasons too strong for me. I keenly felt that this job belonged to someone else, someone like Nico's Julie, his daughter. I could not perform all the world's jobs and of this one I wanted no part. It was, forgive me, the anger in me. I also had Javier to think about and Hector's instructions to carry out.

Nico cooled his scraped palms on the beer bottle and asked me to open it so that he could drink while healing his hands. "Your point about the chaos of individual consciences, Tree, is well taken. But it's a price worth paying because religion is the only thing that allows us to approach truths that are absolute."

"Absolute truth may be a beautiful thing, Nico, but the only absolute truth about religion is that it's all relative. The best argument for situational ethics can be found in the study of religion. As religion unfolds over recorded time, the changes in absolute truth make you dizzy as good whiskey. Don't like the number of gods you have, change it. Don't like the number of wives you have, change it. If you wake up of a morning and find bacon wonderful but scripturally forbidden, just take a red pencil to that rule."

"People of sincere faith..."

"You can tell when people are sincere? Only a judge would be arrogant enough to think that. You would have loved my father. You get indigestion, and he snatches out your appendix on the notion that you don't need it anyway so where's the harm? Never was there a fake doctor with more sincerity—he sincerely liked the appendix business and made right smart of a living at it. He would have enjoyed medical school, but it was hard to find the time when there were so many folks crying out for an appendectomy. Sincerity, Nico? Like when Lear gave his kingdom to the two daughters who most kissed up and said they loved him more than moon and stars? That kind of sincerity? Like Lear, you need to give your head a good slap, the head that let judgment out and folly in. You can tell when people are lying? Just by how they say things? Please tell me you don't believe that."

"No one has said…"

"Nico, put a sock in it." I wanted to turn the knife to satisfy Javier and Hector, and, forgive me, my own rage. "You're not smart enough to be part of this conversation. Leave this to me and Pharaoh."

Truth, that felt nice to say. Sublime. In the firelight, it was hard to read Nico's face, but a fair guess was smoldering, awaiting only a vagrant zephyr to explode into flame.

"More mockery. And I thought you were a friend of Jorge's."

"I never claimed Jorge was smart enough to be a Supreme Court justice, a thing you two have in common. Jorge's at least kind to the poor. Passing mean to women, though. There are lots of Catholic women, so they must like the back of the bus, or be some confused. Go figure. You, Nico, are kind to billionaires but mean to the poor—some poor people like that, too. I grant you that there are so many mysteries in life it does cry out for explanation. How about we set some bushes on fire to see do they sound like God? Or maybe a burning camper will do?"

"Tree, you're a damn fool."

"I already told you that I was the King's Perfect Fool."

213

Nico looked weary, perhaps because he was having to listen to me, and I could find in my heart no room to blame him.

"There's one beer left, Nico. I want it. My burning bush tells me it's mine. You may think I have a blind spot about beer, that I have, in the words of Jesus, a beam in my eye. It's for sure that one of us does. But my friend Pharaoh is actually a pet bloodhound with droopy eyes. He's a student of both Socrates and Lewis Carroll; he and I spent many a night in the lonely woods talking across the darkness. Pharaoh may see one of those blind spot motes in my eye, but this could be because of the beam in his own eye. It's my own poor thought that we spend our lives squinting, trying to peek around, over, or under the beams in our eyes. Regardless, I am satisfied that Pharaoh thinks any day I spend time with him is frabjous, and that I will always be his beamish boy. I like that, sometimes more than I can say with a steady voice."

I was right about Nico's face because it burst then into flame. I calculated he was about as mad as my poor powers were capable of making him. It came at me that he was mad as a rattlesnake striking at its own broken back.

"Fuck you, Tree. I got my letter back. And we're done. You're done. Just so you know. You're still a janitor, and I'm still Associate Justice of the Supreme Court Nicolas Grasso, a legal legend. So, go back to pushing your broom, and I will go back to a marble hall of justice. And you know all that bullshit you were talking about Jorge saying I was on the take?"

"Yes?"

"Jorge doesn't know the half of it. He can't even begin to imagine all the clever ways Willard Jordan and his friends have to funnel money and favors to the right people. And I earn every penny. All you have to do is hide the money from the IRS and not let them catch you spending improbable sums. There's a mansion in Central America that is owned by a trust whose sole ultimate beneficiary is my oldest son. The trust pays the taxes and will for a hundred years. I've never even been there. Almost everything, anyway, is completely legal. What's a bribe, if not a political opinion? And, happily, the Founders intended that political speech should be free. My children get free rides to the best universities. They get outstanding jobs. Sometimes they get generous gifts just because they're nice kids. It's perfectly legal to hide money in quiet places. Anonymous. Ridiculously legal. The rich make the rules, Tree. The Grasso family swims in a river of money, thanks to my foresight, and my understanding that my highest calling is to help my friends. By doing that I also help my country, Jemmy Madison's country. There is no river of money in the janitorial business. There are only campers that fall victim to the mysteries of spontaneous combustion; I believe Al is the local expert on that. I could have gotten you started, Tree. Into a school somewhere. Taught you to swim in the river of money, like I taught you in the Rolling River."

"Be glad, Nico, that Hector loves you and loves the law and keeps you safe. And that I am his obedient servant."

Chapter 19

Nico stood and yelled up the hill to Al. I could see Billy moving around their small fire and then I saw Al's smaller figure up and stretching. A powerful flashlight appeared with Al, and the flashlight walked a crooked path through the small rocks and boulders. Billy lagged and no longer seemed to be trying to stay close to Al.

"Let's get out of here," said Nico when Al arrived.

"You got what you wanted?" asked Al.

"More than I expected."

"Sorry about your camper," Al said to me. "You should be more careful with fire safety." He said this with that way of smugness and smirk that the Sheriff of Nottingham most like used when he had the upper hand on Robin Hood. Al was, after all, practicing up to be the Sheriff of Summit County.

I had promised Hector not to hit Nico, but I wasn't sure this applied to Al, and this loophole looked fetching at that moment, but I considered and decided to check first with Hector. As though conjured by my thought, Hector scuffed his way out of the shadows behind the shell of my camper. Trailing behind him was a tall, thin, uniformed deputy with a rifle in the crook of his arm. The deputy had fancy goggles pushed up on his forehead. In a bit, George appeared from a slightly different path. As was fit for a man who had hiked the Appalachian Trail, George simply glided out of the darkness with no flashlight and no sound. As was fit for a newspaper publisher, he carried a briefcase. Billy walked over, put his hand on Hector's shoulder, nodded, and then faded into the background.

"What a happy meeting," said Hector.

Nico appeared, to my untrained eye, unhappy. "What the hell are you doing here?" he demanded of Hector. When Nico talked, Al beamed the flashlight on his face. "Get that damn light out of my eyes." For a surety, unhappy.

"Working. I hate working this late. But what are you gonna do?"

"Working at what?" from Nico.

"Crime prevention. You're an important public official. You seem to have sent your marshals home. I had to be sure Tree didn't hit you. I believe he has been tempted."

"I don't need you. I have Al," said Nico.

"And you're in good hands," said Hector. "But that's another thing. I'm also investigating an arson. So, I've got my hands full."

"OK. What's he doing here?" asked Nico, pointing at George. "I hate the press."

"You ever think how the press feels about you?" asked George. "I don't like working late any more than Hector. Although I do like tramping around the woods in the dark. I may just decide to walk home. I'm here because Tree invited me."

Nico turned on Al. "I thought you checked this place out. Nobody here but us. That's your job."

"I'm sorry, Your Honor. I checked. I could've sworn…"

Hector laughed. "Judge, there's an old movie, can't remember the name. Paul Newman, the older guy, says to a kid, 'I taught you everything you know, but I didn't teach you everything I know.' Funny line. I had to fire Al before I got done teaching him. It's not his fault."

Al said to George, "What's in that briefcase?"

"Tools of the trade. You got that big pistol strapped to your hip; me, all I've got is a briefcase. I'm just scared it makes me look like a lawyer. What do you think, Al?"

From Nico, "You need a briefcase to keep a notepad in?"

"Not using a notepad tonight. Can't see to write in the dark."

From Al again, "What's in the briefcase?"

George did not answer but asked me for my pliers, which I fished again from my pocket. George went over to the same slot in the coffee table that had held Nico's letter. He knelt and then reached his hand up to Hector, who handed him a small flashlight. George fished in the crack with the pliers and extracted a tiny microphone, which he held to the light and then dropped in his pants pocket, along, I noted, with my good pliers.

"Goddamn it," roared Nico. "Give me that."

"OK." George reached in his pocket and handed the microphone to Nico, who threw it down and stepped on it, stomped more like. The plastic and metal parts made a popping sound as their molecules sheared apart.

"Your Honor," said Al. "That's just the microphone. We need the recorder. That's what's in the briefcase."

Nico turned to Al. "You idiot, you were supposed to prevent this. You were supposed to check the place out."

"That's a pretty small mic. Easy to hide. If there was something, I thought it would be in the chairs."

Nico again, not done with the topic of blame, "And how'd you miss three grown men, hiding in the bushes?"

Al had no answer to this that he felt like sharing, and Nico turned on Hector. "I'll have your job for this. Spying on a justice. Intimidation! An officer with a rifle! Bugging my private conversation with no warrant! What were you thinking?"

"I was thinking what I already told you. I was here to protect you. Thank God you didn't need it. And thanks to Tree for keeping his promise to be good. Slow down and think, Judge. It was George's bug, not mine, but it doesn't matter whose it was. Tree gave permission in my presence to be recorded. That's all it takes to be legal."

"What are you talking about?" Nico was struggling to catch up. I could see him trying hard to remember exactly what he had said in our conversation, what with the beer plus all the irritation just naturally going along with trying to talk any kind of sense with the King's Own Fool. I felt for him because his memory was not a young one, and he had talked a lot and had drunk a lot of beer, which was my job to get him to talk and drink, and I believed I had sincerely done my best.

From Hector, "George was kind enough to let me listen in as we sat in our little hiding place. We didn't get to see much. That was Deputy Raymer's job. So, it was kind of relaxing. I have always enjoyed George's company, and we got to sit back with our headphones like a couple of teenagers."

"I want that briefcase," said Nico. "It's illegal. Don't tell me what the law is. I tell the United States of America what the law is."

"Give me the briefcase," said Al. He had his hand near the pistol that was shiny and reflected the firelight.

George handed the briefcase behind him to Billy and said, "The briefcase is now in good hands. Good luck retrieving it from my largest employee." George took advantage of the fact that everyone was standing to sit in my camp chair, to my thinking the sign of an alert mind at work.

Al was at a loss, with his hand wavering over his gun. I tried to think about what he was thinking, to improve my sense of empathy, which had been a favorite theme of Julie's. Al was having a difficult day. It did not seem to me such a big deal to overlook a tiny microphone—it's a big place, the Rocky Mountains, hard to thorough search. But I did take Nico's point that to overlook the presence of three grown men, it would be a stretch to call this competence. George, OK, he was short and a skilled woodsman, but Hector and Deputy Raymer? Even I had spotted Raymer, when it was still light, as he peeked between two boulders. I had started to yell at him to keep his head down but immediately decided that this would be working contrary to purpose.

More than this, though, much more, was the fact that Al had been shown up. Law enforcement officers and baseball umpires hate this, just hate it, perhaps also true for Supreme Court justices. And Al was hating it more every second. My guess, it did not help his disposition that most everyone was ignoring him. Nico was looking at him like Nico expected Al to do something, anything, and, me, I was just working on my empathy. It was nice not to be in charge.

Al cracked under the pressure and pulled his gun, to my mind, a superfast draw. He completely had the drop on everybody, even Hector. And the only thing Hector did about it was to put his hand on Raymer's elbow and shake his head. I was still concentrating on Al, and he was suddenly, deliriously, in charge.

"I'll take that briefcase now," Al said. He was back to smirking, which always made me want to hit him, but it was Hector's show. Nico was speechless; my belief was that he did not have a lot of practice with the Wild West, which me likewise.

And Hector said, "Why would we want to give it to you?"

"How about because I've got a gun pointed at you and just might decide to shoot you. For old time's sake."

"So, not the right time to arrest you for burning Tree's trailer?"

That darned Al smirked again. "There's never going to be a right time for that. The justice here will tell you that you have to have evidence for that."

"You were a deputy, Al. I have your fingerprints on file."

"Gloves don't leave fingerprints."

"Maybe you forgot and took them off just for a moment. To pry open Tree's locked drawer?"

"I didn't need to take them off for that drawer. You're bullshitting, Hector."

Hector said, "Ah, I thought you might say that." Hector stepped towards Al and reached his hand towards the gun. "I'll take that."

"No, you won't. You think I won't shoot? Defending Grasso? With him to testify for me? Don't be a fool."

"I'll try. But life's difficult, and it's hard not to be a fool sometimes. Here's what you need to know, Al. Billy has the recorder, which is still recording because the actual live mic is taped to Tree's ankle. The one the judge stepped on was a decoy. Hasn't worked in years, so I could sacrifice it without my budget taking a hit."

Al's gun wavered from Hector and pointed towards me.

"Point the gun where you like," said Hector. "It's a pretty gun, but it doesn't work without bullets and Billy has those in his pocket. I knew you'd doze off up there. Billy knew it. Hell, everybody that ever knew you would know it."

Hector gently took the gun out of Al's hand. Deputy Raymer handed his rifle to Billy and went around to handcuff Al, who had lost the will to fight, also his prospects for being sheriff.

Nico went back to his camp chair and sat down. He seemed old and tired, but also, in fairness, still thinking hard and still used to winning. Raymer had helped Al sit on the coffee table, which there was plenty of room because it would have held, my own estimation, half a dozen of those lively clog dancers you see at county fairs. Hector crouched, pulled my pants leg up, and removed his precious mic. He took the briefcase from Billy and opened it on the coffee table. He dropped the mic in the briefcase. He took the recorder out, conspicuously turned it off, returned it to the briefcase, and snapped it shut. He was then careful enough to hand it back to Billy, who was good at keeping things safe.

"You seem to be holding the cards with your illegal tape," said Nico to Hector.

"Colorado allows single party recording. The only thing that matters is that Tree gave consent to be recorded."

"I don't know," I said. "Maybe Nico has discovered a new right to privacy in the Constitution. Sort of a ghostly penumbra. Right, Nico?"

"Fuck you, Tree."

"Does this mean I don't get to be your law clerk?"

"I liked that part," said George. "Tree's only real job was to keep you drinking and talking. I had no idea—I just figured he would tell you stories about Alabama hogs for three hours. Who knew he could talk about the Constitution? I may have to rethink Tree. I've already got one uneducated columnist in Billy. Maybe there's room in the budget for two. They're both so poor they'll work for peanuts, which is fair because that's what I work for."

"I want that tape," said Nico.

"That's not entirely how it works," said George. "I'll tell you how it works as far as I've got it worked out. It's my tape. It's a big story, especially that part, Nico, where you got angry and got to talking about Willard Jordan and money. I think you let Tree aggravate you a little. Mind you, I don't judge because I've had some experience with Tree. Something I believe Hector counted on. In any event, all this has thrown me into a crisis of the soul. I believe this could put me back in the game. A big-city paper. If I got crazy, I could start thinking about prizes. On the other hand, the hiking in big cities sucks. And I would miss my *gente*, who happen to live here. I'm getting old and maybe losing my ambition. I would miss the view of the mountains from my front porch, where I have a woodpile and a rocking chair. It's where I smoke cigars because my wife draws the line."

"So, sell me the tape," said Nico.

"Well, that could be nice. I've got you on tape saying you've got the means. I could build a bigger house with a bigger woodpile and an even finer view. But the same rocking chair, I think; I like that chair. My wife works, and she's of an age where she'd like to quit. There is one thing, though. When money changes hands like that it could seem just the tiniest bit like blackmail. You and Hector would have to be the judge of that. But here's my thing. I'm just having a late midlife crisis, and it comes to me that the thing I want most in the world is what I've got, even if it means putting up with Billy and Hector. And my wife wishing she could quit her job, which is the hardest part. But she and I both like to smoke some quality cannabis and that seems to make things better. And then, come to think, she would have questions about where I got the money; questions she might not like the answer to; she can be real righteous on some things. So, no deal. I keep the tape—in a place where Al can't burn it up. There's no quid and quo here, since I don't plan to publish the tape. But there are some things I like besides the rocking chair, simple things. Things that would make me happy. I like Marcos and Maria and that little Javier. I'd like to see them back here, without being interfered with. Billy speaks highly of them, and I have had in the past the experience of trusting Billy with my life."

There was a silence then and Hector cleared his throat and George looked at him and Hector nodded slightly in the direction of my camper and George went smoothly on as though he had taken only a mental pause to deeply contemplate the verities.

"I also like Tree because he's interesting to talk to—his mind just runs off in the oddest directions—a rare thing. Up here in the mountains, Justice Grasso, we're maybe more use to odd characters, of whom I'm told I'm one. I would also be happy if some billionaire made Tree whole for his camper. The damn thing can't have been worth much, but then Tree doesn't have much. That's it. That's all I need to be happy, taking care of Marcos and Tree. And a personal favor. Nobody tells my wife. She's unpredictable, and she really does want to retire."

"That's easy," said Nico. "Tree?"

"The only happiness I want you can't give me. But I do worry about Jorge."

"Jorge!"

"You have a letter in your pocket from the actual pope of the Catholic world saying what would make him happy. He's an old, silly man, with a good but sad heart. You are going to have opportunities to make him happy. Do it, goddamn it. You're also an old, silly man, with what I have come to think of as a white heart. It might be your last chance. And think on this: What if you are right? There's the big rub for all you good Christians. What if you're the dog as actually catches up to the Christian bus? What if it turns out you bet right on that wager of Mr. Pascal, that odds-loving Frenchman and Christian philosopher. Turns out after you die there is a Heaven, a Hell, just like you and Pascal bet the farm on. Except there's another bet you're making that you've got a blind spot on. Because there was this other Christian philosopher, came earlier in time than that smart Frenchman. And this earlier Christian oddsmaker laid out the chances for rich folk like you, Nico, to get into heaven. Camels have a tough go squeezing through the eye of a needle. What if your three gods really do exist and in their mysterious way really do love most the poor? Love most a little kindness? Is that a bus you really want to catch up with? If I were you, Nico, I would think on the terrible consequences of being right about your Christian belief. That's the message, the real message, of this troublous letter from your sad pope."

In that same way that Jesus simply wept, Nico simply sneered.

"And that leaves Al," said Hector. Al seemed to be out of small talk and out of smirks; he still wasn't likeable but was more tolerable this way.

Hector said, "I have some evidence against Al on the tape, but I'm embarrassed to say I lied about the fingerprints, and that lie is also on the tape. And then, both with Al and the judge, anything that happens legally just runs into a tidal wave of Willard Jordan's money. Just a great big towering wall where my district attorney, a nice guy who likes to ski, is looking across the table at a billion-dollar busload of legal talent, whose only goal is to disturb the peace of my little county. They could twist the meaning of what Al and the judge said on tape to where a jury would swear that all they were doing was saying three Our Fathers and two Hail Marys. I'm with George—I don't want it. I think Al walks. I would be happy if he walked to a far place, maybe someplace where Jordan owns another ranch. The gift of Al's absence would be *muy bien*. And the last thing is I'm going to make a present of Al's treasured gun, and the bullets that go with it, to Billy. Just for the hell of it. Just to be doing something right even though I have no right to do it. Those that don't like it, my advice is to get over it."

That was the end of the interesting stuff, and I asked George if I could walk home with him. He seemed surprisingly pleased. But before we left, I started picking up the litter of Nico's empty beer cans, and George jumped in to help. George retrieved his briefcase and took us down the road, pale in the darkness. He even slackened his ferocious pace so I could have a hope of keeping up. It was downhill and easy going. We walked maybe a mile before he spoke.

"Are you who you claim to be?"

"Are any of us?"

"Don't give me some thumb-sucking answer. Are you a lifelong janitor and high school graduate from Alabama? No other formal education?"

"Yes."

"I'll be damned. It was fun listening to you take Grasso on. I learned some stuff. From both of you. Some of it I still don't have straight in my head. I may study that tape. Why didn't you take Grasso up and become his law clerk?"

"Are you kidding?"

"Yes. But any such goal for you is possible. Why not? I wasn't kidding about writing for the paper. Can you write as well as talk?"

"I can't say. I always liked Homer's way, where those old Greeks memorized the story and walked it down the road to the next campfire. That way seems real companionable. Julie tried to get me to write down some of my campfire stories, but she despaired of my erraticism on paper. On the other hand, she was sometimes pleased, as I dare to believe, with my eroticism."

"Maybe we can work with that."

"With which?"

"The erraticism."

"Maybe. Julie thought sometimes I should go to school where such things are taught, and sometimes we went back and forth over it. Mostly she didn't care what I did for the unaccountable reason that she loved me. She was an educated, professional teacher. She was from money. She was beautiful. She never felt she needed a show dog of a husband. It was all luck to me."

"I wasn't kidding about the mountains collecting odd ducks. Think about staying."

"I have been."

"What was the deal with you and Grasso talking about your father? That part confused me. He was a doctor? A surgeon?"

"He was a quack...a surgeon who never went to medical school."

"And he got away with that? Never caught?"

"Not that I know of. He left my mom and me when I was very young. So far as I ever knew he always stayed one step ahead of the posse."

"That's impressive...that he got away with it. Must have been smart."

"I guess."

"But you never heard from him? I had one of those, a father who skipped out. Hard to forget."

"Memory does run on."

"You could try to find him. I did with mine. You could look him up."

"I used to think I wanted that. I was fascinated by the question of whether, when I once laid eyes on him, I would kiss him or hit him. Know what I mean?"

"That is the question."

"What did you do with yours when you found him?"

"Oddest thing. I couldn't think of a thing to say. I just stared at him until he got scared and started crying and then I walked away."

"That sounds about right. Crazy to expect an old man to change. My old man couldn't change thirty years ago. If you're a scoundrel, like my dad, I think it must get harder, not easier, to change. Look at Nico."

"As scoundrels go, a prime one."

"Were you telling the truth about not using that tape?"

"Just to give it a listen, for my own amusement."

"After you do that, would you destroy it?"

"Sure...I guess...if you want. It's more yours than mine. Isn't that risky? It's the only thing we've got on Nico."

"That's why I want it gone. I don't want to have anything on Nico because one day I might decide to use it. He's too far along in his peculiar life to change. Maybe, for my peculiar life, I'm not...not too old...to change. Burn it up."

"OK. Done."

"You thought I did OK with Nico? Kept up OK?"

"You were great."

"Who knew that was possible for an Alabama kid? Some things you can't dream of because you've never imagined them; they're like the sounds only dogs hear. It's not something I ever thought about in Alabama."

"Tree, you did great. Amazing. I see what you mean, though. That's a big jump from the backwoods of Alabama. Another thing, maybe he's not as smart as he's cracked up to be. The press, me, we anoint people with some description, say, smart—'the brilliant Justice Grasso.' And then we all just repeat the smart business endlessly because it's the approved shorthand and saves time."

"Thanks, George. It's going to take a while to sink in. My mother—when the excitement turns me loose, I have to think of what it might have meant to her. And Julie. She's the one got me into this mess with Grasso."

"Which is part of what I'm saying about whether you should try to do more."

"Maybe, but I don't think so. What if I get all formally educated and turn out like Nico? I have liked being a janitor. Learning is my hobby, like my dogs. Like your rocking chair on the porch, like your hiking. I don't want to ruin my hobby by turning it into work. That happened some with Julie, an English teacher. She complained sometimes about the job forcing her to read, to teach, some book she didn't like. If I don't like a book, I put it down and go flying to something else. I was tempted...by Nico. By the smart world. By being smart and looked up to and paid a lot of money. But I have work I like and a beautiful hobby. I mostly hated my teachers because they took a book I had read and messed up the purity of the song I had in my head. A good hound, on the scent, running hot, as we say in Alabama, runs a pure line and sings a pure song, with no confusion in it. That's the song I have, on rare occasions, found, and, who knows, if my ear is ready, maybe again."

Chapter 20

I will stay for the while that I can see.

In August, there was a wedding, a thing beloved of storytellers, a thing based on hope, based on turning from one time to another. I got to go (to the wedding). The sky was blue, the grass green, and the bride wore white. I started to ask Cleopatra about the propriety of her choice of color, but a voice spoke to me, from some untrammeled brain frontier, and said, nay, Tree, nay. I listened to the voice, so I believed there was yet hope for me. Not only that, I felt hope tugging loose, peeking around. Sometimes I was afraid of it because I thought it a trick, but mostly not. Mostly I just thought it was hope. Hope didn't feel the same as before, though; now it was sort of a knitting bone, bound to mend, but bound also to mend crooked. And to ache with the changing weathers.

There was both a wedding and a reception, two separate things, two separate locations. The wedding was in Hector's backyard, with the celebrants and the officiant standing on the deck and a small group sitting on the grass below. The reception was to be in a public park because these were public figures, local royalty—with any luck, in need of a Fool. There were no invitations to the reception except that everyone was welcome who knew Hector and Iris, and who, after all, did not? Billy and Marcos and I had wrestled tables and chairs and beer and more beer to the park in the morning. Billy's boys were left as the honor guard for the beer, and they could (possibly) be trusted.

The guest list for the wedding was exclusive, and I was on it for no obvious reason, but I was happy for gifts, deserved or not. I was a friend, as I strongly felt, to the bride and groom, but, still, a new friend. Hector and Iris went back with the people of the valley for all their long lives and were loved, liked, honored, and felt by some to be overrated jerks; this is what happens when you have settled in and made some marks.

At the wedding, before the ceremony, I sat back under an aspen tree because I wanted to watch the bride and groom without being distracted. Iris was tall and slender and regal with her black and graying hair. She had been up early for her daily run. In lieu of a bouquet, she carried a longnecked bottle of beer as she wandered among the guests. Hector wore ostrich cowboy boots and a black suit with a bolo tie, and his hair was also black and gray. He wore a royal blue baseball cap with gold braid and gold stitching that read, Sheriff; he wore this because Iris made him, to protect his balding forehead from the sun. I sat under the tree and thought how magnificent they looked (and were).

There was a rocking chair on the deck with a big pink bow on it, which no one sat in. I had learned in the kind time about Iris's daughter, who had died a few years before. She had physical problems and mental disability problems. After Buster died, and after she was an adult, she lived sometimes with Iris and sometimes in a group home in Denver, depending on her wishes. She was fragile and finally overtaken by a stroke. Iris told me that Laurie loved to have her father tickle her feet and groaned for his presence after he died. The rocking chair was hers, and people that passed it reached out a nudging hand, so it moved with the remainders of a life.

When Iris told me I was invited, I went to Denver and bought a suit. It was dark blue with a skinny gray stripe and nicer than anything I had ever owned, even the one I wore to my own wedding. I also had to buy shoes and socks and shirt and tie and a black, skinny belt. I bought a pocket handkerchief but then left it home because it seemed above my raisin. I made do with my old underwear, and no one the wiser. The night before, Maria had made sure all the pins were out of the new shirt, and she ironed out the creases from the packaging.

When I was dressed, head to toe, she laughed at me and could not stop. Javier got mad at her because he thought that she was making fun of me, but I knew and she knew and Marcos knew that she was not. She was moved (and moved to laugh). They were back and living with me in my strange new abode.

We were renting Iris's house, where she lived before she moved in with Hector. It was an old, Victorian house, far too big and expensive for any ten of us. It was furnished with some expensive stuff and some banged up stuff, but it didn't matter because Maria rarely let any of us sit down for fear that we would get something dirty and Iris would visit and Maria would be shamed. The rules were more complex than Marcos or Javier or I could grasp. We could, however, grasp that it was necessary to obey Maria. Marcos said the rent we were paying was certainly too low, for the simple reason that we could afford it.

Even though she would not let me sit on the furniture, Maria had grown more patient with me. She regularly taught me a few words of Spanish before she put her hands over her ears and said, *no más, no más, por favor,* Sweet Jesus, *no más.* More evidence for my belief that there is something about Alabama that fights off foreign languages, including proper English, like an invading virus.

Maria could not believe the story that Billy told her that people like Hector and George had insisted on the return of her family. She kept repeating this story to me, as if I had not been there myself when it happened. I saw no special change in Marcos; he was dignified before and after and will forever be. The first thing all of us did after moving in was to painfully reclean an already clean house, driven like whipped donkeys by Maria's pride, and by her gratitude.

The next thing Javier and I did was build another fort in his room. We sat under the bedspread roof of the fort and read books and told stories and sent toy soldiers into carnage, stuff, of a surety, I had wished for from my father. My mother had gamely done some of this stuff with me, and it was fun, but of course she had the wrong chromosome. I was glad she tried, and I would not have made it through otherwise, and thanks, Mom. Playing with Javier, wreaking destruction on the soldiers, I was happy.

Without by any stretch seeing it coming, I had for the moment a family. Understand that I did not for even a quick second forget about Eunice and the two little ones, Edna and Ethan, back in Muscle Shoals. Eunice took me in after my mother died and again after Julie died and let me sit under her magnolia tree. After Julie died, I did nothing, could do nothing, but watch that tree live, and try and try to think why it was doing that. Lying in the early quiet in my bed in my new house and Iris's old house, it came to me that Eunice let me leave Alabama because she knew I had survived the loss of a father named Vernon, a kitten named Mouse, a mother named Corrine, and I would find a way to survive the loss of a wife named Julie. Eunice took me in, and I planned to try to talk her into moving here with me if she saw it fit. There might be room for her and the kids in this large house if we squeezed some.

Marcos was whisked back into his old job so smoothly that I felt the moving hand of Willard Jordan behind it. Maria was back cleaning houses (other than our own). I was not working but was useful in seeing after Javier, as he, in his solemn moments, also watched over me. Willard Jordan paid for the camper, or, technically, a nameless cowboy came in the dark to the door and handed me a manila envelope that contained ten thousand dollars in cash. Old, worn, hundred-dollar bills. So, thanks, Willard. I put the money in the bank. Which, somewhere up the chain, Willard probably silently also owned the bank. That's OK, I guess; and if it's not, I can't say I know what to do about it. Leave me alone to have a little life.

I was not actually as poor as I looked. My mother had left me the home place, which I sold when I married Julie. And Julie left me some money. It wasn't like she had a will, but I was the only one in line, and there was an insurance policy came with her job. So, I was OK with money, the stuff I've tried never to take an interest in. If Maria ever says *sí*, then I believe I can stake Marcos and me to that cleaning business. In the kind time, I have a job that starts in two weeks as a janitor at the hospital. The high school had no openings. I will miss cleaning a gym, but I can dream, so maybe someday.

Beside our house there was a smaller house that Iris's friend, Ben Wallace, lived in. He had been traveling on his summer vacation as a history teacher but was now back for the wedding. Iris had said she would not have it without him. Marcos and Maria and I had him over for a beer, and I believed that he especially liked Javier, as who would not. Ben spoke good Spanish, and was good looking, and, like me, had lost his mate, so Maria made clear that he would never need to cook for himself again so long as he lived next door, or until she could find a way to dump Marcos. Marcos suggested a couple of women into whose arms he would not mind being dumped, but Maria failed to see the humor.

Ben and I did not talk much because there was not the space although I was pleased he knew history because who is not interested in history? He was also from the South but was polished in his talk and I thought that worthy of study. It was a thing I was mixed up on because, as I said, I did not want to get above my raisin. I feared losing who I was, losing the understanding of things bound tightly in Southern language, and of somehow letting slip Julie and my mother.

I had noted what Iris told me before about Ben, that he would not leave the house that his fiancée had been killed in. It put me in mind of another Southerner, Mississippi John Hurt, who sang the spiritual, "I Shall Not Be Moved," and Mr. Hurt surely was not moved from Avalon, Mississippi, but his voice carried out from there, and there was no doubt in that quiet voice. Besides, why would you want to move when you're already in Avalon, waiting only to be buried beside King Arthur? Assuming it's the same Avalon as in the Arthur legend, and I doubt it not. Arthur—fitting, royal company for Mr. Hurt. Ben and I for sure did not talk about our losses because it was not a thing, like baseball, to want to have in common.

George officiated at the wedding. Somebody sang a song first. The singer was OK, but she was not as sure of music as Mississippi John. I liked sitting back under my tree because Buddha had some success with that and because I did not know many of the people and because I was shy about my new suit.

I could hear George with no problem because of his booming voice. As a newspaper man, he was good with words, so good that I mostly did not remember any one turn of phrase, but the thoughts came clear. I remembered from his ceremony speech that George loved Hector and Iris. That would have been true for many years because their stories traveled far back. In the stories, they had fun. And hard times, too, as will come. And, in George's telling, Hector and Iris loved their peeps, including, despite everything, George. So, it was fit that Iris and Hector should love each other and marry and have hot sex. Iris grinned but did not blush, and Hector the opposite. The two of them said promissory things, and George pronounced them husband and wife. George looked out over what he had done and pronounced himself well pleased, and he rested while Hector and Iris kissed, and then George demanded a cold beer.

Lena came to me under my tree, and I stood to greet her. She looked stunning, still and forever short, but stunning. She had on a sort of blue-hued dress with part of it yellow. Sorry, I can't do a better description. As I think on it, I don't believe the yellow was the color of objects on the dress, like parakeets or daisies. It made me think of the cheerful colors of Renoir, as I studied them in a book from the high school library. I stood up when Lena approached, and we were both embarrassed because we were so dressed up.

"We will have you over for pot roast," she said.

"I would love it. I have not seen enough of you and Billy lately."

"You've been busy, getting settled in. I'm glad you're staying."

"Me, too, more so since it means seeing you and Billy and the boys."

"Tree."

"Yes."

"I don't really have a crush on you."

"Oh."

"I like you. But I was just trying to make Billy jealous because he was spending too much time reading and hiking around in the hills. Is that OK?"

"Sure. Thanks for telling me. We will go on from here all together."

She tilted her head up and I knew to lean down so she could kiss my cheek. She turned to leave.

"Lena, that's a happy dress."

"Me, too."

Hector and Iris wandered over after making many mingling rounds. I stood and kissed the bride and hugged the groom.

"You guys are beautiful. I have not been able to stop looking at you."

"I hope," said Iris, "that we make you think of a wedding you could have some day."

"Iris," Hector cautioned.

"Tree and I speak our minds to each other."

"Do we not," I said.

Iris said, "Tree, don't kill that man in prison. I won't have it."

"I won't have it, either." I answered up prompt and easy, but, truth, it was not as easy as I made it look.

"Is this something I should know about?" asked Hector.

"No," said Iris.

"Iris likes you," said Hector. "We both do. But Iris has her own sense of people. She adopted Ben, and he became her best friend."

"You, Hector, are my best friend," said Iris.

"No, I'm the person you have hot sex with."

"And don't ever stop," I said. I kissed them both on both cheeks and thought of myself in my new suit as suavely Continental (the European continent, specifically).

237

George brought me a beer and motioned me down when I started to stand; he sat beside me in the lush grass. He talked. First about migratory butterflies. This reminded him of a trail outside of town through mixed spruce and aspen where in the autumn the gold aspen leaves fell into the blue-green spruce fronds and rested there like a dense swarm of monarch butterflies. He talked about once backpacking a long stretch of the Colorado Trail, and it was chilly and rainy and sleety up high, so on the evening of the third day he built one of his bonfires to warm up. A few passing hikers hissed at him as he sat, warming up and simultaneously drinking cognac and smoking a joint. His fire was in violation of the backpacker "leave no trace" rule, and in the luxuriant heat of bonfire and cognac and cannabis he gave them all, each and several, the finger. He had a lovely, long footnote on his tricks for finding dry shavings to get a fire started in the wet. I was happy listening, but I could see his wife eyeing him, and I knew she was thinking it was time for him to move about among the guests, and I understood. He had found a good listener, which I could be, and a listener was more desirable to him than gold, and sweeter also than honey.

Before he could be fetched away, I said, "Thanks for what you did with Nico."

"What did I do?"

"You gave up your big scoop. Your chance for fame and glory. I don't exactly know why, but thanks."

"Tree, I have no clue what the fuck you're talking about." Whereupon his wife, who wanted to retire, came to fetch him, and he went in peace.

And last there was Billy. When I tried to stand, he pushed the top of my head down. It was a marvel to watch him sit on the ground because I always expected awkwardness from someone so big.

"Wonderful day," he said.

"Yes."

"They are two of my favorite people. Hector arrested me once just to save me from a motorcycle gang that I really wanted to fight."

I had heard this story before, but I believed that repeating stories made them stronger. "How was jail?" I asked Billy.

"I don't know. Hector just drove me home, and Lena chewed me out and sent me to my room. Are you guys getting settled in your fancy new house?"

"It's great. More room than the camper."

"And there's Maria's cooking."

"And there's Maria's cooking."

"And Marcos's sister, Irina. Has she been over much?"

"Once is all. I think Maria has warned her away."

"Good."

"You don't approve?"

"No, she's fine. Looks great. But not your type."

"What's my type?"

"Julie was your type. What would you talk about with Irina?"

"Maybe I'm not after talking."

"Coming to life, are you? Good. But after that, consider that Irina has never willingly read a book."

"That works for you and Lena."

"Only because we fell in love when we were kids. We had to make it work. It wouldn't be that way with you and Irina."

"You're right. Remind me if I forget."

"I'm happy you're taking an interest, though."

"Me, too."

"Maybe someone will come along."

"Someone did—Julie. I'm learning a little bit to be happy for that."

Billy glanced over his shoulder at the wedding throng. "Lena didn't like it that George performed the ceremony. She thought there ought to be a real preacher."

"OK, but a real preacher might not know them and love them as much as George."

"Lena, lots of people, good people, hold ideas from God, church, to be dear."

"I know. It's really Nico I'm talking to. And God bless him, anyway, as we like to say in the South. Lots of folks take knowledge by revelation and turn it to good. My mother. My only wish is that these good folks would treat their personal revelations as exactly that. God has blessed you by telling you a secret. This is your private relationship with God. Treasure it. Tell no one. Freely exercise your beliefs as you think best. But be proper humble. There should be a wall of separation between your divine revelation and the person sitting next to you. If God wants to share your revelation with others, He will do so; He does not require your help, what with being omnipotent and all. Trust God on this, and please shut up. All religions can't be true, but all can be false. This is easy stuff. Eventually, a plodding long eventually, most people will figure this out. Lots already have. But the Constitution and the Bible, sacred documents, teach us that, by definition, our blind spots are hard to see."

"Do you ever miss having religion?"

"You know, the truth is I really don't. What I miss is having dinner with my friends. I talked to Lena earlier, and she said she was going to fix that. And she said she loved you madly."

Billy's round face gave up smiles slowly but entirely. "Good," he said. "That's a good thing." He got up the same way he got down, by pushing on the top of my head, a little harder than I would have liked, but he was, after all, a man of such strength that he could not know it all.

I was hiding a partial bit from Billy. I had lately received a revelation, and it was to me divine. I had come to think that it was possible for good things to happen, perhaps even unto me. I kept repeating this to myself, the way I repeated over and over the words when I married Julie. She had written the words, and in her part of the ceremony she said she would not have found me, loved me, if she had not caught me reading aloud from Mr. Charles Dickens as I pushed the broom across the empty gym at Muscle Shoals High School. Good things can still happen, perhaps even unto me. Some of these good things were happening now. I also had this fanciful notion, bubbling from a sweet well, that these good things, perhaps the best of them, like Julie, were going to be a surprise, completely unimagined. So, was I going my own illogic circle and saying that a surprise would be surprising? Yes. And joy joyful? Yes. Guilty. For the while that I can see, this will have to do, and more than good enough for someone with a raisin the likes of mine. But from it, I take some hope, some eagerness to see the possibilities of this new place, of these new people, of me.

End

About the Author

Mac Griffith lives in a small mountain town in Colorado. Mac skis from winter to spring. In summer and fall, he hikes and runs and casts flies in the rivers where trout live. In between, he reads and writes and sometimes works.